P9-DEL-189

BROGNOLA NARROWED HIS GAZE

"We heard through the grapevine some CIA people got killed. Is this related?"

The President nodded. "Three. Shot down in cold blood during surveillance on the deal I mentioned."

"You want Stony Man to take this on for you?"

"Damn right I do. No stonewalling, Hal. I want this mess cleaned up, from the CIA mole, through to the people handling these deals, and the Chinese. If Beijing is sanctioning the purchase of U.S. technology, I want it stopped. What's the point of having superior firepower if it's being taken from under our noses and sold down the road to use against us?

"This is a direct threat to national security," the Man went on. "Put an end to it. We're being taken for a ride here, Hal, and I won't let it go on. If the Chinese want down and dirty they can have a taste for themselves. Do we understand each other?"

"No restraints, Mr. President?"

"When was the last time that worried you, Hal?"

"Just wanted to hear you say it, sir."

DON PENDLETON'S

STONY

AMERICA'S ULTRA-COVERT INTELLIGENCE AGENCY

MAN®

CHINA CRISIS

A GOLD EAGLE BOOK FROM

WORLDWIDE®

TORONTO • NEW YORK • LONDON
AMSTERDAM • PARIS • SYDNEY • HAMBURG
STOCKHOLM • ATHENS • TOKYO • MILAN
MADRID • WARSAW • BUDAPEST • AUCKLAND

If you purchased this book without a cover you should be aware that this book is stolen property. It was reported as "unsold and destroyed" to the publisher, and neither the author nor the publisher has received any payment for this "stripped book."

First edition October 2007

ISBN-13: 978-0-373-61975-7
ISBN-10:   0-373-61975-8

CHINA CRISIS

Special thanks and acknowledgment to
Mike Linaker for his contribution to this work.

Copyright © 2007 by Worldwide Library.

All rights reserved. Except for use in any review, the reproduction or utilization of this work in whole or in part in any form by any electronic, mechanical or other means, now known or hereafter invented, including xerography, photocopying and recording, or in any information storage or retrieval system, is forbidden without the written permission of the publisher, Worldwide Library, 225 Duncan Mill Road, Don Mills, Ontario, Canada M3B 3K9.

This is a work of fiction. Names, characters, places and incidents are either the product of the author's imagination or are used fictitiously, and any resemblance to actual persons, living or dead, business establishments, events or locales is entirely coincidental.

® and TM are trademarks of Harlequin Enterprises Limited. Trademarks indicated with ® are registered in the United States Patent and Trademark Office, the Canadian Trade Marks Office and in other countries.

Printed in U.S.A.

CHINA CRISIS

PROLOGUE

Second Department, Intelligence, Beijing, China.

"We are nothing if not versatile," Director Su Han said. "Industrial espionage is something we have excelled at for many years. At this juncture it can serve us well. Rapid advancement can be ours simply by jumping a generation as it were. The Americans have devoted years and millions of dollars developing the current technology. Now we can reap the benefits."

"I fully appreciate the concept," Dr. Lin Cheung said quietly. "My only concern is that this kind of illicit dealing will only increase American hostility toward us if they discover what we are doing."

"The Americans would like nothing better than to see China remain a backward nation where weapons are concerned. It suits them if we were to remain singularly weak and unable to fully defend ourselves. It keeps us in our place, which would be behind both the Americans and the Russians. That imbalance sits well with the American military. They would breathe easier if we stayed in the background. It would allow their expansion in this part of the world." The Director leaned forward. "Our voice must be heard. Through military strength we cannot be ignored. If we fall behind, then we have no one to blame but ourselves. This must not be allowed. I will not allow it."

Director Han waited for his words to take effect. He looked around the table, seeing the approving nods coming from the uniformed military presence. His words were what they had been hoping to hear. He turned his attention to Lin Cheung. He sat quietly considering the director's statement. Han allowed himself a slight smile. As always, Cheung considered every facet of any proposal before he took it on board. It wasn't that he was a weakling. Cheung possessed a fertile mind, brimming with originality, but always tempered by caution, and though he might never vocalize it, Han appreciated Cheung's input. He was almost Han's conscience.

"Cheung? You are quiet," Han said, gently prodding the man with his words.

Cheung, slim and reserved in contrast to his superior, turned his full attention to Han.

"We will need to work very carefully. Be certain that whoever we deal with can supply what we need without exposure. Once the Americans become suspicious, they will increase security on all projects and suppliers that we might find all avenues closed against us. If we are shut out before we have all we need then the whole project will falter."

"Exactly why I have entered into a partnership with an organization that will handle that part of the deal for us," Han said. "They will gain the major technology for us. And we will pay them for it, leaving us clear to simply handle the hardware and adapt it for our own use."

"Who are these people?" an air force colonel asked.

"They call themselves Shadow," Han said, smiling indulgently. "I find these people amusing with their little code names. But in the instance of this group they are extremely proficient. I have had excellent reports from previous users of their services."

"Have you met them?"

Han nodded. "I have had successful meetings with the man who heads Shadow. He calls himself Townsend. His background is the U.S. military. Many of his people are also ex-military."

The Chinese army representative, a heavyset man in his sixties, registered alarm.

"You make deals with the Americans? The nation we are competing against?"

"Who better to understand the intrigues of the military industrial complex? Townsend has contacts, people in place, the means and the motive to provide what we need."

"Motive?"

Even Cheung understood the response to this.

"Money. The driving force behind the American psyche. It is what keeps the U.S. living and breathing. It is their god."

"Nicely put, Cheung," Director Han said. "Shadow operates like any American company, providing a service we pay for. They are not going to risk damaging their own reputation by trying to cheat us. There is a whole world out there willing to hand over large amounts of money for their expertise."

"Is this entirely wise?" another dissenting voice questioned.

"Do you think I would contemplate such a venture without extreme investigation?" Han asked. "I understand your reservations, but be assured that the security constraints I have raised to shield us will defy any and all attempts at penetration."

Cheung said nothing this time. He had past experience of so-called impenetrable security protocols. He did not trust them. As secrets were often betrayed, so were loyalties and promises. People were simply people in the end. Whatever nationality, whatever regime, there were always those who harbored weaknesses that could be exploited. Bought and paid for by any number of means or combination of means. Monetary, sexual, politically motivated, or through misguided reasons. It was extremely difficult to maintain total security, and the Chinese were no different than anyone else. He was well aware that the reigning Chinese regime had many enemies, both out of and within the country. The hard-line, Marxist style of government was held in contempt by many of its own people. That the government came down hard on any form of dissention only added fuel to the flames of resistance and simply pushed those dissenters deeper underground where they continued to work on their own manifestos. Director Han had to be aware of such counters to the Chinese administration, and in light of that he had to accept that the covert acquisition of American technology was open to exposure by those who sought to get their hands on anything that might cause embarrassment to the Beijing masters. Whatever he felt on the matter, Lin Cheung kept it to himself.

A short time later, when the meeting had been concluded, Han beckoned Cheung to stay behind. When they were alone he gestured for Cheung to take a seat next to his at the table.

"A quiet word, my friend. This undertaking has the problem of being an unqualified success for us, or a rather messy failure. You agree?"

Cheung inclined his head. "All matters we involve ourselves in have their plus and minus sides."

Han smiled.

"Lin Cheung, the master of understatement. I sensed during the meeting a faint air of disapproval. Does my intuition serve me well?"

"Only from the point that I can see that gaining this technology could take us forward, but with grave repercussions if something goes wrong. The Americans would orchestrate great political profit if they exposed our intent. Even more if they had names and faces to go with that exposure."

"Then we will have to be certain nothing does happen to put us in the spotlight."

"Easy to say, but difficult to put into practice."

Han leaned back in his seat. "Yes. I will not deny that. But we must take the chance. We need this technology. China needs to maintain its place alongside America and Russia. Too much is at stake to allow us to slide into a weak third place. If we are not careful, North Korea will overtake us and that is something Beijing will not tolerate. Can you imagine how Pyongyang would crow if they gained superiority over us?" Han shook his head. "We must regain the lost ground, Cheung. If this is the only way, then we pursue it with all our might."

"You have my support as always," Cheung assured the director.

"I never doubted it. As soon as you have concluded your business here I want you to return to Guang Lor. I have the authority to give SD-1 anything you need. Work your people day and night on the prototypes. I am already in discussion with Shadow to start supplying us with hardware as soon as they obtain it. Have your technology sections ready to commence work once we receive consignments. And be ready to initiate a test launch as quickly as possible so that we can show we are capable of giving them what they want."

Six months later

DOCTOR LIN CHEUNG HEARD the knock on his office door. He continued pouring the pale tea from pot to cup before he raised his head and spoke.

"Come," he said.

The door opened and Major Kang stepped into the office, closing the door behind him. Kang was young, ambitious and had an elevated sense of his own importance. He strode across to Cheung's desk and stood rigid while Cheung turned, cup in hand, and sat down.

"Tell me, Kang, do you sleep at attention?" he asked casually.

Kang's expression failed to register any emotion. Sighing inwardly, Cheung tried to imagine what it had to be like to go through life without a shred of humor in his body. He was unable to grasp the concept, except to realize that Kang had to be a miserable individual. Being dedicated to the State was a laudable ambition but allowing it to turn the individual into a humorless drone was going too far. When he looked at Kang he felt sorry for the man. He understood Kang's problem. The boy had been indoctrinated almost from birth, taught nothing but ideological dogma to the total exclusion of everything else.

Cheung sipped his tea, placed the cup on the desk and turned his attention on Kang.

"Your call suggested a problem. Tell me about it."

"The C26-V missile being tested has been lost, Doctor."

"Major Kang, would you define the word *lost* for me."

"Our tracking station was monitoring the performance of the missile."

"I'm aware of that. But you said lost."

"The test firing was going well until a short time ago. All functions were working as expected until the missile stopped responding to instructions."

A small shred of unease raised its head. Cheung leaned forward to pick up one of the telephones on his desk.

"Put me through to Kwok. Immediately." He lowered the receiver and glanced at Kang. "Go on."

"Contact was lost just after the missile was tracked moving in the direction of the border with Afghanistan. Self-destruct failed to initiate. The last thing registered was the C26 almost at the border."

A voice was speaking through the receiver. Cheung put to his ear and heard the measured tones of Yen Kwok, the launch controller.

"…have lost all contact with the missile."

"Give me your best guess," Cheung said.

Kwok's sigh was answer enough.

"I'm certain we lost it close to the border. With its remaining fuel I'd say it traveled at least twenty, maybe thirty miles before it came down."

"Yen, *what else?*"

"I don't know what you mean."

"I have known you too long, Yen. There's something else you haven't mentioned."

The pause was long, heavy with dread, and when Kwok spoke it was as bad as Cheung had expected.

"I just had a talk with Sung. Because of the demand we had from Director Han the missile had to be readied so fast. Sung had no time to..."

"Just tell me."

"The stabilizing and control circuit board we were duplicating wasn't ready in time. Sung panicked."

"Let me guess. He used one of the American boards we acquired. A stolen piece of technology that probably has *Made in the U.S.A.* stamped across it."

"Yes. One of the shipment we purchased from Shadow."

"Foolish."

"Sung is beside himself."

"I mean Han. Always pushing. Demanding so much but denying us the time to develop things correctly." Cheung thought for moment. "Yen, keep things calm out there. See what you can do about locating where the missile went down. If we can find it quickly enough, perhaps we can retrieve it before it falls into the wrong hands."

"And if we can't?"

"We'll worry about that if it happens."

Cheung put the phone down and gathered his thoughts. He suddenly remembered that Kang was still with him.

"Major Kang, assemble a retrieval team. Use the helicopter. If the missile can be located, we have to get our hands on it before anyone else does."

"Who else would..?"

"Any of those damned dissident groups. We know they've been skulking around the district, just waiting for something they can use to embarrass us. Surely you understand that if they got their hands on the missile and found we were utilizing stolen American technology it would be a great propaganda coup for them. It would cause Beijing a great deal of embarrassment having to explain how U.S. circuit boards were fitted in a Chinese missile."

"Deny everything," Kang said, his approach simplistic almost to the border of naivete.

"I truly wish it was that simple, Kang, but we live in the real world, not the fantasy one Beijing sometimes favors. As long as that stolen item exists, there is always the possibility of it being traced back to where we obtained it. If the people who sold it to us found themselves compromised, any kind of loyalty toward us would simply vanish. Survival is the strongest emotion within the human animal when it comes down to choice. And do not forget the money trail. With all the electronic movement in the world the slightest chance of connecting buyer to seller..." Cheung paused, aware of Kang's expression. "Never mind, Kang. I do not suspect that military training covers the world of banking and illegal money laundering. Suffice it to say that our surest way of preventing any repercussions is to recover the circuit board from the missile before anyone else. Do that and we avert complications. That, Major Kang, is your objective."

Kang nodded.

"Leave it to me, sir."

He turned and left the office, heels clicking on the

hard floor. Cheung sighed. He returned to his pot of tea, pouring himself a fresh cup. There was nothing else he could do at this precise moment. He would have to depend on Kang's devotion to duty. He had no doubt as to the young officer's skill in his chosen career. Kang would pursue his mission will fervent zeal. Cheung felt a moment of pity for anyone who got in Kang's way and did not give the answers the man wanted to hear.

CHAPTER ONE

CIA Field Surveillance Unit

Agent Arnie Trickett was starting to get nervous. It showed in the way he was pacing back and forth in the surveillance truck, constantly peering at the monitors. He was downing paper cups of black coffee as if the stuff was going to go on ration.

"Arnie, sit before you wear a hole through the bottom of the truck," his partner Jack Schofield said. "It's going to go down."

"Yeah? Well we're going to look like a pair of prize dicks if it doesn't. We only got the go-ahead because of our input. All the intelligence is ours."

"And it's sound." Schofield swung his seat around. "Arnie, what's wrong? Why the jitters?"

"This isn't the first time we've tried to catch that bastard Townsend with the goods. Every time he's slipped through the nets free and clear. We can't touch the guy without evidence that's one-hundred-and-one-percent solid. I don't see that happening. The guy is laughing all the way to the bank, and there's nothing we can do about it."

"Patience, my boy, patience. We'll catch him. Even Townsend has to slip up sooner or later. When he does, it's payday."

The third member of the observation team snapped his fingers.

"We got contact," he said. His name was Zach Jordan. He was younger than both Trickett and Schofield, with only a few years' field experience. "Looks like Riotta. Yes. Confirmed. Joseph Riotta."

Trickett leaned over to scan the monitor.

He saw that a dark sedan had parked outside the deserted warehouse where the exchange had been arranged. A man was already out of the vehicle, standing beside the front passenger door, gazing around the abandoned industrial site. Jordan zoomed in with the camera and brought the man's face into full view. Even in the gloom Trickett was able to recognize Joseph Riotta. He had looked at dozens of images of the man over the past few weeks, along with other members of the group Riotta was in with.

"What'd I tell you," Schofield said. He leaned forward to open a switch and spoke into his headset mike. "First contact made. Stay alert, people. We should be getting more visitors anytime now. Will advise. Nobody moves until I give the word. Let's get these people in one spot before we net them."

There was more to it than that. Getting Townsend's people and the sellers in one place was nothing on its own. They needed an actual exchange to take place, with goods and money in evidence before a conviction could be guaranteed. Schofield's years with the Agency had taught him one thing: total, unbreakable evidence was required before any case could progress. They needed more than simple knowledge of a crime. They had to have the whole package, which was why he understood Trickett's nerves were strung so tight. His partner was a born worrier. He liked every detail nailed down before he could relax. That wasn't a bad thing in their line of work. It was only that it made life difficult for anyone working with him. Trickett's insistence on overplanning sometimes bordered on the irritating.

"Hey, this looks like what we've been waiting for," Trickett said, pointing at one of the monitors. It showed a dark-colored SUV cruising along the service road that would bring it to the warehouse where Riotta had parked.

"Be advised," Schofield said. "Second party has shown up. Be ready."

He left his mike open to avoid any delay when he gave the order to move in. Now he turned his attention back to the monitors, studying the people under the eye of the CIA cameras.

"They going ahead?" he asked.

Jordan shook his head. "All they seem to be doing is standing around talking."

Something stirred the back of Schofield's mind. Both parties were present. There was no logical reason why they should stand around passing the time of day. Unless they were waiting for something else to happen.

But what?

The faint stirring took on an uneasy edge as Schofield allowed his mind to permutate the options, and even as he did, a disturbing thought entered his consciousness.

In was then that he heard the door to the surveillance truck click as the handle was turned. He felt a rush of chill air and he turned to look over his shoulder....

THE PEOPLE LISTENING to the tape later heard Schofield say, "What are you doing here? I didn't see your name on the roster for—"

There was a subdued cough of sound, easily identified as the chug of 9 mm bullets exiting the muzzle of a sound suppressor. It was stated in the written report that the weapon had most probably been a 9 mm Uzi on full-auto, expending its entire magazine in seconds. The end result was inevitable. Arnie Trickett, Jack Schofield and Zach Jordan were all killed in those fleeting moments. They weren't given a chance to draw their own weapons, and from the way Schofield had greeted the assassin, it was obvious he knew and recognized the individual.

What the killer hadn't realized was that Schofield had left his com line open and everything said in those final moments was relayed back to the field office and caught by the tape machine monitoring the entire operation.

By the time the office contacted the tactical team waiting for Schofield's go and ordered them to check out the truck, the killer had left the scene, the buyer-seller had been alerted and fled. Nothing was found at the rendezvous point, but at the surveillance truck the tactical team found bloody slaughter.

White House—three days later

"I'M REACHING THE POINT when I don't trust my own shadows," the President said. "Trust. Hal, that word is becoming a joke around here. I get a new version of events depending on who I talk to. The CIA excludes the FBI. The NSA has the lead when it comes to paranoia. None of them wants to cooperate with the others, and they only give me versions they believe I can handle."

Brognola waited in strained silence. He knew what the President's final request would be. He wouldn't have been summoned to the White House if it didn't need the attention of the Sensitive Operations Group.

The Man sat heavily, the weight of his burden showing for a moment on his face. Then he gathered himself and directed his gaze at the man seated across the desk from him.

"I truly believe you're the only man in the damn country who wouldn't betray me," the President said, studying the big Fed closely. "Tell me I'm right, Hal."

"No problem, Mr. President. You know how I feel about this office and you especially. I work for *you*. No one else. The SOG is *your* security arm. We don't compromise on our mandate and that goes down the line."

The President relaxed a little. He reached out and placed a hand on a file.

"Are you up to date on this?"

"I read your memo."

This time the Man managed a laugh.

"Memo. Well, that cuts it down to size. Then you'll know the defense community has been losing top-secret electronic hardware. Computer software has gone, too, specifically items developed for current and developing missile applications. Guidance and stabilizing systems. Inflight circuitry boards. God knows what else. From what I've been able to gather, the suspicion is the stuff has been stolen to order and sold to the end user—namely the Chinese.

"I have been reliably informed that the Chinese are currently engaged in an all-out program being developed so their military can keep pace with the latest in missile capacity."

"China? Our emerging Asian trading buddies?" Brognola asked.

"Exactly. Don't let all that twenty-first-century business expansion fool you, Hal. The Chinese will play the market for what it's worth. They'll build our TV sets, washing machines and DVD recorders. Automobiles, too, if we let them. And they'll undercut prices, sell by the shipload and collect their pay in dollars. Then they will use those dollars to buy military know-how by the back door."

"What's behind all this?" the big Fed queried.

"Survival. Our defense program has always been ahead of theirs, because we put in the money and the time. No one has the capacity to match the Slingshot satellite system, and once we get the Zero platform fully operational, that will put us even further ahead. The Russians only pushed the knife in deeper when they announced they were going to update their own ballistic missile arsenal again. For *home defense,* they quoted," the President stated.

"And there's no way the Chinese are going to stand by and let that happen."

"Precisely. China sees itself as number one in their neck of the woods and a major player on the world stage. They aren't going to lose face and end up the poor kid on the block behind the U.S. and Russia."

"Full circle," Brognola said. "Back where we started."

"If we allow it to happen. The Chinese are aware that starting from scratch means years of development and testing. Buying in technology, to be copied and reproduced, will give their armament community one hell of an advantage. They let us do all the research and development, spend the billions, then buy the goods from their U.S. supplier. All they need then is to analyze the components and start to build their own."

"Suspicions?" Brognola probed.

"Nothing we can move on officially. It's believed an organization called Shadow run by a man named Oliver Townsend may be the culprit. The CIA got close to a deal being brokered but the whole thing went to the wall at the eleventh hour, so we're no closer to the truth at this time," the President told him.

"We heard through the grapevine about some CIA people getting killed. This the same incident?"

The President nodded. "Three. Shot down in cold blood during surveillance on the deal I mentioned. Early indications suggest it might have been one of their own who pulled the trigger. There's a transcript of the tape that recorded the last words of one of the agents."

"Anything on the shooter?"

"No admission yet. Personally I don't believe they know. But the CIA is embarrassed that the killing may have been by one of their own. They were caught off guard. The Agency has closed ranks. There's an internal investigation being carried out, but every time I ask questions I don't get much. I have the feeling the CIA is confused by what happened and they don't know themselves who to trust. I'm the President, Hal. I should be able to get to the truth."

"You want Stony Man to take this on for you?"

"Damn right I do. No stonewalling, Hal. I want this handled. Top to bottom. I want this mess cleaned up. From the CIA mole, through to the people handling these deals and the Chinese. If Beijing is sanctioning the purchase of U.S. technology, I want it stopped. What's the point of us developing superior firepower if it's being taken from under our noses and sold down the road to use against us? This is a direct threat to U.S. security. Put an end to it. We're being taken for a ride here, Hal, and I won't let it go on. If the Chinese want down and dirty, they can have a taste themselves. Do we understand each other?"

"No restraints, Mr. President?"

"When was the last time that worried you, Hal?"

"Just like hearing you say it, sir."

"No restraints, Hal. Get our hardware back, or destroy it so the Chinese can't use it. Go the whole damn mile and however farther you have to go. If the Chinese are running this deal, give them a bloody nose and shut the operation down."

"Repercussions?"

"I'm sure there will be, but we'll field them if and when. Be interesting to hear the mitigating circumstances from Beijing." The President slid a file across the desk. "Main points. All the detail I've been able to collect. I'm sure your Mr. Kurtzman's cyberteam will find out more."

"They like a challenge, sir."

"Usual terms, Hal. If want anything, just pick up the phone and ask me."

Stony Man Farm, Virginia

THE ACTION TEAMS and support staff sat at the War Room conference table.

The meeting was headed by Hal Brognola, with Barbara Price, mission controller, at his side. Aaron

"The Bear" Kurtzman was checking out the monitor setup, ready to reveal his findings.

The members of Phoenix Force and Able Team were spaced around the table, all of them eager to get the proceedings under way.

"Let's have the light show," Brognola said to Kurtzman.

Kurtzman tapped in a command and the large wall monitor displayed a series of photographic images, the first one showing Oliver Townsend. The other shots were of people known to be associated with him and working out of the ranch he operated in South Texas, close to the border with Mexico. The sequence was short. No one recognized any of them, until T. J. Hawkins asked if Kurtzman could backtrack.

"That one," he said.

The image was held. Hawkins leaned forward to make certain he had been correct, then nodded.

"That's him. Vic Lerner."

"He's right," Kurtzman said, checking his list.

He brought up Lerner's detail.

"Where do you know him from, T.J.?" Gary Manning asked.

"We served together. He was with me in Somalia. I lost track of him after that."

"Records show he left the military about a year ago. Seemed to drop out of sight, then he was seen with a couple of people tied in with Townsend." Brognola glanced at Hawkins. "Impressions?"

"Nice enough guy face-to-face but I always had the feeling there was something going on under the surface. Vic always had his eye out for the main chance. Did a little dealing in 'lost' equipment if I remember.

He could always get his hands on whatever you wanted. That kind of guy."

"He'd be up for this kind of deal?" Brognola asked.

"Vic? If it paid cash money, he'd trade his sister's puppy dog."

"High-tech hardware is a lot more expensive than a dog," Manning said.

"And stuff like that doesn't just casually fall into someone's hands," Calvin James pointed out. "I mean, these boards aren't lying around like crackers spilled from a box." He stared around the table. "Well, are they?"

"Let's hope not," Brognola said. "That means the gear is being systematically stolen by an organized group. It looks like we've hit on something deep and dirty here. From the information we've already got, the Chinese have started in on their missile regeneration bigtime. Interagency data points to a concentrated program."

"So why now?" Rosario Blancanales asked.

"This didn't happen overnight," Brognola said. "The Chinese have been feeling out in the cold for a few years now. Kind of like the poor relation peering in through the window at all the goodies on show. And they see the neighbors being invited in and not them."

"Sounds like paranoia to me," Carl Lyons said.

"The Chinese are into saving face," Brognola said. "No chance are they going to let other nations stand tall and leave them in the shadows. Remember last year when the Russians announced they were going to beef up their own missile program? It was soon after that the Chinese stepped on the gas and started to improve their own missile program."

"Are we into 'if you have a big stick, I'm getting me a bigger one' territory here?" David McCarter asked.

"That's a simplistic way of putting it," Brognola said, "but it pretty well sums up the problem."

"See, simple is best," the Briton offered.

"And you're the expert when it comes to simple," Manning agreed.

McCarter leaned forward, wagging a finger at the big Canadian.

"And also the boss, chum."

"China isn't going to let itself be pushed into the background," Brognola agreed, choosing to ignore the banter. "They have to been seen as the strongest force in Asia and being able to dictate terms if the need arises. This Russian desire to be able to rattle the saber again isn't going to go down well in Beijing. So it's in China's interest to become a major player. They want parity with all the other big powers."

"Back to the old cold-war syndrome," Price said. "Full circle."

"Not exactly," Brognola said. "The President has green-lighted this as priority. Bad enough China upping its weapons capability, but it's like being given the finger when they start using our technology to let them jump-start and draw level."

"Government loses technology, we're handed the baton and told to get it back?" Carl Lyons said.

"That's what we can't allow to happen." Brognola turned his attention to Hawkins. "T.J., hear me out on this."

McCarter caught the inflection in the big Fed's voice and was way ahead of Brognola. "I smell an undercover job coming up, young Hawkins."

Hawkins glanced at the Briton, a slight frown on his face.

"You've got history with this Vic Lerner," Brognola said. "If you can make contact, maybe it could give us a way into Townsend's organization."

"I guess so."

"No pressure, T.J."

"Don't you believe it," McCarter stated. "Turn him down and he'll cut your credit-card rating and stop your subscription to the *Buffy* fan club. By the way, you still got that life-size cardboard cutout?"

Price barely concealed her snort of laughter. She raised a hand to her mouth as she feigned a sudden cough.

Brognola allowed a wisp of a smile to touch his lips before he moved on.

"Able Team will shadow you on this. Find anything we can pin on him, and they'll move on Townsend."

"Get me into his computer system," Kurtzman said, "and we can dig out all his dirty secrets."

"Tell me how and I'll do it."

"I love enthusiasm." Kurtzman grinned.

Hawkins drummed his fingers on the table. "Sure. Let's see what we can work out. I need some kind of hook to get me involved with Lerner."

"You are in the hands of the masters of guile and deceit," Blancanales said.

Price extracted a file from the stack in front of her.

"Phoenix, you handle China," she said, and handed the file to McCarter. "That's your mission brief, guys. Everything you need to know. We want our technology returned or at least destroyed so it's useless to any potential hostiles. You can bring yourselves up to speed while you're on your way to Andrews. There's a C-17 transport waiting to take you to Bagram airbase. Jack's already on board with *Dragon Slayer*. He'll make the insertion into China. The flight will give you the chance to update with Mei Anna. An incident has occurred directly tied in to this whole affair."

"Whoa," McCarter said. "Mei Anna? How did she get caught up in this?"

"David, she's been back with her group for the past few weeks."

"Didn't she tell you?" Lyons asked.

"Lover's tiff maybe," Blancanales suggested innocently.

McCarter's dark scowl indicated he wasn't seeing the humor.

"You forgot where I've been the past few weeks? A little busy."

"The important thing is, David, that Anna has background that bears directly on your upcoming mission. We flew her in from Hong Kong so she could join up with you and go into Xinjiang with you. Read the file and you'll see why," Price said. "Hey, I'm sure she would have let you know, but it might have been difficult getting a message to you at the time."

McCarter slumped back in his seat. "I suppose so."

"Part of Anna's Pro-Democracy group has been monitoring the facility the Chinese set up some time ago," Price said, quickly moving on. "Aaron?"

Kurtzman keyed up a series of images, showing the facility. It was set in rough terrain, with low mountains far to the north. The shots were mostly taken via long-range lens.

"The place is called Guang Lor," Kurtzman offered.

He brought up a map. "Northwest China, province of Xinjiang. It's close to the border with Afghanistan. Well isolated, away from any populated areas so Beijing can keep it under wraps as much as possible. Intel says this is where they're developing their new generation of long- and short-range ballistic missiles. There's a small settlement grown up in the vicinity for workers at the facility."

"Anna's Pro-Democracy group has been working the area and picking up what they can," Price went on. "They have to be careful because the area is pretty well controlled by the Chinese. Current intel says the missile testing has been increased lately. The group has a man inside the facility now, and he's been feeding them what he can. Pretty thin, but at least it indicates just what the Chinese are up to."

"Take a look at this," Kurtzman's said. "The Pro-Democracy group took these shots a couple of weeks back in Hong Kong."

He brought up a series of shots that showed a group of men talking together.

"This was shot in Hong Kong. The Chinese is Sammo Chen Low. No surprise that he comes from the facility at Guang Lor. He's a negotiator *and* a financial specialist. The Caucasian here is Joseph Riotta, and CIA intel has him linked to Townsend's Shadow organization. Same with this guy. Ralph Chomski. Ex-Air Force. I managed to filch that information from military data banks. Make of it what you will, folks."

McCarter leaned forward and poked a finger at the image of another man in the group, sitting a little back, but listening intently to what was being discussed.

"Well, well," the Briton muttered. "Our old chum from Santa Lorca. Jack bloody Regan."

James studied the face of the man in the crumpled suit and old Panama hat.

"You are not wrong, bubba," he said, using the man's favorite expression.

"Still in the business," McCarter said. "Regan has good contacts for moving ordnance. Looks like he sub-contracted to Shadow."

"That going to be a problem for T.J.?" Brognola asked.

"No. He never met Regan on that mission. T.J. was backup on a warehouse roof. They never even saw each other."

They spent a few more minutes tossing facts back and forth until one of the phones rang. Price picked it up and took the message.

"Phoenix, your ride is ready to take you to Andrews."

McCarter stuck the file under his arm and stood, the rest of his team following suit.

"We're gone," the Briton said. "Hey, hotshots, you look after my mate. He's a pain in the arse, but he's my pain. We'd like him back in good working order."

Lyons nodded. "He'll be fine. You know our rep."

"That's what worries me," McCarter said, grinning.

"Take care, guys," Price said.

"Easier said than done," Manning replied.

"You sure you old boys can manage without me?" Hawkins asked.

"You really sure you want an answer to that?" James asked, a wide grin on his face.

CHAPTER TWO

The aircraft waiting to ferry them to Bagram was sitting on the end of a runway, engines already warmed up. The vast cargo space of the C-17 housed the Stony Man combat helicopter, *Dragon Slayer*. Jack Grimaldi was inside carrying out detailed preflight checks that would go through everything from the twin-turbine power plant, electronics and computer aids. He would also run thorough checks on the chopper's impressive ordnance capabilities. *Dragon Slayer* carried an awesome catalog of weapons, multibarrel chain gun, missiles and pilot-activated aim and fire through a slaved helmet array. Within the electronic heart of the machine were sensors and range-locating instruments. The satellite-linked communication setup enabled Grimaldi to call Stony Man at the flick of a button and also connect in to air-traffic feeds so he could maintain instant locations. Where they were going on this particular mission his sources would be the U.S. Military Communications Net.

The men of Phoenix Force, carrying their gear,

crossed in driving rain and climbed on board. Grimaldi raised a hand in welcome as he watched the team arrive, then returned to his checking procedures. As they stowed their gear, McCarter spotted a familiar figure sitting patiently on one of the benches the far end of the aircraft.

It was Mei Anna. She wore a camou-pattern combat suit and boots, the same as Phoenix Force, her jet-black hair pulled back from her face. A backpack lay on the floor at her feet, along with her P-90 assault rifle. She carried a 9 mm Beretta pistol in a shoulder rig. She offered McCarter a brief, silent acknowledgment when he met her gaze. He nodded in recognition, then turned and made his way to the flight deck and immersed himself in the technicalities of the pre-takeoff discussion with the flight crew.

While he did that, James, Manning and Rafael Encizo secured their equipment, then joined the Chinese operatives.

"Where's T. J.?" she asked.

"Working undercover on another piece of the mission," Manning said. "We thought it was time he had a grown-up job."

"It's good to see you," Anna said, standing and greeting them all with a quick hug.

They responded warmly. There wasn't one man among Phoenix Force who didn't hold Mei Anna in great esteem. Since their first encounter during a previous mission to China, she had proved herself to be a formidable young woman. Her dedication to her Pro-Democracy group was intense, and her fight against the repressions of the Chinese government and the often brutal suppression of civil and personal rights was something she believed in with a passion. Her fight had taken her all over China, and she was a wanted woman by Beijing. She accepted it without making a point over the matter. Her courage was something Phoenix Force was fully aware of. Her being back in action didn't surprise them. It had been something they had all accepted as inevitable now that she had recovered from the aftermath of a wound that had taken its toll and forced her into a long recovery period.

"We had no idea you were involved in this until a short while ago," Manning said.

"Things happened fast" Anna told him. "We've been monitoring the activity at Guang Lor for some time. This particular incident has given us something definite we can focus on, and it seems to have happened just as you became involved."

They felt the aircraft vibrate as power was applied to the powerful engines. After a few seconds they felt the plane start to move, the whine of the engines increasing.

"Is David okay?"

James grinned. "He's being David," was all he said.

Anna touched his arm. "You don't have to say any more."

They braced themselves as the aircraft gained speed, the sound of the engines filling the cavernous interior, and then the deck beneath their feet tilted and they felt the momentary hollowness in their stomachs as the aircraft lifted off.

"No going back now," Manning said.

McCarter appeared and made his way along the plane.

"Talk to you later," James said.

They nodded to McCarter as they passed him halfway down the length of the plane and took their seats, leaving the Briton to join Mei Anna.

The woman had sat again and made a point of looking out the window. She kept up the pretence for a couple of minutes before turning to face McCarter.

"What do you want me to say, David?"

"Hello would be a start. Might make up for vanishing the way you did," he stated.

"I had no choice."

"Bloody hell, Anna, we all have choices." McCarter controlled his outburst, lowering his voice. "What do you think I would have done? Locked you in the cellar and hidden the key?"

"Something like that," the woman replied.

He moved to sit beside her. "Am I that much of an idiot?"

She laid a hand on his. "Of course not. You're a caring man I have learned to trust and have affection for."

"So why the disappearing act?" the Briton queried.

"You know why. If you had found out you would have tried to persuade me not to go. I was afraid you might succeed, so I decided the best thing to do was to just go. The last thing I intended was to hurt you. You have to understand my feelings in this. I was doing this kind of thing before we ever met. You know that. I would never change the times we have together, and I want that to go on. Truly. But what I do in China is something I can't turn my back on. If a matter comes up and I'm needed, I have to respond. That was what happened, and it was why I had to go. Don't hate me for that."

McCarter put his arm around her shoulders.

"Hate you? Not going to happen, love. You are the best thing to happen to me in a long time. It's just bloody hard to watch you haring off on some dangerous trek with a gun in hand and that look in your eyes. Honestly? It scares the pants off me. And I miss you."

"Really? I haven't given *you* a single thought since I boarded that plane out of England."

"Comforting to know."

"And not true. It was nice having you around. London can be a dangerous place."

"Don't I know it. Talking of dangerous places how was it going back to HK?"

"We have to be so careful now. The authorities have been coming down hard on any kind of antigovernment groups. Beijing is showing its tough face right now. Harsh penalties for anyone getting caught. It doesn't show them in a good light when corruption or repression is exposed, so they use any means to strike back. Every so often they have a purge. Round up suspects, jail them without trial. Send them off to labor camps for reindoctrination. There are public executions, too. It doesn't stop the groups though. Just makes the survivors more determined to carry on."

"What the hell is it with Beijing?"

"The government is scared. They see the people getting restless, wanting change and being prepared to suffer, and die, to get it. The ruling group is terrified of allowing China its freedom because it would signal *their* end. They cling to power so desperately, the country pays the price."

"So this missile deal is part of that paranoia?"

"Exactly. America is still the most powerful nation on Earth. Now Russia is updating its missile system, claiming it's for defense. Beijing sees all this and has to respond, to bolster its own strength and to convince the people they are safe in the government's hands. It's all to do with saving face and maintaining the balance of power. No one has learned a thing, David. The wheel goes around and comes around."

"More or less what we talked about back at base when we got the mission brief."

"So we're all after the same thing," Anna said. "Only for slightly different reasons."

"Not that different." McCarter smiled. "I only said yes because I knew I'd see you."

"Flatterer. But don't stop, I like it."

"Tell me about Xinjiang."

Anna pulled a folded map from her pack and spread it. She pointed out locations.

"Northwest China. Close to Afghan border here. Some pretty harsh country where we're going. Some desert areas. Rocky terrain. Desolate and isolated. Which is why China's nuclear test site is located in the area. Here at Lop Nor. It's a long way from where we'll be operating, so don't worry about picking up anything to make you glow in the dark. The missile research and development facility is here at Guang Lor, with a village close by to house outworkers. There is also a military presence in the area because the indigenous population, the Uygur, want autonomy from the rest of China. The Uygur maintain their Islamic religion, and they refuse to relinquish it. Some years back Beijing decided to send in Han Chinese to bring the area under control. The Uygur opposed that, believing it would erase their ethnic identity, which is probably Beijing's intention. So there is unrest, resistance, military repression."

"So there'll be more military than we might normally expect?"

"Not necessarily where we're going."

McCarter frowned. "I don't know whether to take that as a yes or a no."

"Take it as an 'I'm not certain either way.'"

He smiled at her firm reply. One thing he had learned about Mei Anna was her refusal to be intimidated in any way, as slight as the intention might be. At her strongest, she took no prisoners.

"Here, take this map. I have another. Use it to work out what you need to do," the woman stated.

McCarter folded the map and tucked it under his belt. "Okay. Let's talk about your people. How many? Where are they and can we get to them without ending up with the local militia coming down on us?"

"The latest report we had said they're on the run from the military. They located the downed missile before a search party from Guang Lor could get there. They extracted the circuit board and took photographic evidence. But they were spotted and the military pursued them. From what I managed to pick up, there had been a running fight. Hung and his surviving team took refuge in the foothills. Something about a deserted village. It was shelled by the army during one of the strikes against the Uygur. Planes razed it to the ground, the people relocated. In real terms it means many of them were killed and buried in a mass grave."

"Do they know we're coming in?"

Anna nodded. "We managed to get a short message through to Loy Hung. He's our team leader in the area. He understands we have people coming in to help and to collect the evidence because he's been prevented from delivering it to Hong Kong."

"The board and the photographs?" McCarter queried.

She nodded and pulled a group of photographs from one of her pockets, handing them to McCarter.

"Loy Hung, Dar Tan and Sammy Cho. They are all that is left of the team. The others died during the escape into the hills."

"And what about this Major Kang character?"

"He is head of security at the Guang Lor site and for the region. A very ruthless man. He will not have taken this incident well. It will reflect on him personally, so he will be doing everything in his power to regain possession of the board."

"Okay." McCarter paused as a thought intruded. He realized it had been niggling away at the back of his mind, kept at bay by more pressing matters, but it was suddenly demanding his full attention. "Anna, the information that came out from Guang Lor said the only reason the U.S. board was used for the trial was that the copies weren't completed yet?"

"Yes. Why?"

"If we get the original back, that isn't going to stop Lin Cheung's development people from finishing what they started. They'll go right ahead and complete their counterfeit boards, and still have what they want."

"In other words, they'll still be on a par with the U.S."

"Not much use the President waving the genuine board and shouting, 'We got it back, Beijing.' All they'll do is smile and rattle their newly equipped missiles at him and yell, 'So what?' They'll do their best to stop the news leaking out about what they've been up to, but in the end they aren't going to pack up developing their missile system, using technology they stole. And they probably still have other hardware they've bought under the counter."

McCarter leaned back against the bulkhead. He could feel the power of the aircraft vibrating through the metal skin of the fuselage. He focused on the information Anna had given him and the implications of his own thought process and what it meant. Whichever way he turned it around, it looked as though Phoenix Force's incursion into China was about to have its stay extended and its mission upgraded. Whatever lay ahead, it wouldn't be a walk in the park. Phoenix Force was going to drop in on a potential minefield of problems just waiting to jump up and bite them.

He paused in his thoughts. There were never any guarantees of an easy time. Stony Man didn't exist to take on peaceful missions or easy tasks. It was here to handle situations that required on-the-spot-down-and-dirty solutions to ugly scenarios. When in doubt, send out Phoenix Force or Able Team. It was what they did best, and they were the best at what they did. He smiled at his own clichés.

He felt Anna's eyes on him. She had a wistful smile on her lips, head slightly to one side as she observed him.

"What?" the Briton asked.

"I was just imagining what I'd like to be doing right now if we were back in London. Maybe breakfast in that café near the flat," Anna told him.

"You just fold those thoughts up and store them away, love. Keep them safe until we get back."

"Okay. I have something else for you. Loy Hung has a man inside Guang Lor. He's been established for some months. It's why we got the information on the circuit board and the downed missile. Hung's man has also passed him detailed information on the security setup and locations within the site. Could be helpful."

"Will we be able to depend on this man if we hit the site?"

Anna shrugged. "We can't say. The last time they spoke, Hung's man said he was concerned Major Kang might be on to him."

"Let's hope he's okay."

Anna glanced at her watch.

"David, I'm going to get some sleep. It feels like I've been in the air for the last week."

"You do that. And I'd better go have a chat with the lads. Tell them what a pleasant spot we're going to drop into."

He pushed to his feet and made his way along the aircraft to where Manning, James and Encizo were checking equipment.

"Briefing session over?" Manning asked.

McCarter joined them. "Oh, yes. You want the good news or the bad news?"

"What's the bad news?" Encizo queried.

McCarter couldn't resist a wide grin. "The bad news is, there's no good news."

"I hate it when he gets that smug attitude," James said.

"He likes to think he has comic timing," Encizo said.

"I do," McCarter announced.

"Miss-timing more like," Manning said.

"I just talked to Anna," McCarter said. "Her people are on the ground and hiding out, waiting for us to make contact, haul them out of trouble and take this circuit board off their hands."

He passed the photographs Anna had provided so the team would know Hung and his men.

"These are the people we have to locate and lift out," the Phoenix Force leader said.

"But?" James asked, waiting for McCarter to drop the bombshell he was keeping to himself.

"Collecting one board isn't going to make the problem go away. And the problem is that the Chinese will still have the copied version of whatever they stole from the U.S."

"I feel something's coming that I'm not going to really want to hear," Manning said.

"Along the lines of we have to neutralize the missile center," Encizo guessed.

"And make sure all the stolen technology is destroyed," James added.

McCarter didn't respond until he felt three pairs of eyes on him.

"Well, yes, something like that."

"Let's take a stroll in the park suddenly turned into a rumble in the jungle," James said.

"We have to be flexible, chums. This was part of the mission brief so we had to expect it."

McCarter produced the map Anna had given him. He spread it out, and his teammates leaned in closer as he pointed out the various locations.

"So we concentrate on Anna's group first?" Encizo asked. "Get them clear before we go take a look at this missile base?"

"That's the way we run it. Once we have them sorted, we can decide if going on to Guang Lor is feasible."

"Does Anna have a figure on the kind of resistance

we might face if we do try for the base?" Manning asked, tracing routes across the map with his finger.

"We won't get that information until later," McCarter admitted. "But Anna's group has a man on the inside. He's already passed on some information about the place, so hopefully we'll have some data."

"Oh, that *will* be helpful," Manning said.

"I do understand the sarcasm," McCarter stated. "And I wish we had better intel. If we can't pin it down to numbers, we're not going to walk in like a bunch of amateurs."

"Can we have that in writing?"

The question was posed by James and Manning in the same breath.

McCarter glanced at Encizo, who simply shrugged.

Kai Chek Village, Guang Lor, Xinjiang, one day earlier

LOY HUNG CAUGHT the man's sleeve and pulled him inside, closing the door.

"What is so urgent?"

The man's face blanked. His gaze wandered the room, in itself an admission he was nervous.

"Kam Lee?"

Lee hung his head, hands nervously toying with the wide straw hat he held.

"Kang..."

"I know about Kang. You have had to deal with him all these months."

"I think he may have suspicions about me."

"After all this time? Why?"

Kam Lee shook his head. "A feeling. Loy, I think my time at Guang Lor may be finished."

"Then we will have to bring you out," Hung said.

Lee seemed relieved. "I will complete this assignment, then we will do it."

"So what is you need to tell me?"

"The missile test went wrong," Lee said. "Something to do with the stabilizing system. It sent the missile off course and it crashed close to the border."

"My people will have been tracking it," Hung said. "I haven't spoken to them during the last couple of days."

"There is one more thing," Lee said. "I was nearby when Controller Kwok was talking to Kang. One of the circuit boards on the missile was a stolen one. It came from America."

"Truly?" Hung asked.

"Yes."

Hung smiled. "Just what we need to prove what Beijing has been up to."

"And because of that, Kang will be working hard to get it back," Lee stated.

"Have they sent out a search party yet?"

"It's being organized now."

"Then we don't have much time," Hung said. "You are certain about this stolen board?"

"Yes. Orders came from Beijing for the test of the new missile to go ahead immediately. No excuses. The technicians were still working on the copies of the board, and they knew they wouldn't get them ready in time. Mau Sung fitted one of the stolen boards so there would be no delay. If the test had gone as planned, the board would have been destroyed when the missile hit its target and detonated."

"We have to get our hands on that board. This is better than we expected," Hung told him.

"I should return. If I stay longer, someone might notice," Lee said.

Hung nodded. "You go. I'll make contact with our team to locate the missile and retrieve the board. If we can clear the area before the search team arrives, we have a chance."

"Hung, be careful. Major Kang will be leading the search team personally. If he learns of your involvement…"

"Don't worry. I know all about Kang. His reputation doesn't alarm me," Hung replied.

"Be careful," Lee advised.

Hung waited until Lee was well away from the house. He closed up and made his way out to the rear of the building where a battered panel truck was parked against the wall. He climbed in, started up the vehicle and drove out of the settlement, picking up the dusty road heading north. Once he was clear he took a cell phone from inside his tunic and switched it on. The cell was Tri-Band and worked through a satellite signal. Hung tapped in a number and waited until his call was picked up.

"I've just learned about the missile crash. Have you found it?" Hung asked.

"Yes. We know it landed miles off track. We have it on our monitor."

Hung explained about the stolen circuit board and the need to get their hands on it.

"I'm on my way," he said. "Get the team moving. If they are close they should be able to reach the missile well before the team from Guang Lor can assemble and take off. If we locate this board, it has to be moved out of the area quickly before Major Kang can pin us down. Make sure that everyone is armed in case Kang does show up."

THREE HOURS LATER Hung met up with the group. There were five of them, all armed and ready to move. He parked his truck alongside their vehicle.

"Have you located the missile?" he asked.

Dar Tan, heading the group, nodded. He led Hung across to the team's 4x4. The rear door was open and one of the team sat over an electronic tracking system.

"Show Hung where the missile is, Sammy."

Sammy Cho, a thin, young man wearing a faded denims and a baseball cap, indicated the readout screen on his tracking station.

"We had the missile's flight path locked in from the moment it was launched," he said. "It was easy to follow the flight path. It left enough of a signature from its engines that we were able to keep it on screen. Even when it went off course we managed to keep tracking, and after it went down I was able to work out the location." Cho leaned out the door, pointing in the direction of low hills to the northeast of their position. "No more than thirty miles from here."

"Good. Can we reach it by vehicle?"

"Should not be a problem," Cho told him.

"Then we go now. I want to try to be out before Kang shows up. We'll take your 4x4. That old truck of mine isn't fit to tackle those foothills."

THE MISSILE LAY at the end of a shallow furrow it had gouged in the dry ground, coming to rest straddling a wide stream. The moment the 4x4 stopped, Hung, Tan and Cho went directly to the missile. Cho had a tool kit slung from his shoulder. The rest of the team spread out to form a protective shield, keeping watch while Cho went to work.

Hung took out a digital camera and started to take shots of the missile, following the actions of his team and what was being done.

Cho knew exactly where to go. While Tan held the open tool kit the young technician used a power-pack-driven tool to remove the flush retaining screws holding the access panel in place. The whine of the power tool was the only sound to break the silence of the desolate location. Once he had the screws out, Cho used a steel pry-bar to break the seal holding the access panel secure. With the panel free Cho leaned inside the body of the missile, probing the shadows with a flashlight until he located the section he wanted.

"Can you see it?" Tan asked.

"Wait. You know how much equipment is packed inside one of these things?"

"Cho, you can explain when we're safely back in Hong Kong with the evidence. I'll gladly listen while you present me with a detailed thesis on missile technology."

Cho made no reply. He was concentrating on getting hold of the circuit board. He had to free a number of retaining clips before he could lift out the board. Finally he had it.

Cho inspected the twelve-inch-square circuit board.

"Well?" Hung asked.

"It's the one," Cho affirmed.

Hung, who had kept taking shots as Cho worked inside the missile, focused in on the board, shooting it from both sides.

"Good. Now let's move out of here."

"Cho, take this," Tan said, handing the tech a solid, brick-shaped package. "Push it down out of sight. I've set the timer for twenty minutes, and it's activated."

Cho took the explosive device and leaned back inside the missile, sliding the package deep inside the interior.

"Time to go," he said.

They all returned to the 4x4 and climbed in. Loy Hung took the circuit board and the camera and packed them in a small backpack after wrapping each in lengths of cloth to protect them.

"Now all we have to do is deliver it."

KANG HEARD the explosion and saw smoke rising from the site.

"Sergeant, get the men moving faster."

The five-man squad broke into a trot. Kang swung around and returned to his combat vehicle. He leaned inside and spoke to the radio operator, who was also operating the tracking equipment.

"Did that come from where the missile came down?"

"Yes, Major. The signal has ended. That explosion must have destroyed the tracking device inside the missile."

Kang called his sergeant. "Spread out. If the missile has been destroyed there may be a good reason."

"Sabotage?"

"Exactly. I can't believe the missile has been down for so long and has only just exploded. That traitor Kam Lee must have passed information to the group he was spying for."

"Pity he died before he gave us any more information."

Kang shook his head. "He died because he made us kill him. It was pure luck we caught him trying to reenter Guang Lor before we left. My suspicions were simply confirmed that he was the one working undercover."

"And he had discovered the American circuit board was used in the missile? Passed it to his people?"

"A logical conclusion. Which is why they were heading for the crash site. If they got their hands on that board, it could cause Beijing great embarrassment." Kang waved an arm in the direction of the WZ-11 helicopter that had flown in to join them from Guang Lor. "Sergeant, take command of the squad. I will fly over the crash site and relay anything we see from the air. Stay in radio contact."

"Yes, Major."

Kang took his seat in the helicopter. "Get this thing airborne. Take me to the site."

Over his shoulder he instructed the door gunner. "If we see anyone moving in the vicinity, don't waste time waiting for orders. Shoot. If we are correct and Kam Lee's friends have been at the crash site, they have most probably located and removed that circuit board before sabotaging the missile. I want that board back. Understand?"

"Yes, Major Kang."

THE HELICOPTER MADE a direct flight to where the dark coils of smoke stained the sky. It took them less than ten minutes. The pilot took the chopper over the crash site. Looking down, Kang saw that there was little left of the missile. The explosion, powerful in itself, had also detonated what had remained of the missile's fuel. The resulting detonation had torn the missile apart, scattering debris in a wide circle. The actual spot where the missile had landed had been turned into a blackened crater. Kang felt his anger rise.

Damn those dissidents, he thought.

They were causing major problems. If their fate had rested in his hands, they would have been rounded up and executed long ago. Beijing hadn't been strong enough in its actions against the Pro-Democracy groups. Perhaps now they would admit the error of their ways and strike a harder blow against these people. The longer they were allowed to survive, the more popular they became among the masses. Hero status had the strength to increase their appeal.

"Take us lower," Kang instructed the pilot. "Let's see if we can spot any tracks. They won't be on foot."

The helicopter began to make wide sweeps, covering an ever-widening circle out from the crash site.

Over the next hour Kang and his ground troops checked and cross-checked the area. It was starting to reach late afternoon before they spotted anything. It was Kang's sergeant who was the first with a positive report.

"Vehicle tracks, Major. Fresh. Heading in a easterly direction. By the condition of the tire marks they can't be more than a few miles ahead."

"Good. Keep moving after them. I'll fly over and check ahead."

DAR TAN SAW the helicopter first.

"It's coming this way."

"Military?" Hung asked.

"In this part of the country, what else would it be? No one else is allowed to fly here."

"Try for cover," Hung said, "before he spots us."

"We may be too late."

Cho's remark was punctuated by the harsh rattle of a machine gun. A stream of slugs curved down from the pursuing chopper as it dropped lower to line up with the 4x4. Loy Hung watched, almost fascinated, as the line of slugs slapped the dry earth, moving closer to the speeding vehicle. Then the solid thump of the slugs hitting the ground changed to metallic sounds as they rose and peppered the rear of the 4x4. A startled cry rose from one of the team sitting in the rear as ragged slugs, deformed by the thin metal, drilled into yielding flesh. The man slumped across the rear floor of the vehicle, clutching his bloody side where the ragged chunk of metal had torn into his body. The 4x4 veered from side to side as the driver tried to escape the hovering bulk of the helicopter. The problem was the lack of escape routes. The foothills offered little in the way of substantial cover.

The helicopter dropped even lower, aligning itself alongside the 4x4. Turning his head, Hung saw the black muzzle of the 7.62 mm door-mounted machine gun swing around. He tried to shout a warning, but his words were lost in the harsh rattle of the machine gun. The heavy stream of slugs tore into and through the bodywork of the 4x4. Window glass shattered, shards hitting exposed flesh, Hung himself felt a sudden burn of pain across his cheek, then felt the warm stream of blood. The lurching 4x4 hit a rough stretch of ground, and the wheel was being wrenched from the slack hands of the driver. Only now did Hung realize the man had taken a number of the 7.62 mm rounds down one side of his body. He was slumped back in his seat, sightless eyes ignoring the hazards ahead. More machine-gun fire sounded, bullets clanging against the sides of the vehicle as it ran out of control. It made a sharp right turn, careering over a steep ridge, and bounced its way down a long, rocky slope, finally coming to a jarring stop at the bottom of a gully.

THE GULLY was too narrow to allow the helicopter access. All it could do was hover while Kang screamed into his handset for his ground troops to locate the stricken vehicle. It would take them almost thirty minutes to reach the base of the gully, where they found the 4x4 and three dead occupants.

Loy Hung, Dar Tan and Sammy Cho were gone.

And so, too, was the circuit board.

IT WAS near dark, freezing cold with food or water, and Sammy Cho was wounded. He had taken a couple of bullets in his right side.

But at least they had their weapons and the circuit board.

Loy Hung hoped that was enough. They were alone in the foothills, being pursued by Major Kang and his squad, which was as bad as it could get. At least, Hung thought, the major was denied the use of his helicopter until dawn. The machine was of little use in the dark, so Kang was having to depend on his ground troops.

It gave Hung and his men something of a chance to stay ahead. Not much, but at least a little advantage.

"Loy, we have to stop," Dar Tan called. "Sammy's wounds are bleeding again."

They crouched in the semidarkness, able to see only what the thin moonlight allowed. While Hung kept watch, Tan did what he could for Cho. Tan had managed to rescue the first-aid bag from the 4x4 when they had been forced to abandon it. The bag held only basic first-aid items, certainly not advanced enough to deal with two bullet wounds. Tan had used some of the sterile pads to cover the holes, then bound them in place with some of the bandage from a roll. For his part Sammy Cho made no sound, offered no complaints and managed to keep up with his partners.

That had been three hours ago. Now Cho was showing signs of slowing down. He kept stumbling and when Tan had a look at his bandage he saw it was oozing blood heavily. When Cho fell to his knees this last time, he couldn't get up.

"You should leave me. I can hold them off for you."

"So you can be a hero?" Tan smiled at his friend. "You'd love that. So all the girls can flock around you while you tell the story?"

While he spoke to distract Cho, his fingers loosened the sodden bandage. Peeling back the inner dressing, he saw that the bullet wounds had swollen around the entry points. They were still bleeding, too. Tan feared they had become infected. His problem was that he had little idea what he really needed to do. The bullets needed extracting and the wounds cleaning and sealing. For once in his life Tan felt utterly helpless.

"That bad?" Cho asked. "Must be to stop you talking, Dar."

"Sammy, I wish I could do more for you. But this is something I can't deal with."

Hung knelt beside them. "Can you keep moving? I

think we're not far from the village now. If we get there we only have to wait for Mei Anna and her friends. They'll surely have someone experienced to deal with your wounds."

"Well, I don't have many other choices, do I?"

Tan dressed the wounds and replaced the bloody bandage with a fresh one. They stayed for a little while longer, giving Cho more rest.

Hung took a look around, checking the direction they had come. If it had been daylight, he might have been able to spot Kang's men. The semidark, layering the terrain with deep shadows, made it impossible to identify anything. He decided they would just have to keep moving, hoping the encroaching night would slow Kang as much as it had them. He preferred that way of thinking rather than imagining everything was running smoothly for their pursuers.

Their luck seemed to be holding. Despite the fact they had to move slowly, they spotted the village just after midnight. The temperature had dropped even further. The wind coming down from the higher slopes of the hills dragged at their clothing, pushing them around, and with the ground underfoot being unsafe, it made travel difficult.

"Will Kang know about this place?" Tan asked.

"He might, but what else can we do?" Hung said. "If we stay in the open, we might freeze. Out here we're too exposed. If we can get under cover, we'll be out of the wind and at least have a place to defend."

"When you say it like that," Tan remarked, the trace of irony in his voice not lost on Hung.

"I didn't expect it to turn out like this, Dar. This wasn't the plan."

"I'm not blaming you. We all knew what we were letting ourselves get into when we joined the group. I don't regret it. I just hope we have the chance to make something out of this. It would be a shame if we lost everything after getting this far."

They reached the village a short time later, making their way past the razed buildings until they reached the one remaining that would still provide some shelter. This semiderelict house still had a couple of rooms and a door they could close against the bite of the wind. Pushing open the door they got the semiconscious Cho inside. Hung secured the door, then crossed to the single window slot that allowed him to look back the way they had come.

Tan had Cho propped up in a corner. He found some discarded, dusty blankets and covered the man as best he could. Then he joined Hung at the window.

"It's the best we can do. Pity we can't risk a fire to get a little heat in here."

Hung squatted with his back to the wall, hugging the backpack that contained the circuit board to his body.

"The only thing we can do now is wait."

CHAPTER THREE

Townsend Ranch, South Texas

Oliver Townsend, former Major Oliver Townsend, U.S. Army, retired from active service for the past three years, was the driving force behind the covert organization Shadow. Depending on your stand, Shadow was either an inspired business enterprise or an illegal operation.

As far as Townsend was concerned, his operation was pure genius. In a world dominated by global enterprises, many of them partly funded and under the protective umbrella of federal government, Shadow might have been small. It did, however, cater to a specific need—that of providing military ordnance and technology to the specific requirements of its clientele. In essence Townsend did his business with those customers who, by whatever misdeed, were considered untouchable by the legitimate suppliers. There was a great deal of hypocrisy in that. It was a well-documented fact that overseas regimes once favored by government could fall into the black hole of becoming non gratis due to political expediency, power change or not adhering to nonspecified rules. The delicate balance in the political game was easily tipped. Today's friend was tomorrow's enemy. It was a simple equation that highlighted the power struggles and the watch-your-back mentality.

Townsend had been a spectator to much of this during his military career, his final two years spent at the Pentagon, and he had realized that there was much to be made from the infinitely complex machinations of the strategy game. He had acquired a great deal of insight, background knowledge and, importantly, contacts, a number of whom were instrumental in backing his enterprise and working behind the scenes. They were powerful men, their influence running deep in financial, industrial and political circles, and Townsend was well versed in the way they operated behind closed doors.

With his backers on board, Townsend began to formulate the operation that would both fund his retirement and occupy his time. He saw an opportunity and he reached out and took it. There was a certain irony in his decision. His retirement had been forced on him through one of the manpower cut-back initiatives the military machine had devised. Men of his age were being offered early retirement because they no longer fitted into the scheme. The Pentagon wanted younger blood, officers who would slot neatly into the new technological era. Townsend made little fuss. He saw the writing on the wall and figured he might as well go quietly, taking with him all the information he had gathered and channeling it into his own personal data pool.

Within twelve months of the parting of the ways Townsend had his organization up and running. With his backing secured, Townsend recruited his team of specialists and his newly formed Shadow was already doing business. His first clients had been based in Asia. He had taken on the contract and supplied them with the ordnance they needed. The deal was conducted efficiently, the funds placed in a Swiss account Townsend's moneyman had set up, and the client suggesting Townsend get in touch with a number of other groups who needed similar deals processing. Shadow's efficiency was noticed, and over the next year Townsend saw his turnover increase substantially. The people he was dealing with had an urgent need for what he could supply, plus there was the added advantage they paid well and needed anonymity.

Now Shadow was not only operating from a strong business base but had expanded into another area entirely. Townsend was being asked to supply not just ordnance, but technology centered around advanced weaponry and electronics. He had done some research and found that industrial espionage, as it was designated, had a higher premium comeback. One deal in this sector would net him more than his entire income since he had started the enterprise. He discussed this with his people and the consensus was it had extreme possibilities.

Shadow had its contacts within military and government research communities, and once Townsend started to look further he realized that obtaining sensitive material was not outside his scope. He used his knowledge of how the military-industrial setup worked to his advantage. As well as employing monetary enticements, Townsend got his people to look into the backgrounds of people in top-secret areas. It wasn't long before there was a stack of files on a number of key players, containing details of gambling debts, infidelities both financial and sexual, anything that could be used as a lever was employed.

Townsend learned something about himself during this stage. He found he had no conscience or moral restraint when it came to blackmail, coercion or downright threats. It was a part of his makeup he hadn't been aware of before. Now it had surfaced he found he liked that side of his character. He was enjoying his new career, the money, the power and the sensation that he was defying the odds each time he went into a new venture. The illicit thrill engendered by the whole risky game was as much of a high as the money. The expansion of his organization, moving into something far beyond selling a few crates of automatic weapons, really hit the right spot for him.

The call from an intermediary asking for a meet in Paris with his main client had intrigued Townsend. The initial conversation hinted that any possible arranged deal would be worth an extremely high fee. This part of the conversation interested Townsend even more. His trip to Paris was to be paid for, as was his accommodation in a five-star hotel in the city. Townsend agreed to the meeting. A return ticket and hotel reservation were delivered by courier two hours later. The flight was due to leave that afternoon. By the evening of the next day Townsend was sitting in his hotel suite awaiting the call that would summon him to his meeting with his yet-to-be-identified client.

He had no idea just what he was going to be asked to provide. The hinted-at amount of his fee, being so astronomical, suggested something extremely high-tech and of great importance.

What was he going to be asked to do? Steal the latest U.S. Air Force fighter plane? Hijack a Navy submarine? He leaned back in the comfortable armchair, toying with the glass of fine French brandy, and let his imagination run wild. He hoped that when he did get the request it wouldn't be a disappointment.

He was picked up an hour later and driven in a comfortable limousine to the outskirts of Paris and a château on the edge of the Seine. The house was more than four hundred years old, beautifully maintained and very private.

Townsend was met at the massive front entrance by an unsmiling Chinese in an expensive suit and immaculate shirt and tie. He was led inside the château, across the marble entrance hall, and shown into a pleasant, sunny room that looked out onto smooth lawns that led to the river. The door closed quietly behind him and Townsend found himself in the presence of a powerful-looking Chinese in his forties.

"Please take a seat. Do I call you Major, or is it now Mr. Townsend?"

"I left the rank behind when I left military service," Townsend said.

"Mr. Townsend, my name is Su Han. I am director of the Second Department, Intelligence, of the PLA, and I would like to commission your organization to procure certain items for me. These items will be held in the strictest security by the U.S. government and will not be easy to get to."

"Director Han, that is why you have come to me. My organization is dedicated to providing what our clients ask for. I'm sure you have done your checks on Shadow. If you have, then you will have seen we haven't failed once to fill our obligations."

"Quite so, Mr. Townsend. I am extremely impressed by your record of successes."

"All praise is gratefully received."

"From what I have learned, you have no problem relieving the American government of weaponry, electronics and the like."

"Why not? Like all governments, the U.S. administration has no hang-ups when it comes to selling its wares if it decides a certain regime suits its purpose. As far as I'm concerned, Director Han, we are in a global bazaar. Supply and demand. It was what America was born for."

Han reached down to a folder resting on the small table beside his chair. He opened it and offered it to Townsend.

"You may find my needs unusual. They are, however, strictly in accordance with current trends in defensive weaponry. In brief, China has an urgent need to bring herself in line with the present level attained by America and Russia. Our leadership cannot tolerate the advances made by Russia especially. The stalemate is too biased in favor of the U.S. and Russia. We need to redress that balance."

"And to save time on development you need samples of the latest U.S. hard and software?"

"Exactly, Mr. Townsend. As for example, the circuit board on the first page. If we could have one of those, our technicians would be able to reproduce it and we would have saved two maybe three years of trial and error."

"Very astute, Director." Townsend smiled. "Let me work on this list. I need to do some checking. Get my people to assess how we could do this."

"I take it you are interested in a deal?"

"As they say in my country, you can take that to the bank."

"Take your time, Mr. Townsend. Anything you need should be available here. We have a communications room so you can confer with your people in the U.S. All lines are secure."

"I would expect nothing less from you, Director Han."

Han called out in his native tongue and the man who had met Townsend at the door entered the room.

"Show our guest to the communications center. He is to have complete privacy. No disturbances of any kind."

The man nodded.

"Director Han, I will try to have some positive answers for you by midday."

Neither man had broached the subject of money. It seemed to Townsend that it would appear churlish if he brought up payment at this time, and Han was plainly from the old school, where payment remained hidden discreetly out of sight until everything else had been cleared.

The communications center was situated in a room at the rear of the château and contained telephones, computers and a fax machine. Everything was the most up-to-date on the market, and Townsend noted wryly that it was all of Japanese origin. The door closed behind his escort, leaving the American on his own. He sat at the desk and used one of the satellite phones to call his U.S. base. Within a couple of minutes he had Ralph Chomski, his second in command, on the line.

Chomski, ex-Air Force intelligence, had been with Townsend from day one. He was a man who existed for life's challenges. His contacts were legion, stretching from the military through both civilian contractors and even a number of covert agencies who handled a great deal of what was known as black ops. He hated being defeated by any problem and would do anything to make sure he came out on top. He had a small but influential list of people within government who could be persuaded to help. He would never divulge exactly what he had as leverage, and Townsend didn't push him on that, content to accept that Chomski could deliver when required. Chomski listened as Townsend sketched in Han's needs without being too specific.

"I'll e-mail you the list in a few minutes. I need confirmation we can get what the man requires as soon as possible. Ralph, we could do extremely well on this."

"Sounds interesting," Chomski said, and Townsend could sense the rising excitement in his voice at the thought.

"Calm down, Ralph. Don't wet your pants too soon. Look at the list first."

As soon as he finished his conversation, Townsend used the computer setup to scan Han's list and forward it as an attachment to an e-mail he sent to Chomski. He received an acknowledgment within a minute and knew that his second in command would be checking the list and working on ways to obtain the goods.

Townsend returned to find Han, informing him that urgent attention was being given to the list and he would have an answer within a short time. Han nodded, content, and invited Townsend on a tour of the house and grounds.

Two hours later Townsend had a call from Chomski, guaranteeing they could fill the order. Townsend informed Han, confident that if Chomski said yes they were in business.

"Excellent, Mr. Townsend. I hope you will dine with me this evening before you return to the U.S.A."

"My pleasure, Director. Then I must leave. I have a lot to arrange."

Townsend was back at his hotel by nine that night. He retired early and by midmorning the following day was settling in his seat on the plane that would take him to the States.

That had been six months ago...

Longhorn Bar, Landry Flats, South Texas Border Country

T. J. HAWKINS CAUGHT a glimpse of Carl Lyons as the Able Team leader paused in the doorway, scanning the bar's interior. The moment he spotted Hawkins, Lyons made directly for him, coming to a halt at the table.

"You think I don't have anything better to do than chase all over the damn place? I told you once before, Hawkins, nobody skips on me."

Hawkins carried on drinking, aware of every eye in the place focused on his table.

"Playing dumb isn't going to buy you a ticket home."

This time Hawkins sat upright, leaning against the rear of the booth. He faced Lyons.

"And am I supposed to be worried? What are you going to do, rooster? Crow loud enough so everyone can hear? All I'm doing is having a quiet drink. There's no law against that. I haven't broken any rules, so back off, Jenks. I'm not in the fuckin' Army no more. I don't have to listen to you."

"Listen, asshole, we had a deal. It's time to settle."

Hawkins shook his head. "Deal's off. You didn't come through on your end. Or have you forgotten that?"

Lyons reached out and caught hold of Hawkins's coat, hauling him upright. He swung the younger man around, slamming him against the wall, then pinned him there with one big hand.

"You could die right here, Hawkins."

"Then are you going to shoot all these witnesses? I don't think even you could cover that up, Jenks."

"Maybe I'll risk it. Be worth the sight of you with your guts spread over this floor. I don't like people going back on a deal."

"Yeah, right. Jenks, you screwed up. You lost the merchandise and now you expect me to bail you out. Open your eyes, pal. It don't work that way. We both know you're trying to put the squeeze on because your boss is going to be pissed at you." Hawkins slapped Lyons's hands from his chest, then stiff-armed him away, pushing the man across the floor. "Go tell him what happened. Get the hell off my back. It's not my problem. Now fuck off before I find my gun and put *you* down."

Lyons made a show of bluster, but eventually backed away. He jabbed a finger at Hawkins.

"You and me got this to settle. This isn't over, Hawkins." He stared around the bar, face taut with anger.

"Jenks, this *is* finished."

Lyons backed off a step, refusing to meet Hawkins's eye. After a moment he spun around, glaring at the rest of the bar's customers.

"Seen enough, you assholes? Get back to your bottles, losers."

He turned and barged his way out of the bar, slamming the door behind him. A long silence ensued until a single voice broke it.

"Still bucking the odds, T.J.?"

Hawkins turned and watched as Vic Lerner moved away from his stool at the bar and crossed the room. He peered at Lerner, pretending he wasn't certain he recognized the man.

"Vic? Where in hell did you spring from, buddy?"

"I was here awhile. Didn't pay much attention until you made your little stand against the bully boy." Lerner threw out a hand and slapped Hawkins on the shoulder. "Hell, T.J., how long has it been?"

"Too damn long. Hey, where's the uniform?"

"I dumped that a while back. Had my belly full of being ordered around."

"Yeah, I been there, done that."

"I haven't forgotten. Man, they really did the dirty on you in Somalia."

Hawkins shrugged. "The system always gets you in the end. Let me buy you a drink, Vic."

Lerner had already turned, gesturing to the bartender. He had quickly sized up Hawkins's shabby appearance, figuring his former Army buddy wasn't exactly walking around with too much in his pockets. When he returned with a couple of beers, Hawkins had taken his seat again. Lerner placed the chilled bottles on the table, pushing one across to Hawkins.

"Here's to when we did have some good times, T.J."

Hawkins lifted the bottle and drank. He brushed at his creased shirt. "Seems you caught me on an off day, Vic. I need to do my laundry."

"Got to admit I've seen you looking better in the middle of a firefight, T.J."

Hawkins gave a vague shrug, reaching for his glass again. "To better days."

"So what happened after you left the service?"

"Things kind of went on a downward spiral. What the hell, Vic, I was trained as a damned soldier, not a brush salesman. Tried different things but nothing lasted. Money was scarce. I wasn't pulling much in, so I started looking around for anything where I could put my training to use. You know what? Ain't much there. Almost hooked up with a mercenary group going to Africa. Missed the boat there, too. Funny, I heard a month later the whole crew were wiped out by some local militia. So I guess my luck stayed with me that day."

"And now?"

"I scratch around. Do a little social drinking, if you know what I mean. But I'm not eating too high off the hog, and that old pickup outside on the lot is the best I can afford right now."

"What you working on now?"

"Now? Right now I'm drinking with an old Army buddy who looks like *he* won first prize."

Lerner smiled. "Can't complain." He hesitated for a moment. "T.J., you up for a job?"

Hawkins toyed with his glass. "Is it legal?"

Lerner laughed. "Does it make a difference?"

"Hell, no. That deal I had with that jerk who was here wasn't exactly tax deductible. Anything that kicks the honest and upright's ass is just what I need. Walking the line didn't do me any good. I did the right thing and the Army booted me out. Honorable discharge— that was their way of getting rid of me."

"How about we get out of here? Let me buy you a decent meal and make a call. Could be I can find you a place with the people I work with. Hell, T.J., you got the credentials we're looking for."

"Sounds good to me."

Lerner led the way out of the bar. His vehicle was parked at the edge of the lot. A dark metallic-gray Blazer.

"Cool-looking truck," Hawkins said.

"What about yours?"

Hawkins grinned. He pointed across the lot to a battered and sad-looking Chevy pickup. The once-red paintwork had faded to a dull pink and numerous scratches showed rust.

"Some set of fancy wheels."

"You said it, Vic."

"Where did you buy that?"

"Let's say it's kind of borrowed. I don't even have insurance, or papers for it."

"That kind, huh?" Lerner grinned. "You bothered about leaving it lay?"

"Hell, no, the tank's about dry anyhow." Hawkins hesitated. "You mind if I pick up my bag?"

"Go fetch it."

Lerner used his remote to unlock his truck and climbed in. He waited until Hawkins returned with a scruffy duffel over his shoulder. Opening the passenger door, Hawkins tossed his bag on the rear seat and settled in the passenger seat as Lerner fired up the powerful engine.

"Sweet sound." He patted the leather seat. "I might move in. This is better than the trailer I'm living in right now."

"Don't worry, buddy," Lerner said, "if this works out, you could be running around in one of these."

As Lerner drove out of the lot, dust spewing up from beneath the heavy tires, Hawkins sank into the comfort of the seat, almost closing his eyes.

"Who do I have to kill to get one of these?" he asked. "Just remember that I got my own fantasy list to work through first."

"That bad?"

"Fuck, Vic, look at me. One step off being a tramp. Man, I've been so long on the downslide I forgot what it's like to walk tall. Be honest? If you can get me something I'm in. Man, I just want to climb out of this damn hole I been stuck in for too long."

"OUR TWO-DAY STAKEOUT paid off. Looks like Lerner took the bait. He and T.J. just took off in Lerner's truck. They headed west. That's in the direction of the Townsend ranch. We'll hang back. Give them some space until we know if it's taken."

"Keep us updated, Carl," Price said. "Just don't let anything happen to T.J. or we'll have World War McCarter on our hands."

Lyons smiled bleakly. He wasn't a man to be fazed by anything, but given a choice between a room full of cobras and David McCarter on the prod, he admitted he would go for the snakes.

"Talk to you," he said, and broke the cell phone connection.

He picked up the transceiver on the seat beside him and called Blancanales. "T.J. and Lerner in a metallic-gray Blazer heading your way, Pol." He recited the license number. "Give them room. All we do now is watch and wait."

"Understood."

Lyons called Hermann Schwarz.

"The Politician has them under surveillance. They took off west from the bar."

"Okay. What do we do?"

"Head back to the motel for now. We'll coordinate once we hear from Pol or T.J."

"MR. TOWNSEND, THIS IS T. J. Hawkins, the feller I called you about. We were in the service together until he got in a jam."

"Heard about your trouble," Townsend said. "You're not the first to end up on the wrong end of military injustice. Might make a man want to get even. How do you feel on that score?"

"I think you already know that, Mr. Townsend. Since Vic called earlier, you probably have most there is to know about me."

Townsend smiled. He jerked a thumb at the computer setup on the corner of his wide desk.

"We live in the age of information, Hawkins. Press a button and a man's life spills right across your monitor."

Don't I know it, Hawkins thought. And now I also know I'm looking at your own information bank.

Hawkins waited. He wanted to see how Kurtzman's data implants had colored his files. It was surprising, and a little scary, to realize just what could be done to someone's background in the hands of a man like Aaron Kurtzman.

"Seems you've had quite a ride since you quit the military. Close scrapes with the law. What was that little fracas you had down in Albuquerque? They pulled you in for suspected dealings in illegal weapons. How come you walked away clean?"

Hawkins gave an embarrassed shrug. "I was kind of expecting problems, so I made sure I was well covered before the Border Patrol moved in. They searched, but they didn't find a damn thing. While they were busting me, my deal was going through somewhere else."

Townsend smiled. "So how come you're walking around like a bum?"

"The deal was small-time, Mr. Townsend. By the time I paid off everyone it didn't leave me with much, and the cops were still dogging me. I like making money. Problem is, I'm not too hot when it comes to working the financial side. So I had to move on. Since then, well, I guess my luck kind of went south."

"With your guns by the sound of it," Townsend said. "Your latest deal kind of bit you in the ass I hear."

"Something like that."

"Hawkins, I don't deal small," Townsend said. "You sound like the kind of man we could use. But don't be fooled into thinking I tolerate any stupidity. Fuck around with me, and you'll wish the Border Patrol *had* caught you. A stretch in Huntsville would be a vacation compared to what I could do to you." He met Hawkins's unflinching gaze. "Are we clear on that?"

"Yes, sir, Mr. Townsend. Understood. I might not be too smart with finance operations, but I know how to take orders."

Townsend visibly relaxed. "Fine. Vic, can you make room for Hawkins?"

"Sure. Plenty of spare rooms in the bunkhouse."

"Get him some clothes and whatever he needs. Hawkins, there's something coming up shortly. You can handle it with Vic. Let's see if you're as good as your rap sheet says."

When Hawkins and Lerner left the office, Townsend turned to Ralph Chomski, who had been standing quietly to one side, observing. "Do the usual, Ralph. Keep an eye on him. See if he does anything we should be suspicious of. If he behaves himself, fine. If there's anything, *anything,* that doesn't sit right, you know what to do."

"Oh, I know what to do," Chomski said, his mood lightening at the thought.

"Now let's have Mr. Kibble in here. I have a feeling I'm not going to be too happy with what *he* has to tell me."

Chomski left the room. He was back a couple of minutes later, accompanied by a sandy-haired man in his early forties. Townsend indicated a seat in front of his desk.

"You have a good flight?"

The man nodded, his expression indicating he was in no mood for small talk.

"Sit down, Mark, and tell me what the problem is."

Mark Kibble took the offered seat. He sat on the edge, refusing to allow himself to relax, and Townsend took that as a bad sign. The man was so tense he would snap in two if he bent over.

"The problem is, I can't complete the arrangement."

Behind Kibble there was movement. It was Chomski. He already had his hand inside his jacket. Townsend caught his eye and gave a slight shake of his head.

"Take your time, Mark. Tell me what the problem is. Would you like a drink?"

Kibble raised a hand in a gesture of refusal. "I need to get this said."

"Fine. Go ahead."

"There's been some kind of security initiative. I don't know where it came from, but the entire setup has been upgraded. New people running things. All codes changed and a fresh protocol put into place. They're even installing some new hand-print identification procedure. One of those gizmos where you have to place your hand on a pad and it scans your fingerprints against records held in the computer. They took mine yesterday, and they have introduced more frequent stop and searches. There's no way I can risk taking anything out now."

"And you haven't had any directives telling you why all this is happening?"

"Not a thing. Someone did ask, and they were told it was none of their business and to carry on with their work."

"Do you think it might have to do with the missing items?"

Kibble shrugged.

He was running scared, Townsend realized, and a frightened man might easily let something slip.

"What do we do?"

Townsend smiled. He knew what *he* had to do. But not here. Not now.

"Mark, let's not get ahead of ourselves. We need to take stock. Stand back and look at this calmly. There will be a way around it."

Kibble shook his head. "No. I'm out. If I got caught, I'd end up in some federal facility and I won't risk that. Jesus, it would ruin my family. I have a wife. Children."

"And you have a great deal of money hidden away in that special account we help you set up."

"I'll give the money back. It isn't worth all this risk."

Kibble was sweating now. He was ready to cave.

The next step could be running to the Feds and telling them everything if it would help to pull him out of the deep, dark hole threatening to swallow him.

"I don't see there being any need for that, Mark. You already earned that money for previous transactions."

Townsend took a long moment to consider his next move. He wanted Kibble out of his house, well away before anything happened, because that was the next move.

"I just can't do this anymore," Kibble said, pushing to his feet.

"Okay, Mark. Leave it with me. I understand your position and I won't push you into anything you can't do. Perhaps it's time to back off and let things cool for a while. Give things a chance to settle down. You agree?"

Kibble nodded, a little of the tension draining from his face. He watched Townsend stand and cross over to face him.

"I'm sorry this had to happen," Kibble said.

"Like I said, Mark, don't worry. We'll figure a way around this mess. Go home. Be with your family. Someone will run you back to the strip and the Lear can fly you back to Dayton."

Chomski waited until Kibble cleared the room before he spoke.

"He'll do it," he said. "Somebody gives him a hard time, he'll spill his guts and point the finger. We can't let that happen."

"Nicely put, Ralph," Townsend said. "You'll never win prizes for diplomacy, but you head straight to the heart."

"So?"

"Send a couple of the boys with him. Make sure they deal with it quietly. Just make sure there are no tracks that lead back to us. Fly him back home as excess cargo. Let his body be found by his local cops."

Chomski turned and left the room, closing the door.

Townsend sat, staring out the window.

"That boy sure likes his work," he said, voicing his thoughts.

Now that Kibble was out of the loop, he needed to work on his second string at RossJacklin Inc. He had to have the secondary circuit board. It was necessary if he wanted to deliver the full package to Director Han. Necessary and, more importantly, it would demonstrate Shadow's ability to always complete its contracts. Since taking on the Chinese client, Townsend had profited greatly. His initial deliveries of vital components to the facility at Guang Lor had resulted in six-figure cash amounts being deposited in his Swiss account. There had been no delays, no complications. Han, as if to prove a point, had made immediate deposits, and had followed up with calls to Townsend to make certain the money had arrived safely. The man certainly knew how to maintain customer-client relations on an even footing. Townsend understood the courtesy. It was part of established Chinese custom. They understood the need for both the hard and the soft approach to negotiating a deal. Strict lines of communication, with everything handled quietly, resulted in a harmonious relationship. The American also knew there was another side to Director Han. It would only be revealed if Townsend failed to live up to his promises. The claws of the dragon would show and persuasive words would be lost in the roar of chastisement.

He was in no doubt that Han would exact severe retribution if matters fell below his exacting standards.

Townsend assessed the situation. He realized why the security upgrade had happened. It was because of the CIA's surveillance of the recent transaction. Bad enough that the Agency had gotten close enough to be on the spot during an exchange. Townsend's CIA contact had prepared Townsend beforehand, allowing him to put on a display and had enforced the setup himself, leaving the Agency in no doubt as to what they could expect if they tried to interfere. They had nothing solid to move with and as long as Townsend could stay one step in front he would survive. It was all to do with keeping the balls in the air at the same time. Risk management came with the package. All Townsend had to do was to move the lines of engagement.

He picked up his telephone and punched in a number. He let it ring until a message clicked in. He waited until he was requested to speak.

"Call my number, Raymond. We need to talk. And it is urgent. I'll expect your call back soon. Don't make me wait too long."

WHEN HE THOUGHT BACK to the night of the killing of the three CIA agents, it had taken a couple of hours for Pete Tilman to take in the full realization of what he had done, that there was no going back. He was fully committed now, even more than he had been before pulling the trigger. Yet even with that acceptance of having stepped over a line that wouldn't let him go back, he felt little in the way of remorse. He lived in an uncaring world. One that decreed a man stand or fall by his own actions, and if he wanted to survive he had to make his stand for what he believed in. His actions had been dictated by that need for survival and his fear of being discovered.

His desertion from the path of loyalty to his chosen profession had been easy at first. The illicit thrill of playing a dangerous game had become a narcotic, fueled by the financial rewards and the closeness to men of power and influence. There was, too, the choice he made to kick back against the hypocrisy of the administration that preached one line of policy, while at the same time consorting with the devil. Government within government was no fantasy. Infighting and self-advancement created strange partnerships. Hidden agendas and the lust for power and wealth layered the administration with secret alliances and back-door dealing that would have astounded the naive and the innocent. As an agent within the CIA, Tilman had been privy to certain aspects of the Agency that had surprised him at first, but as his own experiences clouded his clear vision he began to see the world in a different light. What was good for America became blurred within the twists and turns of policy, and there were those in power who were working, not for the elected administration, but for their own goals. And with these insights Pete Tilman's disenchantment soured his view of what was good and what was evil.

His move from the path he had walked initially to his crossover came about painlessly. He hadn't realized that his casual remarks at an embassy party in Washington had been overheard by someone from a group influencing illicit operations from the corridors of power. Within days of the party Tilman had been approached by a young woman he had briefly met that evening. It wasn't until later that he realized he had been drawn into a relationship with her. By then he was so smitten he would have denounced the President himself. Tilman already lived beyond his means. He owed money. He wanted more money. It was as simple as that. And he was fast losing faith with the agency, tired of being pushed around by younger, lesser men who were rising rapidly while he seemed to be standing still, despite his impressive record. She had suggested he meet someone who could offer him a promising future, someone who could use his skills and his position in the Agency. His desire for her sucked him even deeper. He was addicted, and there wasn't a thing he could do to break the habit. In his private moments he accepted his weakness. It scared him a little, but he quickly got over that feeling. One phone call, hearing her voice, a few minutes of being with her and drinking in the sweet scent of her, and he was a total devotee and would have committed murder at her suggestion.

In the end he did just that, gunning down three fellow agents in a moment of desire to maintain his new lifestyle and his position within the organization that now called the tune he willingly danced to.

Financial rewards were offered and taken without consideration of possible repercussions. Tilman had taken on board the full package. The people he was secretly working for, while maintaining his position within the CIA, expected results and he found he was able to comply comfortably. His Agency classification gave him access to high-level data. It allowed him to view sensitive material, check operational dispersement and gain advance warning of upcoming operations. Once he had carried out a number of these clandestine procedures with no comeback, the illicit excitement had made him eager for more. It was almost a secondary sexual thrill, this dangerous game he was playing, but it was *so* addictive. It gave him back the buzz he had almost forgotten, the kind of feeling he used to get in the old days when he'd run his own team and was involved in covert operations.

By this time Tilman was well involved with Townsend and his operation. He worked closely with the man, manipulating Agency information leaks and making sure that Shadow remained just that—a whisper of a murmur, kept discreetly out of the limelight and always just beyond the reach of the authorities.

The information concerning the Agency operation intended to gain evidence against the Oliver Townsend organization raised concern with Tilman's employers. Townsend was one of the principal players within the consortium buying and selling U.S. technology and ordnance. The word filtered down to Tilman that any exposure of Shadow could create a ripple effect that would engulf them all. The cards would fall and they would all be taken down. Tilman, able to access operational details, was given the task of making sure the CIA operation failed. He was told that he had a free hand in solving the problem. Dead men didn't point fingers.

The remark was the last thing Tilman was told as the meeting ended. He repeated those chilling words over and over as he drove home, and by the time he reached his apartment his decision had been made. It wouldn't be the first time he had killed. It had been part of his remit for so long it had become just another facet of his

Agency work. Tilman had done wetwork for the Agency during operations in Central America. The concept didn't cause him any moral problems. The atrocities man carried out against his fellow humans were well documented within the CIA. Tilman had viewed evidence in sound and pictures. He had seen videotapes that made the twisted outpourings of Hollywood look like kid stuff. So the acceptance of carrying out an execution-style killing settled easily on his shoulders. It was a necessity, something that was required to maintain the security of the people and the organization that he had become a part of. The bottom line was Tilman's reluctance to lose what he had gained, including the woman who had first lured him. In an odd twist she had become as attracted to him as he was to her. Their relationship had developed into one of mutual dependency, spiced by lust and a craving for the excitement of the experience.

It had been easy to find out the location of the surveillance unit. Tilman pinpointed where the assault team would be waiting, finding that he would be able to approach the truck free and clear. It would be parked in a secluded position where it could monitor the event planned to go down. Tilman was able to park his unmarked car well away from the location and work his way through the timbered area that lay on the blind side of the parked truck.

Tilman had chosen an unregistered 9 mm Uzi he had obtained a few years back during an operation. The weapon had been brought into the States by some illegals and had fallen into Tilman's hands at an opportune moment. The weapon was brand-new, had never been fired, and he had kept it on an impulse. He'd brought the weapon out of mothballs, fitted it with a suppressor and used it on the night he'd shot the three agents on the surveillance stakeout. The silent kill allowed Tilman to make his retreat without interruption. He had climbed into the waiting car and had driven quietly away, long gone before the waiting assault team became aware something was wrong and the surveillance team was out of communication. The car was one he had from the department pool. It was equipped with CIA plates that were untraceable. And when Tilman returned to his block and parked in the basement garage, he took the Uzi with him to his apartment, cleaned it thoroughly and returned it to its hiding place.

He had been in the shower when the call came in about the killings. Suitably shocked he had readily accepted the order to return to the Agency and assist in the investigation that was gathering momentum. He had, with others from his section, remained on duty over the next couple of days. At the end of it there had been little solid evidence forthcoming. The investigation had been pushed to the higher echelons of the Agency.

It wasn't until some time later that Tilman learned from inside sources of the transmission from the surveillance vehicle that the late Agent Schofield had appeared to recognize his killer. It also came as something of a shock that he learned the murder weapon had been identified as an Uzi. He had experienced brief panic, but had calmed himself with the knowledge it meant little in itself. The sound of an Uzi did nothing to pin down the actual weapon or who had fired it. The added factor—Schofield appearing to recognize his killer—concerned him a little more. He spoke about it to Townsend. The man was more annoyed than overly concerned.

"Okay, so Schofield saw you. That's as far as it goes, Pete. He didn't say your name. He didn't write it in blood because he was dead when you left. He *was* dead, wasn't he?"

"What do you think I am? Some amateur? Yes, they were all dead. I made sure of that."

"So the Agency is walking around in the dark. All they have are theories. Just theories. Quit gripin', Pete. Let's move on. We got bigger things to deal with."

THE LAST TO ARRIVE WAS Joseph Riotta. He was Townsend's negotiator, the man who handled the smooth running of deals and doing most of the financial arrangements. Riotta, a lean, balding man in his thirties, had a natural affinity for organizing money transactions. He was meticulous, sometimes too abrasive, but no one could come anywhere near to matching his skill when it came to working the clients. He came out onto the patio, wearing a neat suit and button-down shirt. His only concession to the informal occasion was that he hadn't put on a tie.

Townsend was already seated at the table with Tilman and Ralph Chomski. They were dressed in casual, light clothing and were already into their second round of drinks.

"Joseph, fill yourself a glass and join us," Townsend said. He turned back to the table. "So what's the latest from our pals in the CIA?"

"Can't put my finger on it," Tilman said, "but the Agency has gone quiet on the killings. Hardly ever mention it anymore. It's weird. Like they've decided not to chase the case any further."

"Doesn't sound natural to me," Chomski said. "Like

the cops shelving an investigation after one of their own gets hit. I've never heard of that ever happening. And I figure the spooks would be the same. You sure you haven't been shut out, Pete? Like it's gone to a higher level?"

"Or maybe they have a suspect and they don't want him to know," Riotta said as he joined them, a tall glass of iced fruit juice in his hand.

Tilman glanced across at him, a faint smile on his face. "It doesn't work like that in the Agency, Joseph. If I was a suspect in the killing of three agents, I wouldn't be sitting here. I would be locked away in a deep, dark place having the crap kicked out of me. Or I'd be sitting on a cloud with my harp, trying to explain to my three dead buddies why I shot them."

Chomski gave a loud hoot of laughter. "I like that, Pete. You know that's the first time I realized you have a sense of humor."

"Yeah? So why don't I nudge Joseph to see if some of it rubs off on him?"

Riotta ignored the gibe. He noticed Townsend smiling gently. It made him bristle. Riotta admitted he had no sense of humor. He took his work, as his life, seriously. It was all business with Joseph Riotta.

"Oliver, I confirmed payment for the shipment to Africa. Full settlement. The delivery should be completed in three days."

"Fine. That should keep our principles happy. Now what about the Jack Regan order?"

"He's still having problems with the local guy, Calvera."

"Is that the Mexican who thinks he's going to put the squeeze on us?" Chomski asked.

Townsend nodded.

"Damned local hood who must have seen too many episodes of *The Untouchables*." He reached across the table and plucked a thick cigar from an open box. "Let's send Vic down to give Regan some backup. Our new recruit, Hawkins, can go with him. Let's see how he operates when the going gets tough."

"New man?" Tilman asked, suddenly alert. "You vetted him?"

"Relax, Pete," Chomski said. "He's ex-military. Served with Vic back when. Got ditched because he got a hard-on over some pussy UN officer who turned chicken and had to shoot some local warlord. I ran a computer check on him. He's been in a few scrapes with the law. Just toughed it out with some redneck trying to run a scam. Looks okay, but don't worry, we'll keep an eye on him."

Tilman picked up his glass and swallowed hard.

"If you say so."

"Ralph, is the Kibble matter settled?" Townsend asked.

Chomski nodded. "Account closed. We won't be hearing from him again. Neither will anyone else."

"Joseph, I'm calling in a backup contact for this Guang Lor deal. We have to complete this order on time. Su Han will start getting impatient if we lose time. And I don't want to upset the Chinese government."

"I understand. Are you talking about Dupont?"

"He works the same research department Kibble was in at RossJacklin. We brought him in and kept him in the background in case anything soured the Kibble deal."

"Did I miss something? Do we have a problem with Kibble?" Tilman asked.

"Kibble backed off. Said there were problems at the plant. Security had been tightened. He wanted out."

"Scared people do things like caving in and talking to the wrong people," Chomski said. "We couldn't risk that, so Mr. Kibble has gone AWOL. For good."

"I'll do some checking," Tilman said. "See if the Agency *is* involved."

"Fine, Pete."

"By the way, our friend from Beijing called earlier," Riotta said. "It appears our Chinese clients have an updated list of requirements."

"Can we handle it?"

"I gave it to Ralph."

"More of the same," Chomski admitted.

"Anything else?"

Chomski smiled. "Only details on deep-cover U.S. operatives working the Asian beat."

"That might come under your wing, Pete," Townsend said.

"I'll see what I can do. It's going to depend on which agency they're with. Leave it with me." Tilman glanced at his watch. "I'd better get on out of here. I'm going to be busy once I get back."

Townsend walked with him inside the house. They were deep in conversation as they crossed the living area and made for the door. Townsend beckoned the driver waiting in lobby.

"Rik, run Mr. Tilman to the airstrip. I'll call ahead and have the plane readied. Pete, have a good flight. Get back to me as soon as you have anything."

Townsend saw Tilman out the door, turning to return to the others. He failed to notice T. J. Hawkins standing just inside the partly open door that led into the games room off the lobby.

CHAPTER FOUR

South of the Texas-Mexico Border

"Hell of a place to hold a ladies' tea party," T. J. Hawkins commented, studying their surroundings.

"Does for what we need, T.J."

Vic Lerner coasted the 4x4 to a stop beside a battered semi-trailer rig and cut the engine. He checked his shoulder-holstered handgun before he opened his door and climbed out. Leaning back inside, he grinned at Hawkins.

"You comin', or what?"

"Don't bust your britches, I'm on my way."

Hawkins exited the vehicle and made his way to join Lerner. He fell in beside the man and trailed after him across the parking strip. They entered the diner, and Lerner immediately made his way to a corner booth and sat across from the man already there. Hawkins slid in beside Lerner, and the moment he laid eyes on the man they had come to meet he recognized him.

The first time Hawkins had been involved with the

man had been on a mission that had taken Phoenix Force to the Central American state of Santa Lorca. Hawkins had never actually spoken to the man, or even come close to facing him. He had only viewed him through the scope of his rifle during the final phase of the operation, but he would never forget his appearance. Since then, he had seen the man's profile at Stony Man, so he knew more about him than he had previously.

Jack Regan.

He was still wearing the soiled Panama hat that appeared to be a permanent fixture. His suit was crumpled, matching the lined features of his tanned face. Regan was tall and lean. As Hawkins sat, Regan's watery blue eyes wandered lazily to examine the newcomer.

"Who is he?" he asked.

"His name is Hawkins," Lerner said.

"What's he doing here?"

"Gettin' ticked off being talked about instead of talked at," Hawkins said.

"Touchy, ain't you, bubba? We delicate or something?"

Lerner chuckled.

"Don't you go thinking that, Regan. This here fella was in the military with me. Local warlord braced him and old T.J. here, he just upped and took him out. Try not to piss him off."

Regan shrugged. "Hell, that's all I need. Another tough guy."

"Don't fret, none, Regan. Townsend hired him. He's part of the team now."

The waitress appeared at their table. "What'll it be, fellers?"

"Coffee all 'round," Lerner said.

The waitress was suitably impressed.

"And there I was thinking the last of the big-time spenders had upped and died."

"Stick around, honey," Hawkins said. "We might even ask for refills."

"You funny all the time, bubba?" Regan asked.

Hawkins leaned back and stared him out until Regan turned his attention to Lerner.

"We ready for this to go down?"

Lerner nodded. "If you have the cash we can finish this deal."

"Okay. Just remember what I told you about the Mex problem. Calvera is still pushing for his piece."

"I thought you took care of that, Regan?"

"Look, bubba, that son of a bitch is pushy. He still believes he's entitled to a percentage just because I've been dealing over the border."

"Calvera?" Hawkins asked.

They waited while the waitress delivered their coffees.

"Luis Calvera is the local heavyweight in the area. He comes down hard on anyone doing business on his turf," Lerner explained. "Figures he's entitled to a cut."

"Does he actually do anything? Or is he just playing the big honcho?" Hawkins asked.

"Bubba, he just holds his hand out and asks for money, and he plays the big honcho because that's what he is."

"So why not move to another area? Away from his turf?"

Regan smiled. "Vic, your boy ain't as smart as I was giving him credit for. Bubba, it doesn't work like that. You realize what it costs to set up an area? All the people you have to buy off? The ones who need persuading? We're not dealing in nickel and dime bags here. You guys have a stake in this, remember. That's your weapons truck in Calvera's warehouse. He doesn't get his payoff, and we can all say goodbye to our deal. Calvera calls the tune across the border. You delivered the truck to me but I can't move it on until Calvera is happy. Guys, I want this settled. Townsend and me, we do good business. This is the first time we ever had problems."

"No offence, Regan," Hawkins said. "Just seemed to me you were being shaken down by a local hood."

"You're not far off that being the truth," Lerner said.

"You'll get no argument from me on that, boys. Calvera is a thug. He's a son of a bitch, but he has this section sewn up tight and if he says the sun don't shine, it don't shine. I need to get that merchandise moving before my people start getting nervous on me. If Calvera doesn't pocket his cut, it could get messy."

"Regan, we'll help. If the deal goes sour, Townsend is out a big chunk of money. And *he* doesn't like upsetting clients, either. Bad for his image."

"Calvera?"

Lerner shrugged. "This time he's shaking down the wrong man."

"When do you want to take delivery?"

Lerner drained his coffee cup and signaled for a refill. "Tomorrow afternoon."

"We need the time to make arrangements," Hawkins said.

Lerner glanced at his partner. "We do?"

"We do, buddy, we surely do."

The following afternoon

HAWKINS WAS UNDER no illusions about Jack Regan. The man put on an act that showed him as a casual down-home country boy, but the man had run his business for a long time, and Hawkins recalled that on the previous occasion Phoenix Force had encountered him, Regan was brokering a deal for one of Saddam Hussein's Fedayeen faithful. Regardless of the fact Phoenix Force had severed that connection, Regan was still tight with the international set. Whatever else he might be, Regan was no fool and would bear watching.

The meet had been set for two o'clock. The rendezvous point was two miles over the border, the location a long-abandoned shoe factory that had once employed a large number of locals. The place had shut down four years earlier and had been set for redevelopment until funds ran out and it was left to slowly disintegrate. Now it had become the main focus of Calvera's business empire. Like the man who controlled it, the site was unimpressive and decaying from within.

The weapons truck was parked inside one of the empty workshops, watched over by a trio of Calvera's hardmen. They were armed with M-16s and carried autopistols in shoulder rigs. Hawkins picked out a couple more armed men in the shadows of the building as he and Lerner made their way inside, Regan just ahead of them.

They had been waiting only for a few minutes when Calvera's stretch limousine rolled into the building.

Luis Calvera considered himself a big man. He didn't walk. He swaggered. It was the only word Hawkins could apply to him. The thing that took the edge off that for the Phoenix Force warrior was the fact that Calvera was big in size only. He had to have weighed in at more than four hundred pounds. None of it was muscle. Hawkins watched as the man levered himself out of the Cadillac's rear door and stood adjusting his rumpled clothing. He dressed the part, in a silk shirt and a pale cream suit that had to have been custom made. Hawkins figured there was no off-the-peg in that size. The clothing flapped and billowed over Calvera's soft body. Even the generous cut of the suit failed to conceal the man's bulk and the stomach that sagged loosely over his belt.

"Hey, man, don't let him get too close," Hawkins said. "He passes out and falls on us, we are goners, Vic."

"No comments about his size," Lerner said. "Regan says he's a little touchy about it."

Calvera stood beside his car and waited for them to approach him. As Hawkins got closer, he could see that Calvera was sweating. His dark skin was covered with a light sheen of perspiration. His dark hair, worn long, was clinging damply to the sides of his face. When he moved his head, his drooping triple chins quivered gently.

A couple of armed men accompanied Calvera, MP-5s hanging from shoulder straps. They made no attempt to conceal who or what they were. Hawkins noticed that the Cadillac's driver was still at the wheel of the vehicle. The engine was running and Calvera's rear door remained open. He was either overly cautious or a little edgy. Hawkins wondered why. The Mexican had everything going for him. They were on his home ground, and he had the advantage.

So why the extremes?

Jack Regan pushed his way between Hawkins and Lerner, holding out a hand toward Calvera.

"On time as usual."

Hawkins scanned the area. He was starting to feel

cautious himself. Something was off center. He began to sense a setup.

"Vic," he said softly, nudging Lerner's side. "Eyes open, buddy. I think we're in deep shit."

To his credit Lerner didn't react overtly.

"What?"

"I think Calvera is playing us for suckers here."

Lerner took a slow look around, managing to keep it low key. "Son of a bitch has a spotter with a scoped rifle up on that catwalk. Your eleven o'clock."

"I see him. Hell, Vic, this guy has a lot of artillery for what's supposed to be a simple shakedown."

Calvera wore a wide, false smile on his glistening face. He spoke to Regan in condescending tones, gesturing with his pudgy hands. Regan looked over his shoulder and pointed to Hawkins and Lerner.

"They represent my supplier," he told the Mexican.

Calvera smiled. "Maybe I should make them pay a premium, too," he said. His English was clear and well pronounced.

"Your choice," Regan told him.

"What does that mean?"

"It means you shouldn't exceed your authority, Señor Calvera," Vic Lerner said.

"Here, *my* authority is absolute."

"Things change, hombre. You know. Big man one day, cut down to size the next."

Calvera's flushed face darkened a shade as he stung from Lerner's words.

"Regan, I do not like your…"

Hawkins saw the slight turn of Calvera's head, the flick of a hand in the direction of the sniper up on the walkway.

The numbers had reached zero.

Hawkins spoke into the microphone clipped to his jacket.

"Now would be a good time, boys."

Lerner caught the words and broke into action. He powered himself forward, slamming his shoulder into Regan's back, driving the man to the dusty floor and hauling his autopistol from his shoulder rig as he went down.

As Hawkins followed suit, he heard the crack of a high-powered rifle. Out of the corner of his eye he saw Calvera's sniper stretch up, then topple from the catwalk.

There was a brief, hot silence and then the whole place erupted in a rattle of gunfire. Bullets clanged off metal and gouged spouts of dirt from the floor of the workshop.

Hawkins rolled, pulling his own weapon and caught a glimpse of Calvera heading for his limousine, his bodyguards hustling his immense bulk at a surprising speed. Dropping the muzzle, Hawkins placed a couple of shots into the front tire. It blew in a spray of black specks, the wheel sinking on its rim.

Regan and Lerner had scrambled for cover behind the limo.

One of the bodyguards swung his MP-5 in Hawkins's direction. Lerner leaned out and put the guy down with a pair of 9 mm slugs from his SIG-Sauer P-226. The Mexican slumped back against the limo.

From their places of concealment, the four Townsend gunners poured a constant rain of fire at Calvera's surprised soldiers. It was obvious they hadn't been expecting such defiance. Townsend's team cut down the hardmen in quick time.

Pushing to his feet, Hawkins faced off the second bodyguard as the man pushed his employer in through the rear door of the limo, yelling orders at the driver, then bringing his weapon to bear on the Phoenix Force pro. Hawkins didn't hesitate. He put two quick shots through the man's chest, laying him out on the floor of the workshop.

The limo lurched forward as the driver floored the gas pedal. There was a scream of fright from Calvera. The man was still only partway in the vehicle and as it began to move his lower half was dragged behind it.

Lerner rolled to his feet, his pistol in a two-handed grip. He began to fire at the driver, drilling him a couple of times. The limo swerved violently, throwing Calvera from the rear door. The Mexican hit the floor, rolling, still mouthing a wild torrent of abuse.

The limo, out of control, smashed into a steel support girder and came to a sudden halt.

"Now that wasn't as bad—" Lerner began.

The sound of a shot from Calvera's pistol blanked out his words. The single slug hit Lerner in the left shoulder, spinning him off his feet.

Before the echo had faded Calvera's body shuddered under the impact of two slugs from the rifle of Townsend's sharpshooter still at his high position in the roof girders. The expensive suit erupted with bloody spurts at the impact points.

"Mission accomplished," the man's voice said through Hawkins's earpiece.

It was Ralph Chomski. And he sounded as if he had really enjoyed his part in the proceeding.

Townsend Ranch

"AFTER THAT LITTLE firefight, buddy, you still want the job?" Lerner asked.

He was lying in his bed, bandaged up after having the bullet removed by Townsend's doctor. Drugs to ease the pain had left him a little high.

"That was nothing after Somalia," Hawkins reminded him.

"You aren't wrong there."

Hawkins picked up movement behind him as someone entered the room.

"You take it easy, Vic," he said. "Catching that slug is going to keep you confined to quarters for a while. Come to think of it, you always were quick when it came to getting out of work."

Lerner grinned amiably.

"Then it looks like you're going to have to double up for your buddy."

Hawkins recognized Ralph Chomski's voice and turned to face the man. Chomski leaned against the door frame, smiling easily.

Standing just inside the door was Townsend himself. He moved quickly to stand beside Lerner's bed.

"How is it, Vic?"

"Hurts like hell."

"It usually does," Chomski said.

"You took one sometime?" Hawkins asked casually.

"Me? Never. I stay out of their way."

"Just wonderin' how you knew what it felt like then," Hawkins said, and turned back to Townsend. "You heard from Regan yet, sir? He get to his contact?"

Townsend nodded. "Called a while back. Made his connection with no more trouble." Townsend slapped Hawkins on the shoulder. "That little arrangement you and Vic organized paid off. Regan got his consignment. We showed those idiots over the border it doesn't pay to fuck around with us. Good day all around. Right, Ralph?"

Hawkins glanced across at the man. Chomski struggled for a moment to hold back his anger. Hawkins's remark had bruised his ego. The Phoenix Force pro reminded himself to watch his back. Ralph Chomski wasn't the kind to let something like that go.

"Sure," Chomski said. "Good day..." A slight pause, no more than a heartbeat, then, "For some."

"Calvera?" Townsend chuckled. "He paid his dues, all right."

Hawkins smiled inwardly. He knew Chomski hadn't been thinking about Calvera. He had been staring directly at Hawkins as he spoke.

After Townsend and Chomski had gone, Hawkins stayed with Lerner until the man drifted off, then made his way back to his own room.

While Townsend and his main team stayed in the big house, the crew lived in a bunkhouse. As far as Hawkins was concerned it was simply a barracks hut. The main difference was that it had been divided into single rooms for each man. There was a large room at the front where the men could watch TV, play pool and generally lounge around when they weren't on assignment. Hawkins had noted there was no telephone in the building. He had mentioned that to Lerner.

"Boss man doesn't like us making outside calls in case somebody says something that might be picked up. You understand what I mean, pal? Kind of operation Townsend is running wouldn't sit too well with certain parties. He doesn't want to take the chance the phones might be tapped."

"Like we took a vow of silence? I mean, come on, Vic, are we celibate, too?"

That had made Lerner laugh out loud.

"Hell, no. We can shoot on down to Landry Flats. I know a few nice ladies we can spend some time with."

Hawkins hadn't pressed the matter. Though he would have liked the opportunity to pass information to Able Team, or directly to Stony Man, he was going to have to tread softly until Townsend felt safe with him around. Being the new boy meant he had to play it cool.

The incident with Calvera added some good points in Hawkins's favor. Even so, he maintain his low profile. One person he would have to stay wary of was Ralph Chomski. Townsend's SIC was no fool, and Hawkins sensed the man was keeping a close eye on him. He was sure Chomski didn't trust him. For that matter, how genuine was Townsend? It was no easy judgment to make. Until he was certain of his ground, Hawkins would need to stay on his toes.

In his room he flopped on the bed, staring up at the ceiling.

Jack Regan showing up as a player was interesting. How deeply involved was he with Townsend's organization? Simply a go-between? Or did his association go deeper than that? Hawkins knew that Regan had global connections. Did they reach as far as China? The consignment of weapons and ammunition Townsend had pushed through Regan was destined for some antigovernment group in Central America. Most probably small stuff compared to Townsend's major league dealing with Beijing. But Townsend was shrewd enough to keep his smaller contracts ongoing in case the big stuff dried up.

Then there were the two names Hawkins had learned on his first day at the ranch.

Mark Kibble. He had only caught snatches of Townsend's conversation with the man, but it appeared that Kibble was part of the technology feed.

The second man held even more interest.

Tilman. The scant fragments of conversation Hawkins had picked up had given him the man's name. A reference about the CIA. Tilman saying something about checking into Agency involvement.

His overhearing these scattered pieces of conversation had been random, pure luck, on Hawkins's part as he had been familiarizing himself with the house while Lerner had left him to do some other chore. He hadn't tried to elicit further information about the two men from Lerner, deciding to keep what he had heard to himself. But he did need to get it to Stony Man. Once Kurtzman had the names, he would run checks, far and wide, and if there was anything in the information he would trawl it out of cyberspace. Until Hawkins found the opportunity, he was going to have to sit on the information.

THE FOLLOWING MORNING he was summoned to the house, and Townsend told him he was going to Landry Flats with Chomski and one of the other men to pick up supplies. It was a preferred way of doing things. Rather than have deliveries to the ranch, which always left them open to curious visitors, Townsend felt safer to have what they needed picked up by his own people. Landry Flats, a crossroads for the outlying community, was used to this kind of dealing so there were few questions asked. And as Townsend always settled his accounts in cash, visits to the small town were always welcome by the local businesses.

They took one of the 4x4s. It had an extended body capable of carrying a lot of cargo. Chomski climbed into the passenger seat, the third man, a heavyset, hard-looking individual who Hawkins knew only as Brandt, sat in the rear cab seat. Chomski leaned out his window and tossed the keys to Hawkins.

"You can drive, hotshot. See if you're good at that as well as everything else."

Hawkins got behind the wheel and switched on the powerful engine. He swung the 4x4 around and along the dusty track that led to the main highway a couple of miles away.

Brandt settled himself and closed his eyes. Hawkins didn't believe he was going to go to sleep for a minute. He drove steadily, aware of Chomski's close scrutiny. As he swung the 4x4 onto the blacktop he spoke for the first time.

"You mind if I have the radio on?"

"Yes, I do," Chomski said.

Hawkins allowed a smile to edge his mouth. "That mean I can expect some scintillating conversation then?"

"You got a real smart mouth, Hawkins."

"People are always telling me that. Gets me into trouble all the damn time."

"And you like sailing close to the wind, too."

"Scintillating conversation," Brandt said from the rear seat. "He uses big words. I don't like asswipes that use big words."

"I can understand that, Brandt," Hawkins said. "Are you two a double act? Like *Dumb and Dumber?*"

"I read your file, Hawkins. Rangers. Delta Force.

Doesn't mean shit to me. I put a 9 mm in your skull right now, and all those fancy badges won't protect your ass."

"Won't prevent you from getting your asses scraped off the highway when this rig turns over, either." Hawkins planted his foot hard on the gas pedal, pushing the 4x4 above 60 mph. "Now we got us a quandary, Chomski."

Chomski held his gaze for a moment longer, then relaxed. He forced a grin, holding up both hands in mock surrender.

"Okay, Hawkins, we both proved we're hardasses. You really think I'd be stupid enough to shoot you out here on the highway?"

"I'll be able to answer that if I can feel the breeze going through my head."

WHEN THEY ROLLED INTO Landry Flats, Chomski directed Hawkins to the general store. Hawkins glanced around the quiet street. There were only a few vehicles present, most of them pickups from outlying businesses. The car Rosario Blancanales was driving stood outside the town's only restaurant. Blancanales wasn't behind the wheel. Lyons and Schwarz were nowhere in sight, but that didn't mean they weren't around. Hawkins turned and followed Chomski and Brandt into the store. Chomski went to the counter and handed his order to the clerk. Brandt located a slot machine and began to feed coins into it, working the lever with his powerful arm. Hawkins moved around the cluttered store, checking the layout.

"Hawkins," Chomski called.

"Yeah?"

"You want to take a walk over to the gun shop and pick up this order? Personal stuff for the boss."

He handed over a folded invoice and a thick wad of cash. Hawkins nodded and turned to go. As he passed in front of the store window, he saw Chomski's reflection nod at Brandt. The big man eased away from the slot machine and fell in behind Hawkins.

Hawkins headed on out of the store and strolled across the street. The gun shop was a few buildings up from the restaurant. Hawkins strode straight inside, not even looking in through the window. He walked by the racks of rifles and shotguns, pausing at the counter until the owner came to serve him.

"Here to pick up an order for Mr. Townsend," he said, handing over the invoice.

"Sure thing," the clerk said. He checked the invoice. "Oh, yeah, that came in the other day." He peered over the top of his eyeglasses at Hawkins. "Can't say I seen you before."

"Only signed on couple of days ago."

"You sound local."

"El Paso."

The man smiled. "Local enough. Now I'll be back in a couple minutes. Got that item out in back. Just need to make sure it's packed well."

"No rush," Hawkins said.

He leaned against the counter, checking out the glass case on the wall. A selection of handguns was displayed on pegs. And Hawkins could also see Brandt's image showing. He was outside the store, watching Hawkins through the front window. It took a great deal of effort for Hawkins not to lift his hand and wave.

He did see Blancanales walk into view, step around Brandt and enter the store. Hawkins turned around, leaned against the counter and made eye contact with

Brandt. His move caught Brandt slightly off guard. Hawkins sensed Blancanales moving around the store, but kept his attention on Brandt, who didn't seem to know what to do. After a time the big man moved away and stopped on the edge of the sidewalk, seeming to decide that the street was more interesting.

Blancanales strolled up to the counter, examining the handguns in the wall cabinet.

"Check out a Mark Kibble and a possible CIA guy called Tilman," Hawkins said quickly. "And Jack Regan is in the loop."

Blancanales made no indication he had heard. He raised a hand and pointed at a particular piece in the display cabinet.

"You know if that's a collector's item or a reproduction?"

"Hard to tell from here," Hawkins said.

The storekeeper appeared then, carrying a long box. He laid it on the counter.

"Mr. Townsend has been waiting for this. His favorite shotgun. Had to send her away to have the engraving done," he said. Then, glancing at Blancanales, "Be with you soon as I finish with this feller here."

"No rush," Blancanales said. "I think I know what I came in for."

Hawkins paid the bill, tucked the package under his arm and walked out of the store.

"Hey, Brandt, nice of you to wait. Makes me feel like part of the family."

He stepped off the sidewalk and made his way across the street, Brandt close behind, still trying to decide whether Hawkins had been genuine or simply making fun of him.

Chomski was standing beside the 4x4, watching closely. He opened the rear door so Hawkins could lay the package on the seat.

"And change," Hawkins said, returning what was left of the money and the stamped invoice.

"Everything okay?" Chomski asked.

He was speaking over Hawkins's shoulder.

"Fine," Brandt said.

"Be a half hour before the order's complete," Chomski said. "Might as well go over and have some coffee."

"If you're paying," Hawkins said. "I haven't had a paycheck yet."

Chomski managed a genuine smile this time. "Don't fret, Hawkins. You'll get what's coming to you soon enough."

Stony Man Farm, Virginia

"YOU WANT TO COME and look at what we found?" Kurtzman said.

"Will I be impressed by your skills?"

"As much as you are by my coffee, Barb."

"Oh? Bad as that, huh?"

"Just get in here and stop trying to be funny."

Kurtzman put down the phone and swung his chair away from his desk. There were only two other members of the team on station at that moment in time, Carmen Delahunt and Huntington Wethers. The third member of Kurtzman's group, Akira Tokaido, was off duty.

"So what have we got on this Tilman guy?" Kurtzman asked as he wheeled his chair across for a coffee top-up.

Wethers finalized what he was doing before he spoke.

"Pete Tilman is a senior operative with the Agency for twelve years. Some of his files were closed, but your sneaky-peek program unlocked them." Kurtzman raised his coffee mug at the last remark. "I downloaded everything I could find. It makes for interesting reading, and some sense. Tilman did some down-and-dirty black ops work in Central America. Wetwork, too. And one of his contacts down there, doing some buying and selling for him, was our old buddy Jack Regan."

"Official or otherwise?" Price asked.

No one had noticed her enter the room, and she stood quietly against the wall while Wethers aired his findings.

"Regan is one of those figures who defines the term shadow warrior," Wethers said. "It's hard to tell if he was on the payroll or just one of Tilman's cash-in-hand employees. But they go back a good few years."

"And now we have Regan handling contracts for Townsend, who also has a connection with Tilman," Delahunt said.

"Keep digging, people," Kurtzman said. He joined Price at his workstation. "Where's Hal? I wanted to bring him up to speed with our findings."

"Off base," Price said. "He had a request to make a house call. The White House. Should be back later. So what do you have for me?"

"You heard of a company called RossJacklin Inc.?"

"The company that develops and supplies technology for aviation and weapons? Rockets and missiles? High-tech electronics?"

"The same."

"They have some long-term contracts with the Pentagon, don't they? Computer-based development of circuitry and…"

"Picture starting to clear?"

"Yeah. Is this the company our missing technology came from?"

Kurtzman nodded. "And Mark Kibble, one of T.J.'s names? Kibble was one of RossJacklin's senior developers."

"Whoa, just back up a minute," Price said. "That a slip, or did you mean to say Kibble *was* working for RossJacklin?"

Kurtzman tapped his keyboard and brought data on screen.

"Kibble's body was found in a ditch outside Dayton, Ohio, where he lived and where RossJacklin is based. His skull had been stoved in from heavy blows. His car was nearby. The driver's door was wide open and the interior ransacked. The local P.D. figured he was the victim of a roadside robbery. He was facedown in the ditch, in two inches of water. Medical examiner found that Kibble's lungs had no water in them, so he was dead before he went into the ditch."

"That could have happened following the crime, couldn't it?"

"Possible, but the autopsy revealed a couple of really odd things. Kibble was facedown, but lividity had started to develop in the *back* of his legs, buttocks and arms, and the back of his shoulders. And it was fairly pronounced.

"That isn't all." Kurtzman flagged up the medical examiner's conclusions. "There were dust and seed particles on his clothing and in his lungs. Dayton CSI also found those same dust and seed traces in the trunk of Kibble's car. The identification of the dust particles has them as grains of a granular species found in South

Texas. The seed particles were of a native sagebrush plant from the same area."

"South Texas? Townsend's ranch is in South Texas."

"Bingo," Kurtzman said.

"Is that a legitimate expression?"

Kurtzman smiled. "No, but it kind of brings it all together."

Price had to agree. "One more thing. There was a single fingerprint found on the steering wheel of Kibble's car that didn't belong to him. The crime scene team checked it out through the IAFIS computer and matched it to a guy named Rik Brandt. I finally got a match through the military."

Kurtzman brought an ID photograph on screen.

"There's a face only a mother could love," Price said. "He's a big one."

"Ex-service. Air Force. Left around the same time as Ralph Chomski. And they were at the same bases every time."

"Old buddies?"

"It's worth sending Brandt's picture over the wire to Lyons. If he spots Brandt in Texas, we could have another connection."

"What's happening about Kibble's murder?"

"Hal has been dealing with that. He's liaised with Dayton P.D. He worked his Justice Department magic and got them to hold off. Asked them not to chase up the Texas connection until we finish our mission. We don't want the cavalry charging in and stomping all over while T.J. is still undercover."

"Townsend is connected to Kibble, Tilman and Jack Regan. RossJacklin is the source of the stolen technology. One of the missing pieces is a high-tech circuit board. The kind Guang Lor put in that downed missile."

"Don't forget Sammo Chen Low liaising with Townsend's buddy Joseph Riotta."

"One big happy family," Price said.

"What about this CIA guy?" Wethers asked. "Anyone considered him as a candidate for the shooting of the three agents?"

"Reason?" Price asked.

"You recall what Agent Schofield said just before he was shot? Something like—'I didn't see your name on the roster.'"

"He recognized his killer?"

"Because he was a fellow agent."

Kurtzman tapped in data and Tilman's image flashed on the screen.

"Well, we do have him linked to Townsend and Jack Regan. Unless we have more than one dirty Agency guy in this team."

"It's worth looking into." Price reached for a phone. "Let's switch Gadgets onto Tilman. Carl and Pol can keep T. J. in their sights."

THE FIRST OPPORTUNITY Hawkins got fell into his lap. Since Lerner was out of commission, Townsend moved Hawkins into his spot and had him conducting ordnance evaluations on some incoming orders. It meant the Phoenix Force pro was allowed a reasonable run of the main house, and Hawkins kept his eyes open for a slot. It came as he completed a part section of the list Townsend had assigned him to check out.

He made his way to Townsend's study-office. He

had expected to find Townsend there, but the room was deserted. Hawkins paused at the open door, the room beyond silent.

Across the far side a large window looked out over the ranch yard, and Hawkins could see Townsend in conversation with Chomski and Riotta. They were standing beside Riotta's silver Mercedes. Hawkins let his gaze settle on the computer setup on Townsend's desk. Even from where he stood he could see that the unit was active, the screen displaying a rolling screensaver.

He stepped into the room and crossed to the desk, moving to stand at the computer. The screensaver floated misty images across the monitor. Hawkins hit the space bar and the desktop flashed into view. Using the mouse, Hawkins selected e-mail and tapped in the address Kurtzman had given him for just this kind of operation. He added his initials as ID, the arranged alert message and sent the mail. He watched it transmit, knowing that the moment it hit, the Stony Man system it would flag up a visual and audio signal.

"OH, YES," Kurtzman said as Hawkins's message came through.

The visual and audio signal had caught his attention, and he glanced at the separate monitor he'd had on permanent standby for just this occasion.

He immediately turned to his keyboard and tapped in the response that would return the e-mail and insert his program into Townsend's database.

His quietly intrusive virus would be immediately absorbed into the entire system, enabling Kurtzman to download Townsend's database in its entirety. The program would remain invisible in Townsend's system, able to be accessed at any time Kurtzman wanted. Once it was established, Kurtzman could activate a stealthy siphoning of data, feeding it into his own system where he would then be able to work his way through the encryptions and firewalls, examining Townsend's dark secrets at his own leisure. It took no more than a couple of minutes for Kurtzman to establish the electronic connection.

STANDING TO ONE SIDE of the window Hawkins was able to see that Townsend, Chomski and Riotta were still deep in discussion. He was waiting for Kurtzman's response to let him know Stony Man had access to the database. When it came, he almost missed the electronic beep. Turning back to the monitor, he cleared his e-mailed message, knowing that Kurtzman would also initiate a hard drive deletion that would scrub the communication from Townsend's system. Hawkins left his checklist on the desk for Townsend to find, then retraced his steps, leaving the room and making his way out of the house. He strolled across the yard, heading toward the bunkhouse.

Out the corner of his eye he saw Chomski glance around. The man watched Hawkins, making no comment. The Phoenix Force commando could sense the man's mind working, maybe wondering what Hawkins had been doing in the house. After a few seconds he was drawn back into the conversation, leaving Hawkins to only guess what he was thinking.

Hawkins entered the bunkhouse and made his way to his room, pausing briefly to check out Lerner. His ex-Army buddy was asleep, the paperback novel he'd been reading still in his hand. Back in his own room Hawkins stood at the window, recalling Chomski's scrutiny. That alone didn't warrant suspicion, but Hawkins knew the way Chomski's mind worked. The man was terminally cautious. He didn't trust anyone as far as Hawkins could make out and judged every move made to be a threat. Especially with Hawkins being the new guy in camp. One way or another Hawkins was going to have to tread carefully.

Pushing to his feet, Hawkins took out his Beretta, checked the magazine and set the safety. He slipped a couple of extra magazines into his leather jacket's inner pocket, then holstered the pistol again.

From here on in he decided to adopt Chomski's rule to not trust anyone.

IT WAS QUIET in the Computer Room as Aaron Kurtzman rolled his wheelchair in through the door. Tokaido was at his post this time, hunched over his keyboard, monitoring data that was flicking across the screens banked on the wall above his station. He wore his earbuds and though he might have been tuned in to some loud music pumping from the player resting on his desk, his attention was on the screens. Every so often he would tap in a command, pulling down some incoming data stream. He would cache it on his own computer and store it in a file. Little got by the young hacker.

Kurtzman left him to it. He trusted the young man, as he did every other member his team.

Kurtzman silently rolled his wheelchair across to the coffee station. He took a thick mug and filled it. The rich aroma of coffee strong enough to buckle Kevlar reached his nostrils. Kurtzman loved his coffee. Not many others did. Kurtzman had to endure endless remarks about it, which he put down to jealousy.

Mug in hand, he rolled across the floor to his own workstation and positioned himself at the desk. He placed the mug in its appropriate spot, squared his chair and locked the wheels. He tapped the keyboard and brought his equipment out of Standby mode. As his screen flashed into action, Kurtzman used his mouse to bring back into play the operation he had left working when he had gone for his break.

He allowed himself a gentle smile when he saw the screen box announcing that his intrusion program had wormed its way in through the protection put in place to stop exactly what he had done. Thanks to Hawkins managing to open a connection, Kurtzman had been able to create a link enabling him to covertly infiltrate Townsend's computer system. Now all he had to do was to confirm the connection and start his surreptitious download of everything in Townsend's memory banks. Once he had that locked down and the information safe in Stony Man's data files, Kurtzman could do exactly what he wanted. He had the option of completely wiping the data from Townsend's computer or locking it by planting a virus that would prevent Townsend from accessing his own information. He could even change the data. Kurtzman debated his options and chose to leave the data untouched for the time being. He didn't want to create any suspicion in Townsend's mind that someone might have tampered with his computer in any way, because there was always the chance it might endanger Hawkins's position with Townsend's organization. But what he could do, without being detected, was monitor any and all data that came and went through the system. His spyware would enable him to look over Townsend's shoulder to see and hear exactly what Shadow was doing.

Aaron Kurtzman dedicated the next work period to analyzing the data he had downloaded from Oliver Townsend's computer system, leaving the rest of the team to their appointed tasks. He checked the surface data and quickly decided what he could discard and leave in the system for later retrieval. He was more interested in the encrypted files. There were a large number of them, held in locked vaults that were protected by barriers designed to hide them from unauthorized eyes. Which only peaked the computer whiz's interest. He loved nothing more than a challenge to his cyberskills, and they were considerable. As well as being skilled in computer terms, Kurtzman was a master when it came to breaking encryptions and the lockouts designed by people who had dark secrets to hide.

"Hey, Akira, Carmen, I'm sending data across from Townsend's hard drive. The guy doesn't want us to know what he's been up to, so I think it only fair we accept his challenge. Drop everything and go to work on this stuff."

Tokaido nodded and waited while Kurtzman transferred a chunk of data to his station. He scanned files as they were listed, smiling to himself when he saw they were heavily encrypted. Puzzles, as he classed them, were his lifeblood. He saw them as adversaries just waiting to be defeated. The youngest of Kurtzman's cyberspecialists, Akira Tokaido, was blessed with the demanding curiosity of youth. He refused to ever accept that any problem was unsolvable. The moment it seemed so, he went into overdrive and would persist until he broke down the walls. He filled his screens with the locked files, initiated Kurtzman's encryption-cracker program and set to work.

The first to extract information, Tokaido alerted Kurtzman and shifted the data to the man's screen.

"Sound bites," Tokaido said. "Townsend has been recording conversations and storing them on encrypted files."

For the next half hour they listened to the open files. They were recordings of face-to-face meetings and also telephone conversations. Townsend always made sure that somewhere during each discussion he verbally identified the individual he was speaking to by addressing them by name.

"He's made records of conversations so he has incriminating evidence against them," Delahunt said. "Clever guy. He's making sure he has them where he wants them if trouble starts."

"Tilman. Riotta. Mark Kibble. Sammo Chen Low. We know these. Run checks on the other names, Akira. Let's find out who else is in Townsend's club."

"Evidence is stacking up here," Wethers said. "We know Townsend had Kibble on his payroll. Now Kibble is dead and evidence points to him having been killed in Texas, then taken back to Dayton and his body dumped in a ditch. Rik Brandt left his print in the car and Brandt works for Townsend."

"One voice we don't have here is Jack Regan's," Kurtzman said. "The question is why."

"Maybe Regan is a trustee," Delahunt suggested. "Even someone like Townsend must have some people he doesn't need to keep checks on."

"How's that list of telephone numbers coming?" Kurtzman asked her.

"Last few are coming through. Whatever else, Townsend has a lot of contacts."

"Get everything you can from the numbers. Names and addresses. The works."

"YOU READY FOR THIS?" Kurtzman asked.

He was in the War Room with Brognola and Price. Kurtzman had sheets of data ready, and two of the wall screens were waiting for the signal that would bring the data on line.

Brognola nodded. He had only just returned from his trip to Washington and a busy meeting with the President. The Man had asked for a situation update and had also wanted to discuss a few pointers with Brognola. The visit had been intense, and Brognola would have liked nothing better than to be able to slump in a chair with a large drink in his hand, his shoes kicked in the corner of the room. He visualized the scenario for a few seconds, then dismissed it as being untenable at this moment in time.

"Okay. Here we go," Kurtzman said, and clicked his hand controller.

The right-hand screen began to list details Delahunt had located for the telephone numbers trawled from Townsend's files. Where possible the woman had added profiles and images on the owners of the numbers. The list ran to almost thirty contacts.

"Townsend has one hell of an eclectic gathering of phone buddies," Kurtzman said. "About the only one missing is a plumber. You've got full printouts in front of you."

Brognola watched the list scroll by.

"Politics, high-tech industry and the military," he commented. "Like you said, Aaron, a hell of a collection."

"When you consider Townsend's business, they all fit the profile," Price said.

"That's what worries me," Brognola added.

"We cross-referenced all the numbers," Kurtzman said. "Checked out who the people Townsend knows know." He smiled. "Give me one phone number I can get you the world."

"So modest," Price said.

"It's why I'm so well liked."

"Really? So it's not the coffee after all?"

Kurtzman swung his chair around and pressed the handset, filling the second screen with more data.

"Townsend's encryption codes were tricky but not impossible to break. He's using a fairly standard form of symmetric block cipher. They can be a headache if you're not into the psychology of encryption mind-sets. Once you know the way these things work it's no real sweat to develop a program to break the code sequences."

"Aaron, I'll take your word for it," Brognola said. "Cut to the part the simple folk can understand."

"Okay. My program has wrapped itself around Townsend's. We pulled out copies of all of his data and broke the encryptions. Townsend has a system for receiving his financial transactions. Electronic laundering. His payments go around the houses, get split up, then pushed back into his loop system and eventually get deposited in offshore accounts or this Swiss bank.

Townsend even has a couple of account locations in London. Every account is under a different name and of course they all have account numbers. Now *I* have those numbers."

"You can do that?" Price asked.

"Neighborhood hackers can get into your bank account once they infiltrate your computer. This is the same once the system has been invaded. Slightly higher on the scale of one to ten, but basically it's still hacking into someone's system."

Price let out a long breath of air. "That is scary. Is there anything this dubious program can't do?"

"Damned if I can get it to place a correct order with McDonald's. I always end up with latte coffee instead of plain and simple black."

"We'd better create a full dossier on all this," Brognola said. "Something I can show the Man. He's already unhappy about the way things have been going. If he sees this list of possible co-conspirators aligned with Townsend, he's going to run up the walls of the Oval Office."

"I'll get it done," Kurtzman said. "Hal, we still have more to break yet. I'll keep the team working. Hunt can run his Phoenix monitoring, as well, and I'll keep tabs on Able and T.J."

Brognola nodded, then turned to Price. "Good call sending someone to keep an eye on this Tilman character. He needs monitoring in case he meets up with anyone interesting."

"I figured sending just one was the best option. I didn't want to leave T.J. without ample cover in case he needs hard backup."

"Problem with these assignments is they're never soft for very long."

"Hal, you'll regret you said that before long."

The big Fed nodded. He knew exactly what Price meant, and unfortunately she was most probably correct.

CHAPTER FIVE

U.S. Air Force Base, Bagram, Afghanistan

While Jack Grimaldi unloaded *Dragon Slayer* from the C-17, Phoenix Force and Mei Anna had a final briefing. When Grimaldi joined them, he was in time to sit and enjoy the meal provided by their Air Force liaison.

"Hey, I see Cowboy got you boys some new guns there," Grimaldi said, spotting the FN P-90 submachine guns Phoenix Force was carrying.

"We ran some test firings over the last few days," Rafael Encizo said. "Stands up pretty well. Good rate of fire, easy to carry and it's got some punch with those 5.7 mm SS-190 rounds."

"You all like them?" Grimaldi asked, filling a mug with coffee.

"I'll give you a full field report when we get back," Gary Manning said.

Grimaldi didn't fail to notice that Calvin James also

had his M-16/M-203 combo slung across his back. There was always a need for the older, dependable weapons.

OUT FROM BAGRAM in the early-morning mist, Grimaldi took *Dragon Slayer* to operational height, skimming low cloud banks and emerging into a pale sky. The rugged Afghan landscape spread in front of them, low hills, craggy mountain slopes. Grimaldi locked the flight course coordinates into the assault helicopter's computerized system and set the chopper unerringly along its path.

In the body-form couch next to Grimaldi, David McCarter used the flight time to upgrade his growing knowledge of the machine. He had already logged a good few hours at the controls under Grimaldi's tutelage. A qualified pilot, McCarter's enthusiasm for a new challenge had him eager to master *Dragon Slayer.* Grimaldi had no problems with that. In his view it was a handy thing to have someone on board with the skills to take over if anything happened to put him out of commission.

While McCarter did his thing up front, the rest of the team took the opportunity to relax or make final checks of equipment and weapons. They ran test transmissions on the communication sets they were all wearing. The units were updates of previous models. Extremely lightweight, they operated digitally and allowed clear, powerful transmissions between the team members, and *Dragon Slayer,* as well.

"Everybody up and running?" Manning asked, and received confirmation from his teammates. "Any problems, let someone know so we don't lose contact."

Sometime later McCarter joined them in the crew

compartment. He sat next to Mei Anna, stretching out his long legs.

"Once again. The plan is to go in and grab Hung's team and make a quick extract. Hustle them and the circuit board back to *Dragon Slayer* so Jack can fly them to Bagram."

"And then we go walkabout?" James asked.

"We take a gander at this Guang Lor site. If it looks like a go, we take the place down, put a stop to this technology scam."

"Let's hope Hung's inside man can point us to the right place," Manning said.

"I'm confident he can," Anna said.

"Well, that's all right then," McCarter said dryly.

He leaned back, folded his arms and closed his eyes.

"HEAD'S UP," Grimaldi called. "I'd just like to point out the local attractions. We're passing through what is known as the Hindu Kush, with the Wakhjir Pass coming up. Next stop the Afghan-Chinese border."

He brought *Dragon Slayer* to a lower elevation, easing the speeding helicopter along the rocky defile of the pass that would bring them to their EVA point.

"Anyone with a return ticket should remain seated," Grimaldi said. "The rest of you hitchers should disembark when I touch down."

"Happy bugger, isn't he?" McCarter said.

Grimaldi eased back on the controls, bringing *Dragon Slayer* to a gentle landing. He hit the side hatch release button. The hatch opened with a soft hum.

"Y'all come back safe now," he said as Anna and Phoenix Force exited the chopper.

They moved aside as Grimaldi closed and sealed

the hatch, then powered aloft again. He eased around full circle and Dragon Slayer retreated along the pass to a spot where Grimaldi would land and wait for the pickup call.

McCarter checked his handheld GPS unit. He pinpointed their current position and indicated the direction they needed to go.

"Should take us about an hour to reach the crossing point. We need to follow this route to get us around the Chinese border patrols. Military intelligence says we can clear the border here. They've marked it as a safe spot. Monitoring has shown the patrols can't cover every inch of this territory and this section is pretty well obscure."

"No guarantees I bet?" Encizo said. "There's always a first time."

"I know. We have the disadvantage of this Major Kang out of Guang Lor looking for Hung, so there could be greater activity than normal. No one said it would be easy. But we have to get to Hung and pull out his team. They're depending on us. Okay, it's no bloody good if we get spotted. So let's not get spotted." He glanced at Anna. "Okay?"

She nodded.

McCarter spoke into his com-link.

"You still picking us up, Jack?"

"Yo."

"'Yo'? Shades of *Fort Apache*," McCarter muttered. "The Duke will be turning in his grave."

"I can still hear you."

THEY MOVED OFF, with Encizo taking point.

The air was still chilled from the previous night.

Underfoot the ground was hard, strewed with loose rock and gritty shale. McCarter had passed the GPS unit to Encizo so he was able to maintain their line of travel even after having to make detours to avoid pitfalls. As they tramped deeper into the inhospitable terrain, the way became harder. It was easy to see why this section was difficult to patrol. The undulating landscape, scored with gullies and ravines, would have been impossible to patrol in any kind of vehicle. Being on foot was barely an advantage. Phoenix Force found itself having to negotiate some precarious sections, with steep rock walls to scale, then having to descend into deep ravines where crumbling rock and thorny brush made even walking a torture. By the time they bellied down on the last hogback before the crossing into Xinjiang Province, China, they were glad for the pause.

McCarter took a pair of binoculars from his backpack and spent some time scanning the area ahead of them. He panned left to right and back again, focusing on specific points until he was sure the way was clear.

"Looks fine from here," he said. "Ten minutes from now we might be seeing a different picture. So we go now, keep on the GPS track and keep our eyes wide open."

"Don't forget they have a helicopter at Guang Lor," Anna said. "Kang will be using everything at his disposal to find Hung."

THEY STEPPED ACROSS the invisible line into China, still unobserved, and as the morning wore on they all knew they were stretching their luck. Too many missions had taught them that the watchword on these occasions was "caution." Right now they were playing in someone else's backyard, moving through country that was foreign in every way to them. It wouldn't do to let their guard down for a second.

They took a break at noon. The sun was blazing, the sky cloudless. The wind that pulled at their clothing was warm. Gritty dust skittered around their feet, making soft hissing sounds. Taking scant shelter beneath a rocky overhang, Manning stood watch while the rest took time for quick drinks of tepid water from their canteens. As soon as Encizo had satisfied his thirst, he took over and sent Manning into the shadow of the overhang.

"Still a way to go," McCarter said after taking a GPS reading. "We haven't got as far as I would have liked by this time. If this bloody place was a bit more foot friendly and flat we could make better time. If we can't do better we're going to have to spend the night out here."

"It's why Hung came to this area," Anna said. "He knew it would slow down any pursuit."

"That part applies to the good guys, too," James said.

They stayed where they were for almost twenty minutes before McCarter ordered them to resume the trek. He returned the GPS unit to Encizo as the Cuban moved ahead to take point.

They had barely moved out when noise intruded, breaking the comparative silence. Everyone turned in the general direction of the alien sound in time to see a band of armed men on tough-looking ponies come into sight from a scattering of huge rocks—heading directly for Phoenix Force.

THE HALF DOZEN RIDERS thundered up to Phoenix Force. As the dust cleared, the only sounds were those of the restless ponies pawing at the ground, snorting in frustration against the hands that held the reins taut. The riders were wiry, seasoned individuals, faces brown and seamed. Bright, dark eyes scanned Phoenix Force, taking in every detail. The riders wore heavy clothing and boots, and thick, round caps. The weapons they carried ranged from old bolt-action rifles to Kalashnikov assault weapons. Two of the riders carried sturdy bows, with quivers full of arrows. Every man had a knife tucked in his thick leather belt.

"Somebody tell me we've wandered onto the wrong set here," James said. "This looks like something out of Genghis Khan the movie."

Anna stepped forward, placing a hand on the P-90 he held. She pushed the muzzle toward the ground.

"It's all right," she said. "These are not Kang's men. They are Uygur. This is their territory, the place Beijing wants to clear them off. They sent Han Chinese here to settle and dispossess the ethnic Uygur."

Anna walked to confront the closest riders. She began to speak to them, her dialect slow at first. But then she gained the cadence and her speech grew familiar. One of the riders replied, raising a hand to point at Phoenix Force, leaning forward to study their dress and the weapons they were carrying.

"David, come and stand by me," Anna said. She caught his sleeve as he neared her. "I have told them you are here from America to challenge Kang."

"That should make me popular."

"These people speak an Altaic Turkic dialect. I know a little but I'll have to improvise," she said, moving to stand alongside him. "The one I'm talking to is Shin Tek. He is their leader."

McCarter stepped forward, catching the eye of the wiry Uygur Anna had spoken to. In her slow, halting version of the Uygur language she told the man why McCarter and the others had come to Xinjiang. How they were here to stand up to Kang and his soldiers because they were doing great harm to the people and the land of the Uygur, and stealing important secrets from the American government.

The Uygur listened intently, nodding when he grasped Anna's words, frowning at the phrases he failed to understand. When she had finished, Shin Tek turned to confer with his men. The moment turned into a busy, animated conversation, with McCarter being pointed at more than once. Then someone in the group laughed. Others followed and a general uproar overtook the whole bunch of mounted Uygur.

"What's the joke?"

Anna failed to keep her smile hidden. "He asked if I was your woman. When I said yes, he decided I would be too much for you to handle and I needed a Uygur."

"Keep grinning like that I might start to agree with him," McCarter said.

"Now you've hurt *my* feelings," Anna replied. "David, they know the village where our people are hiding. They have seen them. And they know a faster route. We could be there by morning if we accept their offer to guide us."

"Are any of Hung's people hurt?"

The answer came back that three of Hung's team were dead, their bodies in the wreckage of their vehicle.

"Will they guide us there?"

Anna relayed his request and Shin Tek nodded. He pointed a finger at McCarter and spoke.

"What this time?"

"He says they will be honored to take the tall one and his people if he will ride alongside them."

"Ride?"

"Yes. They will provide ponies for us all. They have spare ones at their camp not far from here."

"It's better than hiking all over these damned hills," Manning said.

McCarter nodded. "I'm not going to argue that point."

McCarter turned to Shin Tek and nodded. "Tell him we're in his debt, Anna."

THE CAMP HELD about two dozen Uygur men. There were a few of the traditional round tents the Uygur preferred and a number of corralled ponies. By the time Phoenix Force was led into the camp, cook fires were blazing and a two sheep were being spit-roasted over the flames. The air was heavy with the smell of the cooking meat.

"Now I'm definitely hungry," Manning said.

"Shin Tek says we should eat before we leave. There might not be time for food later."

McCarter replied through Anna that Shin Tek was a good leader of men.

"He thanks you," Anna said, "but he already knows that."

"Why didn't I guess he'd say so?"

"Maybe because he's smarter than you," Encizo said.

A copper pot was lifted from the fire and battered tin mugs were passed around. Scalding tea with added goat's milk was poured. The drink was traditional Uygur fare, spiced with salt. It was very hot and strong, and the rich goat's milk gave it a unique flavor. As Mc-Carter accepted his he noticed that many of the Uygurs were watching him intently. They were waiting for him to taste the drink and give his approval.

"Go ahead, *jefe*. You lead and we follow," Encizo said softly.

McCarter raised the mug and took a swallow. The tea burned its way down his throat. The rich flavor almost took his breath away, but the Briton held up his mug, smiling broadly, and nodded his approval.

"Now I see why the Uygur are as strong as they are," he said.

Anna translated. Shin Tek grinned and roared with laughter. He leaned forward and slapped McCarter across the shoulder, then insisted the Briton's mug be refilled.

"I think he likes you even more now," Anna said.

"Just let him know it doesn't mean we're engaged."

As darkness slid in around camp and the fires were built higher, the meal was served—bread, a rich mix of rice and vegetables, and greasy roast mutton. It was all washed down with more of the goat's milk tea.

"They should serve this at fast-food outlets," James said. "Brother, this is pretty good."

"Just don't start quoting it as soul food," Manning said.

"Now that you mention it…"

WITH THE MEAL OVER the Uygur broke camp, clearing the site with speed. The cook fires were extinguished, and what was left of the cooked mutton was sliced and wrapped for later consumption. The tents and other items of comfort were packed on ponies. Extra animals were brought forward and saddled.

James eyed the ponies with a doubtful expression on his face.

"Don't you ride?" Anna asked him.

"I've done some," James said, "but most horses I've known understood English and they tended to be taller than the rider."

Once everyone was mounted they moved off at a steady pace. Shin Tek and his immediate group stayed with Phoenix Force, while the rest took the equipment and spare horses as they set out for another campsite.

"The Uygur keep constantly on the move," Anna explained. "They do it so the Chinese military have no permanent Uygur base to strike at."

It was a couple of hours short of midnight. A pale moon shone in the cold sky. A faint breeze soughed down from the distant foothills. It was silent except for the soft plod of the ponies' hooves and the creak of saddles.

"Man, I got a Beretta in my holster, a P-90 over my shoulder, and I'm riding on a Chinese pony. How weird is that?"

"East meets West," Manning replied. "The classic situation."

"Classic my ass," James said. "All *I* see is my butt meeting horseflesh."

McCarter rode at Tek's side, with Anna close by so she could translate.

"If Kang's men are tracking Hung and his men, I don't want to run into them if we can avoid it," the Briton commented.

Anna spoke to Tek. The Uygur turned and smiled at him, then replied through Anna.

"These Chinese soldiers are like great plodding camels. They make too much noise and they are terrible in the dark. We can ride around them and reach the village. We are quicker on our ponies." Anna grinned. "Tek says you worry too much. You remind him of his grandmother."

McCarter wasn't sure he liked the comparison. "You sure he didn't mean his grandfather?"

"*No,*" Anna translated. "Old woman fits better."

They rode through the rest of the night and into the coming dawn, light sliding down off the higher peaks.

Shin Tek spoke to Anna. "Kang has been our enemy for a long time. He runs errands for his masters in Beijing. They call and like the dog he is, he does their bidding."

"Our only strength is to strike at them and make them see we will not surrender," Anna said.

"Surrender?" Tek grunted in distaste at the word. "The Uygur have held this place for too long to surrender. Better to die still free than to exist as subjects of those old men in Beijing."

Anna placed a slim hand on Tek's arm. "Let us hope not this day, Shin Tek."

He nodded. "Rather we give these toy soldiers a taste of real fighting."

Anna relayed all this to McCarter. He absorbed the sentiments coming from Tek.

"And there I was believing I'm the gung-ho champion."

"I dare say Tek's war has been going on a little longer than yours."

One of Tek's men appeared from the higher slopes, negotiating the rocky terrain with deft flicks of his pony's reins. He pulled to a halt to speak with Shin Tek, and the Uygur beckoned to Anna.

"He has seen the village. There were tracks leading in, left by three men."

"Did he see Hung's people?" McCarter asked.

"He says not," Anna stated. "David, it could be they're simply staying under cover. He does say he spotted some of Kang's soldiers. They are camped a few miles from the village."

"How the hell did they get there so fast?"

"Maybe a forced march," James suggested. "Scouting party sent out ahead of the main squad. There to keep an eye on things until Kang shows up."

There was sense in that, McCarter admitted. An advance team could establish themselves and have the village under observation to forestall any punitive action by Hung and his men. It was forward thinking on Kang's part, but it did nothing to make Phoenix Force's task any easier.

"Sooner we reach the village, the better," he said. "We need to get to Hung and his people before Kang and company increase the odds." He glanced across at Anna. "Tell Tek we need to move out now."

They mounted up and followed Tek's scout as he led them toward the distant village.

WHEN THEY NEARED the village Shin Tek and his scout rode ahead to establish the distribution of Kang's men. On his return he went directly to McCarter and Anna.

"They are there," he said.

"How many?" Anna asked.

"At least eight I have seen. But there could be others. Major Kang's special troops. They wear his insignia." There was a hard edge to his voice. "I know those dogs. They have butchered my people. Burned villages. Destroyed our sheep and goat herds so we might starve."

Anna relayed Tek's words to McCarter.

"If we take them on now, we'll lose our advantage," the Brit pointed out.

Anna understood what he was implying. Engaging Kang's force now wasn't something they could risk.

"Shin Tek, I must ask a great favor. I understand how you have the right to settle your grievances with these men who follow Kang. But my friends need to reach our own people before…"

Tek hesitated only a moment before he nodded.

"I gave my word to the tall one. It would bring shame on me if I did not honor it. We will go around these soldiers and find your friends."

"Thank you, Shin Tek. We are in your debt."

Tek mounted his pony, gesturing with his arm for them to follow.

They were able to see the remains of the village from their concealed position. The ponies had been herded together and tethered out of sight. McCarter crouched beside Anna and Shin Tek, examining the area. Nothing moved. There was no sound. The village looked completely deserted.

Tek spoke quietly to Anna. "Perhaps your friends have gone."

"I do not think so. They have no supplies and probably little ammunition. And they have something they must pass along to us."

"It could be a trap."

"Shin Tek, all things are possible."

He smiled. "Yet still you will go into that place?"

"It is why we came here."

Tek sat with his back to the rock. "Ask your husband-to-be what he would do."

Anna made the request, relaying McCarter's answer to Tek. The Uygur sighed in resignation.

"I knew he would say that. If he goes into the village you may find yourself a widow even before you get married."

"Then it will be a risk I must take."

Tek shook his head. "Ask what he needs me to do then."

McCarter considered for a moment. "Give us cover when we go in. Tell him I don't want him or his men to take risks. I'm grateful for his help getting us here, but I don't want them getting hurt."

"*He* doesn't want *us* to get hurt?" Tek slapped his thigh. "If nothing else, this one makes good jokes."

"He likes your sense of humor," Anna told McCarter.

"Bloody hell, I have to come all the way to China to find a fan." McCarter checked his weapons. "Lock and load, people. This is where we do the dangerous bit. Cal, you and Gary cut around the east side of the village. Cover the back door. You spot anyone who isn't one of us, don't wait for formal introductions. I'd like to do this without attracting too much attention, but if those Chinese spot us, we fight back. Right now our objective is to get Hung and his people clear, move them to the border and extract them."

"We'll give you a call once we're in position," Manning said.

The Phoenix Force pair moved away and began a

wide circle that would eventually place them in position.

Encizo tapped McCarter's arm. "We have movement."

A lone figure had emerged from one of the partially demolished houses, moving lowly, rubbing his eyes. He took a couple of steps away from the front of the house, looking around as if he was hoping to see something—or someone.

"Is that one of Hung's men?" McCarter asked Anna.

"I think it's Sammy Cho. That looks like blood on his clothing. He doesn't look too good."

The single shot cracked the silence, and the solitary figure turned and dropped facedown on the hard ground, raising dust as he hit. A second shot sounded. The downed man's head snapped to one side, dark skull and hair fragments blowing out from the gaping exit wound.

"Bastards," Encizo said. "Looks like they decided not to wait any longer."

McCarter activated his com-link.

"That was one of Hung's men being shot."

"Message understood," James replied. "We'll—"

His words were lost by the sudden crackle of autofire coming through McCarter's com-link.

"Cal?"

No response.

He could still hear the armed engagement.

"Bloody hell," he exploded.

KANG WAS FURIOUS.

He had only just been informed that his scouting party had spotted an incoming group that appeared to be a mix of Uygur and Caucasian. They were all armed and were closing rapidly on the village where Hung and his people were hiding.

"Major, we may lose our advantage if we don't do something now," the sergeant in charge of the scouting party said.

"Then do it," Kang yelled into his microphone. "Just don't let them get away. Any of them." He turned to his pilot. "Get us there quickly. Quickly."

"WATCH YOUR BACKS," Calvin James called through his com-link. "We have hostiles on our flank."

McCarter was relieved to hear James's voice, but not so happy that his people were under attack.

"Let's move," he said.

Shin Tek called to his men and they ran for their horses, throwing themselves into their saddles and heading the ponies in the direction of the opposite side of the village where more Chinese had appeared. As they rode they opened fire, screaming defiance at the enemy. Their weapons crackled as they headed in the direction of the troops. Bullets slashed into the Chinese, at least two men stumbling in shock and pain from being impaled by Uygur arrows. Tek's band rode in a hit-and-run tactic, galloping into and through the troops, then moving rapidly away to regroup for another strike.

McCarter turned his attention to the closest Chinese, sensing there might be an influx of men above the few they had initially seen. Kang's main body of men? Whoever, they added to Phoenix Force's problems. Hostilities had commenced. They were going to have to deal with whatever hand had been dealt.

The rattle of autofire exploded around them. Bullet

hits scarred the rock and spit up spumes of gritty earth. Shell casings glittered in lazy arcs as they were expended from ejection ports, bouncing as they hit the ground.

McCarter, with Anna close by and Encizo bringing up the rear, directed his fire at the Chinese who emerged from cover on his left flank. They were moving down slope toward the semiderelict house Sammo Chen Low had emerged from.

The Briton felt the P-90 vibrate as it spat out 5.7 mm slugs. The burst caught the lead Chinese, dumping him hard on his knees, his muscles suddenly becoming slack. He fell facedown, arms limp at his sides. As the stricken man went down, McCarter turned his SMG on the downed man's partner, raking him side-on. The volley cored in and shattered bones before penetrating deeper to cleave through ribs and heart.

Anna had spotted more gunners and turned her own weapon on them. She touched the trigger and took out the man in the lead, edging her weapon around, hitting the next man in the shoulder. She was about to fire again when the crackle of a P-90 came from close by and she saw Encizo cut the man down, then turn at the hip and loose a volley that caught another Chinese as the man sidestepped his falling colleague.

There was little time for anything else but to aim and fire, picking targets as they showed and hoping to pull the trigger before the opposition could. The immediate area was alive with the snap and whine of crossfiring weapons. The adrenaline surge of no-quarter combat left little time for anything but the individual to struggle to stay alive and cut down the enemy.

And then into the maelstrom of the killing ground

came the rising thwack of helicopter rotors. The swirling downdraft from the swooping bulk of the machine bringing Major Kang onto the scene caused a sudden fog of gritty dust. From his position looking down on the battleground he made a decision and ordered his door gunner to open fire on the enemy.

"On what target, Major? There is so much dust I can't tell who is who."

Kang reassessed the scene below. Despite his annoyance at the door gunner's response, he had to admit the man was right. The dust cloud *had* obscured the target area. He turned to his pilot and jabbed a finger in the direction of the hazy outline of the only village structure still capable of offering shelter.

"There. Put one of your HE missiles into that house. It should bring those damned dissidents into the open."

The pilot, aware of Kang's anger when challenged, knew better than to even think about questioning his commander's orders. He eased the hovering chopper around until he had the target in front of him. He dropped the nose of the helicopter, quickly setting his fire selector to activate the missile pod, and took his shot. The slim HE missile blazed its unerring way from pod to target and took out most of the structure in a burst of flame and smoke. Debris was thrown in all directions.

Kang smiled, a personal satisfaction at having achieved something.

"The only way to deal with vermin. Blow them out of house and home." He turned to his pilot. "Again."

JAMES AND MANNING, choking on the thick dust, hauled themselves to their feet. They had been closing on the house, exchanging fire with the darting figures of the

Chinese troops, when the missile struck, slamming them off their feet. The hot wind of the explosion gusted over them.

"You okay?" Manning asked.

James nodded. "Close but no cigar."

As they stumbled to their feet, checking weapons and themselves, they could still hear the rattle of gunfire from the far side of the house.

"The hell with this rear offensive," Manning said. "Those Chinese have scattered to the front. We need to be there."

"Yeah."

"Let's move, partner."

As they moved forward, James caught a glimpse of the second missile as it burned the air on its way in.

"Gary..." he yelled, his warning lost as the missile struck.

It exploded a split second later. The sudden glare of the blast seared his eyeballs, leaving him momentarily blinded. James felt an invisible force catch him and lift him off his feet. The concussion sucked away sound and sensation, dragged the breath from his body. He knew he was being thrown through the air, but the feeling was so off the scale he had no way of resisting...almost a sensation of freefall...and then he hit the ground again, hard. It left him stunned. The heat washed over him and he caught the thumping roar of the explosion, then nothing.

JAMES SQUEEZED HIS EYES shut, hoping the double-vision effect would fade. When he opened them again the haze had gone and he saw that the battle lines had altered completely.

Kang's helicopter had swooped down and hovered

above the area fronting the demolished house, close to the ground. The swirling rotor wash flung smoke and dust in all directions. Behind the chopper a pair of Multipurpose Combat Vehicles, with swivel-mounted Type 89, 12.7 mm machine guns, had rolled into view. The machine guns, including the door-mounted one in the helicopter, were covering Phoenix Force.

There was a moment when it seemed McCarter might carry on fighting. He had taken in the superior firepower of the machine guns and the Chinese soldiers facing his people, and James could almost hear the thoughts inside his commander's head. There might have been a time, long past, when McCarter could have conceivably defied the odds and gone for broke. Command of Phoenix Force had changed him. McCarter was no quitter, but even the former wild child of the SOG knew the limitations of reckless action. He assessed, deliberated and lowered with obvious reluctance, his P-90.

"For now," he said. "We don't have any choice."

The others followed suit.

James, as had McCarter, saw the mounted Uygur, riding out of sight beyond a distant ridge, away from the combat zone. Shin Tek was taking his men to safety until they could regroup and offer stiffer resistance. In the distance he could hear someone ranting wildly in Chinese. He focused himself toward the sound and saw a uniformed officer directing his armed troops. There was a frightening sense of rage emanating from the man. His soldiers scattered, eager to carry out his orders—or at least to remove themselves from his anger. Whatever else had happened here this man was less than happy with the result.

Glancing around James saw McCarter, Encizo and

Anna in a similar position to himself. He caught Mc-Carter's eyes. The Briton had a bloody gash across his left cheek. Blood had streamed down to soak the collar of his combat suit. He looked, James thought, suitably pissed off.

Kang's soldiers moved quickly to disarm their captives. They bound their hands behind them, then the prisoners hurriedly herded together in front of the man they were to know as Major Kang.

The man walked along the line, studying his prisoners, nodding to himself. There was almost a look of relish in his cool gaze, as if he were congratulating himself on this success. When he reached Mei Anna, his pleasure became even clearer. He cupped her chin with his hand, forcing her to look directly at him.

"Today gets even better," he said.

Anna struggled to free herself from his grip and Kang struck her with his free hand.

McCarter lunged forward and received a hard fist to the side of his head.

"Hey," James called out, and immediately regretted it when one of the Chinese slammed the butt of his weapon into the small of his back. Pain shot the length of James's spine.

The officer, attracted by the incident, came across and stood in front of James.

"Prisoners do not speak unless ordered to. I understand the arrogance of you Americans. Do not upset me. Ignore that and you will be instructed in the ways of obedience." Kang smiled at James's defiant scowl. "Be warned."

James took the command to heart and stayed silent. From where James stood he could see the smoking ruins of the house that had received the full brunt of the missiles launched from Kang's helicopter. The walls were down, the stone and timber construction completely razed to the ground. He thought about Anna's friend Loy Hung and the other survivor Dar Tan. Where were they? Buried beneath the tumbled stonework?

Immediately his thoughts jumped to someone closer.

Where was Gary Manning?

He hadn't seen the burly Canadian with McCarter and the others. His last memory of his Phoenix Force companion had been during those final moments before the arrival of the second HE missile from Kang's helicopter. His warning shout had been drowned in the roar of the explosion and his own reaction to the blast. Was Manning lying back there maybe injured—or worse? James caught McCarter's eye and mouthed the name. McCarter simply gave a brief shrug.

There was a moment when James almost blurted out Manning's name, determined to have an answer to the question, but at the same time he knew he would be doing little except putting them all at further risk. Major Kang would pay little heed to an irrational outburst from one of his captives, and all James would get would be more physical abuse from his captors. He resigned himself to accepting his current position for the time being, in the hope something could be done later. If Kang didn't realize there was a missing member of the team, it would do no one any good to reveal the fact.

Kang was yelling more orders. One of the soldiers knelt beside a scattering of objects on the ground and gathered them into his arms. James realized they were the weapons taken from Phoenix Force. He watched the soldier carry them across to the helicopter and hand them to one the chopper's crew. The crewman took the ordnance and vanished inside the helicopter. Kang was handed a collection of items that he studied carefully. One was the GPS unit. Kang held it up to show them, then dropped it on the ground and smashed it under his boot. He did the same with all the communications units. More orders from Kang and soldiers crossed to the captives and pushed them in the direction of the helicopter. They were herded inside and made to squat on the floor.

Kang himself, along with four armed soldiers, took positions inside the helicopter. Its power began to build. The major looked pleased with himself as the machine swayed off the ground, turned and began its flight.

"We are returning to Guang Lor," he informed them. "There is a punishment block there to hold you until I receive instructions from Beijing. They will be most delighted when I tell them I have American agents caught illegally on Chinese soil waging terrorist acts alongside the infamous Mei Anna."

At the sound of her name Anna threw a scathing look at Kang.

"My fame has spread to your grubby little corner of the world, has it, Kang?" Her words dripped with sarcasm.

"Still defiant? Perhaps we can knock that out of you at Guang Lor."

"That sounds to be your level, Kang. Beating women."

One of the soldiers guarding the prisoners moved

forward, swinging the back of his hand across Anna's face. The blow slammed her against the bulkhead.

"You see what happens when you forget your place, woman," Kang said.

The soldier, encouraged by Kang's words, leaned in to strike again. Before anyone could stop her Anna launched herself away from the bulkhead and rammed the top of her head into the soldier's face, impacting against the man's nose. Bone snapped and a spray of bright blood burst from his nostrils. The soldier stumbled back and Anna went for him again.

It was Kang who intervened before any of his men. His left hand reached out and caught Anna's tunic, swinging her around to face him. There was almost a smile of pleasure on his face as he drove his fist into the woman's face, the blow solid and delivered mercilessly. It caught Anna across the right cheek, spinning her off balance. She stumbled, almost to her knees, then felt herself propelled across the helicopter as Kang used his booted foot to kick her in the side. The blow lifted her off her feet before dropping her to the deck. Kang followed, bending to take a handful of her hair, dragging her head up.

By this time McCarter had lunged forward, yelling out Kang's name. He had taken no more than a few steps before one of the armed Chinese next to him lashed out with his autorifle. The heavy weapon smashed into McCarter's ribs, winding the Briton. The Chinese followed through with a second blow that thudded against the side of McCarter's skull and he sagged against the bulkhead. The soldier used his boots to continue his attack. Anna wasn't even aware of that as Kang yanked her head back.

"Traitorous bitch," he snapped. "Now you will pay for what you have done."

He began to slap her face, back and forth, continuing even after she had lapsed into unconsciousness. Only when he realized she was no longer aware did her allow her to slump to the deck, her face bruised and bloody from his blows.

Kang stood back, breathing heavily. He looked across at McCarter's still form. He snapped a finger at James and Encizo.

"Do any of you want to make a contribution? No? I did not think so."

Snapping orders to his men to maintain a full watch over the prisoners, Kang moved along the cabin until he reached the flight deck and sank into the seat beside the pilot, allowing a thin smile of contentment to etch its way across his face. He congratulated himself on a mission well defined by success, if not completely accomplished, and with far better results than he could ever have expected. The capture of the Americans and Mei Anna would be well received in Beijing. They were a sound political prize. Much would be made of their unlawful incursion into sovereign Chinese territory, the fact they had colluded with the traitor Mei Anna and killed a number of Chinese military personnel. The Americans would be made to look like fools when the captives were paraded in court and displayed on television worldwide. Their protestations would fall on disbelieving ears and their international reputation would suffer a setback. The outcry would drown the arguments that the U.S. was trying to retrieve stolen technology. It would reduce that accusation to a dry whisper in the wind.

For Kang the capture of the American team would help to defer any criticism of having lost the circuit board in the first place. True, he had yet to turn up evidence of Loy Hung and guarantee the recovery of the circuit board, but that was just a matter of time. He had left the bulk of his men in the village. Their orders were specific. Locate Hung and his partners, dead or alive, and find the circuit board, then return to Guang Lor. In the meantime Kang would inform Beijing of his success and deliver his captives to the city where he would take the rewards the Party officials would present him with.

No more than he deserved. His years of service, many of them in such barren places as Guang Lor, would be over. He would receive promotion and be offered a prestigious position elsewhere. For Tchi Chuy Kang this was the start of a new phase in his career. And probably, he realized, ensure some higher promotion than major.

CHAPTER SIX

"This wasn't exactly the way I expected to get inside this bloody place," David McCarter said absently.

He stared around the cold cell, his thoughts not entirely focused on his present situation. He was thinking about Gary Manning, the missing member of Phoenix Force. The Canadian's fate was still unknown, and until he had confirmation one way or the other, McCarter wasn't going to be content. It wasn't in him to mark one of his team as dead until he had solid proof in front of him. While Manning's condition remained unconfirmed, McCarter kept the Canadian alive in his thoughts, and even though escape seemed something of an abstract at this moment, the Briton was far from defeated. When, rather than if, they were free, one of their objectives would be to find Manning.

Calvin James sensed his commander's concern. It was akin to his own. James's last image was of Manning trying to outrun the incoming HE missile. James remembered the blast, his own luck at surviving the detonation, but he was still concerned over his teammate's.

McCarter suddenly slammed his clenched fists against the solid bulk of the cell door.

"And what is that bastard doing to Anna?"

Two guards had come to the cell twenty minutes earlier and had taken Mei Anna away. McCarter's protest had got him a rifle butt in the stomach, the last thing Anna had seen as she was dragged away.

MEI ANNA HAD BEEN escorted along a narrow, dimly lit passage to a bare, windowless, concrete room that held nothing but a sturdy wooden chair. She had been forced to sit in the chair, her wrists and ankles secured by thick leather straps. The two guards stood just behind her. Nothing happened for a while and then the door opened and Major Kang entered.

"I would have expected someone like you to have been harder to capture," Kang said. "I know a great deal about you. Quite a reputation, Mei Anna. But that is over now."

He was extremely pleased with himself. The woman had been an elusive enemy for some time now. She had done a great deal of harm to Beijing's credibility. She and her group were responsible for a number of criminal acts against the state. It was going to look well on his record that Kang had been the one to capture her.

"And *we* know a great deal about you, Kang. All about the things you do. Nothing I would wish on my record."

Kang turned quickly, his right hand sweeping around to slap Anna across the side of her face. The blow was unsparing. It rocked her head to one side, leaving a red welt across her cheek. Tears welled up in her eyes, but she forced back the cry of pain rising in her throat and stared up at Kang defiantly.

"What a hero, Kang. Beijing would be so proud of you. Daring to hit a lone woman all on your own. Of course I'm sure you will omit the fact in your report that I was tied to a chair at the time."

"I have no time for these stupid games. Tell me about your organization. The names of your people. Locations. I want to know."

"Only so you can brag to your masters in Beijing that you have been clever enough to break me. Kang, you are so easy to read. A small man trying to make himself bigger for the men who make him jump through hoops."

He hit her again. This time it was with his fist and the blow split her lips, knocking her sideways with enough force to topple the chair. Anna cracked her head against the floor and lay still and silent, even when Kang ordered her chair to be set upright again. He took hold of her hair and yanked her head back, staring directly into her eyes.

"You are a traitor to your country," he said.

"Whatever I am, Kang, you will never be a man if you live to be a hundred. You will always be a puppet, dangling from Beijing's strings and dancing to their tune."

Kang stepped back, trembling from the harsh words. He deliberately spaced himself from the woman. If he had stayed close, he would have beaten her until she was dead. He knew his responsibility was to deliver her alive to Beijing, so he would have to remain at a safe distance from her. Despite himself he felt the sting of her remarks. She used her words well, knowing just what to say to draw a response. Yet she was an intelligent young woman and had to know she was placing herself at risk by taunting him. Why would she do such a thing? The only reason could be that she wanted him to become so angry he would kill her. If she died, then any propaganda Beijing might gain from her capture would be lost. He credited her with courage on that. She was willing to sacrifice herself to deny her enemy profit from her capture. As Kang reached the door of the cell, he turned to have a final look at her.

Mei Anna returned his gaze with an angry stare. She was bruised and battered, marked by livid gashes. Blood had coursed down her face. More blood had spilled down the front of her combat suit. Yet her eyes, partly obscured by strands of her black hair, seemed to shine with the spirit that seemed to keep her defiant even in this, her most dangerous situation.

No matter how many times we take them on. No matter how many we kill. They still carry on. They still come back. Fight on.

For a fleeting moment, before his ingrained loyalty to the State, to his country washed it away, Kang felt a sense of fear. It lasted only a millisecond and then he turned away. In that fraction of time, through everything else threatening to overwhelm her, Mei Anna registered Kang's doubt at his own vulnerability. In that moment the pain she was experiencing was worth the look in Kang's eyes.

"For your information. Just to prove we are not as stupid as you believe. Your inside man here at Guang Lor, Kam Lee, has been unmasked." Kang smiled. "Unmasked and dealt with. He will not be passing on any more information. I might have his head placed on a stake so everyone can see."

Anna's face betrayed nothing. Internally she stored

the information away. Kang, seeing she wasn't going to allow him any satisfaction at this disclosure, snapped his fingers at the guards.

"Take her back to the cell."

"Do you want one of the others, Major?"

"Later," Kang said. "For now let them worry what is going to happen to them once they are in Beijing's hands."

He strode along the passage. He was angry that he hadn't been able to gain any information from Mei Anna. It would have been pleasing to be able to present names and locations of the Pro-Democracy group to his superiors. Perhaps there would be time yet. First he needed to conclude his business with Loy Hung and the missing circuit board. He made his way to the communications center where he would contact the squad he had left at the village. He needed an update on their progress.

The trouble was he failed to make any kind of connection with his squad. The communications link had been closed down.

Kang strode from the building, heading for the helicopter pad.

"Where is the crew?" he demanded of the ground staff.

"They are—"

"Bring them immediately. Is this machine ready to fly again?"

"We need to complete refueling."

"Do it quickly. I want this machine ready to leave now."

Kang paced up and down the pad while he waited. He couldn't understand why his squad wasn't answering his calls. When he had flown from the village everything had been under control. His men were in charge. All they'd had to do was search out and find Loy Hung. The man had to be in the area. He was on foot. A fugitive. Not even a trained soldier.

So what was going on?

"Kang?"

He looked around and saw Dr. Lin Cheung hurrying across the site. Irritation creased Kang's face. What did the man want now? Kang had enough to handle without Cheung bothering him. As the man got closer, Kang composed himself. Personal feelings aside, Kang needed to remain in favor with the man. Cheung was an important official. He also had the ear of Director Han. Outwardly a quiet, self-effacing man Cheung was also extremely clever and he wasn't the sort to make a fool of.

"Are you leaving us again so soon? Is there a problem?"

"I need to return to the village to take control of the hunt for Loy Hung. Now that the prisoners are settled, I need to get back. It is my responsibility, Dr. Cheung, and I will not forget that. Arrangements have been made for the transportation of the prisoners to Beijing. A plane should arrive for them late tomorrow. Then they will be off our hands. If it is in my power I would like to have Loy Hung go along with them and the missing circuit board back in your hands."

Cheung smiled in his quiet, almost gentle way.

"You are a credit to your profession, Major Kang. Such devotion will not go unnoticed in Beijing. I will make it my business to see that your efforts do not get overlooked."

"I do it for my country, Doctor, not for personal gain."

"Of course." Cheung turned to go. "Major, good hunting."

As he returned to his comfortable office, leaving Kang to bark at the ground crew and his tardy pilot, Cheung's smile broadened.

Did Kang really believe he had fooled Cheung with his oily platitudes? Unfortunately he probably did. Stupid idiot, Cheung thought. If he thinks he will get credit for completing the assignment, he was going to be extremely disappointed. Beijing already knew what had happened.

Cheung had used the time Kang was away to speak personally to Director Han. He had detailed the whole episode, from the moment it had been reported the missile had been lost and that one of the technicians had, without authority, used an American circuit board. Dai Sung, the errant technician, would be dealt with when things had calmed down. Cheung had explained about the exposure of Kam Lee, the inside man working for the Pro-Democracy group and how that matter had been resolved. As to the capture of the American-inspired group caught on Chinese territory, Cheung had made certain Director Han understood *his* initiation of their capture.

"Kang is driven by his dreams of becoming a national hero because he managed to catch these people," Cheung had said. "He seems to overlook the fact that as he is in charge of local security for the area they should not have been able to even set foot in Xinjiang. However, while he is busy finding Loy Hung and the missing board, I see no point in spoiling his moment."

"Of course not, Lin. As long as he believes he is gaining favor he will work all the harder. We can let him down lightly once we have all the pieces of this puzzle gathered together. Unfortunately for Kang once the matter moves to Beijing it will by necessity be taken to a higher level. Far above the authority of a mere major. As you say, Kang will be too busy explaining why, as the man in charge of security at Guang Lor, and the surrounding territory, he allowed all this to take place under his nose. As well as having an undercover operative working inside Guang Lor. It will probably fall to you and I to, er, become responsible for bringing this incident to a satisfactory conclusion."

"Of course, Director. Rest assured blame and congratulations will be distributed to the correct quarters."

"Lin, keep me informed so I am clear on all points. Our stories must tally."

"Just what I was thinking, Director."

WHEN DIRECTOR HAN replaced his phone he sat for some time considering his conversation with Cheung. He was thinking more along the lines of his own survival, rather than his and Cheung's. Friendship was all very well, but if the Guang Lor affair did end in total disaster the falling dominoes would start with Kang, go through Cheung and, without a shadow of a doubt, end with Director Su Han. And in circumstances such as those, friendship mattered little. Individual survival became the watchword.

GARY MANNING LAY where he was for a long time, awake but unsure exactly where he was. He seemed to be in total darkness, covered in heavy clods of earth and lying in cold water that had soaked through his combat gear. When he moved to check the condition of his arms and legs he found he was fine, except for some stiffness having lain prone for so long. His whole body ached, too. It felt as if he had just come through some extreme accident.

That was when he recalled the explosion from the second missile strike. At the back of his mind he recalled someone yelling a warning.

Calvin James.

They had been heading to the front of the house when the missile hit. The force of the blast had picked Manning off his feet, throwing him into the air. It had all happened in a fragmented few moments, and he couldn't even recall hitting the ground again.

Manning sat up, shaking off the earth that covered him. His head and shoulders brushed against objects surrounding him. He reached out a hand. It felt like foliage. Thin tendrils and leaves. He made more effort and gained his feet, pushing aside the tangled brush. As his eyes adjusted to the gloom, Manning was able to take in his surroundings. A round shaft with a couple of feet of water underfoot. It took him a minute to realize he was in a well shaft. The explosion had thrown him through the air and he had fallen down the well as the ground around it and a section of the shaft had collapsed, spilling thick earth into the cavity. It had formed a steep slide of crumbling earth that had served to cushion his fall.

The Canadian tilted his head. Through the debris and the tangle of foliage he could see pale blue sky. He leaned back against the stone shaft, shaking his head at the situation.

He checked his weapons. The P-90 hung suspended from its neck strap and his pistol was still in its holster.

Manning made to move and the well shaft began to spin. He fell back against the shaft and stayed there until the sensation passed. Only then did he feel the pulse of pain down the right side of his face. He explored with his fingers and felt a raw bruise just in front of his ear. He felt the sticky cling of blood. Farther down the flesh of his cheek was scraped and raw. When he felt steady enough Manning continued to recon his surroundings.

He could make out the earth fall and the stone blocks that had broken free. Above that the main shaft of the well seemed to be solid. Manning estimated it to be around twelve to fifteen feet to the rim. It was the only route he could take. He took his time as he negotiated the earth slope, aware that it might collapse before he reached the upper level. Once he felt the earth start to shift, and he paused until it settled again. When he reached the top of the slope he was able to gain hand- and footholds using the stone facing of the shaft. He climbed steadily until he was able to throw one hand over the rim of the well, shouldering aside the tangled foliage wedged in the gap.

Manning remained still, listening for any extraneous sounds that might warn him of human presence. He would have no idea how long he'd lain unconscious at the bottom of the well until he could check his watch. However long it had been he still didn't know the outcome of the firefight that had been under way when the missile hit.

He raised his head above the rim. Taking a look around he saw that the house itself had collapsed from the missile strike. What few sections there had been still standing were gone completely now, reduced to rubble. Manning could feel the warmth of the sun on the back of his neck. It was high, implying it was well into the morning.

He noticed the silence, too. A complete absence of sound.

There were a number of bodies in the open space that fronted the house. Bloody and still. All were clad in Chinese military combat gear. Farther on he saw more bodies. Again Chinese.

Had Phoenix Force done all that? he wondered.

Manning dragged himself over the rim of the well and dropped to the ground. He pulled the P-90 into position as he checked out a wider area. Nothing. The village looked totally deserted. Manning remained in position until he was satisfied the area was clear, then pushed cautiously to his feet.

He took a slow walk around the immediate area. He checked the dead Chinese. They had all been shot—he saw, too, that each man's throat had been slit. There was also an absence of weapons.

Manning knew that Phoenix Force would have had nothing to do with the throat-cutting. The SOG team fought hard but wouldn't have done this. This was more likely to be something to do with the rivalry between the Chinese and the indigenous Uygur. Manning was thinking about Shin Tek and his men. They had made no bones over the feelings they had where the Chinese were concerned. The resentment the Uygur felt had been palpable.

It struck Manning that if the Uygur had done this, they had to have won a victory over Kang's soldiers.

There was a stronger need to know where Phoenix Force was. He knew without question that the only reason they would have left without him was that something had prevented them from searching for him.

A soft sound caught his attention. Manning turned, the P-90 rising.

A man he recognized from ID photographs limped out from behind the cover of scattered rocks.

It was Loy Hung. He carried a Chinese assault rifle in his right hand and a small backpack in the other. Close beside him was Dar Tan.

There was more movement as the Uygur appeared, led by Shin Tek. They and their ponies were loaded with weapons they had taken from the dead Chinese.

But there was no Phoenix Force.

"Your friends are prisoners of Major Kang," Hung said. "He has taken them to Guang Lor."

THREE HOURS LATER they were settled in one of the camps the Uygur used when on raids against the Chinese troops. It was hidden deep in the foothills, with its own natural water supply and even grazing for the ponies. This was larger than the camp Phoenix Force had visited when they had first met Shin Tek.

When they arrived, food was being cooked and hot tea brewed.

Manning took a little time to get cleaned up and do what he could for his head wound and the cuts and scratches that seemed to cover his body. By the time he squatted by one of the fires he was more than ready for the food and drink offered to him. Manning downed the hot tea gratefully. He held out his mug for more. One of the Uygur handed him a chunk of hot mutton.

Wolfing it down the Phoenix Force warrior glanced around the campsite, looking for Loy Hung. He waited until the man joined him.

"Tell me what happened."

"When Kang realized he had caught Mei Anna *and* a team of American invaders—his words—he became very excited. He made it his priority to fly them directly to Guang Lor and secure them in the punishment block.

"He left his squad here to continue the search for me and the circuit board. He would return once he had the prisoners locked up. As soon as Kang had gone and the Chinese stood down, Shin Tek and his men returned. It appeared they had been waiting for the right moment to strike. I believe the Chinese thought they had gone. They were caught unready. The fight was over in minutes. I knew the Uygur had a reputation as fierce fighters but even I was surprised."

"How was it Kang didn't find you?"

"Like you, when that missile struck, Tan and I were almost killed by the house collapsing on us. We were under all the rubble and I believed I might die under there. It was strange. I couldn't move but I was able to see and hear what happened when Kang captured your friends, then when Tek and his men rode back in. After the fight I was able to call out to them and they dug us free."

Manning finished his meal. It made him feel a little better. That and having his wounds cleaned helped. He sat, considering his next move. Foremost on his mind was the fate of his team. Right now *he* was their was their way out of Guang Lor. As long as he was physically able, he would do everything he could to get them out of Kang's lockup.

Manning's contemplative silence caught Hung's attention.

"What are you thinking?"

"That my friends are in trouble. Imprisoned by a dangerous man."

"True enough. Kang is dangerous. And also ambitious. He will consider your friends as nothing more than pawns in his game."

"Kang will want them in Beijing so he can show them off," Manning said. "I can't sit here and let that happen."

"All very noble," Hung said. "But what can you do? Go to Guang Lor and break them out?"

Manning smiled. "Exactly."

Hung stared at him, searching his face as if he were expecting to have everything revealed.

"Are you serious?"

"Loy, you must know why we came here. What we had to attempt. It hasn't changed. And neither has the fact those people are my friends. The same as Anna is supposed to be yours."

Hung's face darkened at the intonation in Manning's voice.

"There is no supposing about it. Mei Anna is very important to me."

"Then you should understand why I have to make this attempt to free my friends."

Hung nodded, relaxing. His expression mellowed when he spoke. "If you go to Guang Lor, you could end up dead."

"At least I'll die knowing I tried."

"But Guang Lor is a hard place to break into. Very risky."

"I know that, too."

"Then why?"

"Because they would do it for me."

The Chinese shook his head. "It seems a shame for so many to have to die. Especially when they are such good friends. In which case I feel I must do what I can to keep you all alive. I will come with you."

"Hung, it looks like I have more friends than I realized."

"You are a lucky man."

"You said you have friends, too," Manning stated.

"Ah," Hung said, "but obviously not like yours."

He turned away, leaving Manning staring after him.

HUNG HAD FOUND ONE of the Uygurs who understood English reasonably well. He had been with the group who had joined Tek to defeat the Chinese soldiers. A young man with his black hair worn long, he listened enthusiastically when Hung had been asking for help. His name was Pak Choy.

"I will go with you," he said. He had one of the Chinese PF-89 rocket launchers slung across his back and carried a canvas bag over his shoulder that held a number of the missiles. "I want to send these rockets back to Kang."

Through Hung, Manning explained to Shin Tek what he needed him to do.

"Just across the border, in the Wakhjir Pass, is a helicopter. It is waiting to take my friends and me out of Xinjiang and back to an American base in Afghanistan. The pilot's name is Jack Grimaldi. Tell him to be ready to fly us out if we are able to reach him. He must understand that we can't be certain when we might arrive. Nor can we radio him to let him know because Kang destroyed our communication equipment. Tell him the Canadian, that's me, has sent you. That you are a friend of Mei Anna." Manning waited until Tek nodded his understanding. "Shin Tek, this is important to us. Can you find this man? Will you do this for me?"

"Of course we will find him. I know this place you speak of, and I will do it for my new friends. You do something for me and my people. If you see this Kang, make sure you kill him. Rid us of Beijing's yapping dog," Tek said through Hung.

Manning commandeered one of the captured multipurpose vehicles. He needed something that would get him to Guang Lor in the shortest possible time.

"We are here," Hung explained, using the tip of his knife to indicate the spot on the map.

"How far to Guang Lor?"

"Fifty, maybe sixty miles. There may be patrols out now. Major Kang will make sure of that. He will be anxious to protect his prize. The capture of foreign combatants on Chinese soil is a great propaganda opportunity for Beijing. Something they can use to humiliate America. And of course it is a dream come true for Kang. It will take him far from Guang Lor. Promotion. He will be Beijing's shining star. A true son of China."

"I already figured on that," Manning said. "Doesn't give us much time to do anything. Beijing will want to fly them all out as soon as possible."

"Then we should leave now."

"Let's go," Manning said, snatching up his P-90 and backpack.

Guang Lor

"DO YOU SEE THE BUILDING that juts from the main outer wall of the site? That houses the punishment block. It's a bad place. A place of suffering for those who displease Major Kang. Workers and soldiers alike. If they break his restrictions, or fail to comply with orders from Beijing, they will find themselves in that place."

Manning turned on his side and glanced at Hung. The Chinese lay on the hard ground beside the Canadian as they studied the Guang Lor facility. Inside the walled compound Manning could see launch gantries, two of them with dark-painted, half-built missiles anchored in place. On top of a squat building he could see radar dishes and electronic antenna.

"Not exactly a welcoming place," Manning said.

He was studying the layout through a pair of binoculars he had found in one of the Chinese vehicles. The wall he was observing comprised the south side of the site. It had the main gate to the site in this section. The punishment block was in this wall, as well. It jutted from the main wall, around sixty feet in length and thirty wide. Heavy double doors were set in the end wall. There were two armed guards positioned at these doors. To one side Manning saw a couple of six-wheeled trucks and three smaller multipurpose vehicles.

"How many military personnel does Kang have?"

"No more than forty," Hung said. "They are divided between the punishment block and also patrol the site interior. Remember, too, that Kang had part of his complement out looking for us and they won't be coming back. But he can call in more if he needs them."

"There's a larger garrison, isn't there?"

Hung nodded. "It was established a number of years ago when civil unrest became a threat to the Han Chinese that had been sent by Beijing. Integration with the indigenous population has never been an easy matter. The garrison is about eighty miles to the south, near the main center of population."

"If Kang sent for help, how long would it take for them to get here?"

"A few hours."

Manning lowered the glasses and leaned his back against the stony outcropping that concealed them.

"First we need to get Mei Anna and my people out of that punishment block. Once that's done we have to destroy the research facility where all the stolen technology is worked on."

"You make it sound so simple when you describe it."

"Believe me, Hung, there's nothing simple about it."

Hung used his knife to scratch a diagram in the hard earth.

"The main research block is housed in the west section of the site. It is actually built against the outer wall. It was constructed from concrete that was strengthened by heavy steel rods. There are two floors. Access is by coded doors here. Once inside, the setup is very well protected by electronics and secured access points. Compared to the research section the rest of the site is crude. Power comes from diesel generators on the far side of the facility. But the research section has its own power from generators housed here on the west side of the block. They are inside a building that is constructed from heavy-gauge steel. Even if the rest of the site was powerless, or destroyed, the research section would still have power and be well protected."

"Sounds like your man did a thorough job of checking this place out."

"He did. It took Kam Lee over six months to gather all his information. Piece by piece. Adding to it every night. Hand drawing the detail and walking every section of the site so he could be as accurate as he could with distances."

"Then we'd better make sure we don't waste all that good work," Manning said. "Hung, I'm grateful for you helping in this. But I don't want you to go in without understanding the danger. This is one hell of a setup, well defended, and there's no guarantee some of us won't get hurt."

The Chinese placed hand on Manning's arm. "As you pointed out, one of our own is in there, as well. Mei Anna is very important to our movement. Even as far away from Hong Kong as we are, Mei Anna's exploits are known to us all. She has never given up. She is the Pro-Democracy group's most wanted person. Every second she spends here on the mainland is a threat to her life. Yet she came to help without concern for her own safety. There is no way we will turn aside now that she needs our assistance."

"I guess that means you're in for the duration."

THEY HAD FOUND an array of ordnance stored in the rear of the multipurpose vehicle. There was a second PF-89 rocket launcher, courtesy the Chinese military, and a box of 80 mm missiles that went with them. A heavy canvas bag held a dozen fragmentation grenades. Hung proudly exhibited some blocks of plastic explosive and detonators, provided by Tek's men. There were no high-tech electronic power units to go with them. Just simple timers that were set by hand.

"They will work," Hung assured Manning. "I have used them before and they have never failed."

"Just telling me that, kind of inspires my confidence," Manning told him, and the Chinese smiled. "The smile helps, too."

"Have you any thoughts on how we should make our attack?"

"We should draw as many as we can away from the punishment block. That'll help when we move in to get them out. Pak Choy and his launcher on that ridge behind us can lay down a barrage of rockets into the site along the southeast section. Go for anything he can see. Make a lot of noise, take down anything he can hit. Those large storage tanks. My guess is they hold fuel for the generators. Maybe even vehicle fuel. He can destroy those missiles, too, if he wants."

"To draw people away from the part of the site we need to go for?"

"That's the idea. Once he starts making the noise, we go for the punishment block and get our people out. It's pretty thin, but we don't have time for grand strategy. We just need to stay alert in case they're waiting for us."

"Something occurs to me," Hung said. "Kang may not be here. He might have returned to the village to take control of the search for me."

"One thing at a time," Manning said. "Let's get into position. Check all your weapons and make sure everything we have is fully loaded. We'll go in once it starts to get dark. We might catch them off guard. Kang might not be expecting a breakout attempt. The way he left things there was no one readily available to mount any kind of rescue. But he's no fool. With the captives he has, he won't dare risk dismissing any possible attempt to free them. If my guess is correct, he'd expect a nighttime strike at full dark. So we go in before that."

"Yes. I prefer to be able to see at least my hand in front of my face," Hung admitted.

MANNING CARRIED HIS P-90 and his Beretta. His Gerber fighting knife was sheathed on his belt. He took a number of the grenades and dropped them into the pockets of his combat suit. He also carried a Chinese Model-56, 7.62 mm semiautomatic rifle they had found among the ordnance in the rear of the multipurpose vehicle. It was far from being a custom made weapon, but it *was* fitted with a scope. This veteran rifle had been standard issue for the PLA over a number of decades. Based on the Soviet SKS, it was a rugged, well-proved rifle, though it had been pushed aside in favor of fully automatic assault rifles for the Chinese military. With an effective range of 400 meters and a 10-round magazine capacity, it was the closest weapon Manning was going to find to a dedicated sniper rifle.

Loy Hung had a number of small bricks of plastique and timing devices in a backpack. Detonators were in a separate pocket. He carried a Chinese Type-56 assault rifle and a QSZ-92 9 mm pistol. Dar Tan had the other rocket launcher slung across his back and carried a satchel holding six missiles.

Pak Choy, armed with his launcher and a canvas satchel holding a dozen missiles, moved to his strategic position where he would be able to fire his weapon into and over the compound wall.

The sun was already sliding out of the sky when they moved off, using every piece of cover available as they closed in on the base.

Their plan of attack was simple but direct, and even Manning had to admit they were shaving good luck down to the wire on this one.

Once they were within range Manning would employ the Model 56 and take out the two guards at the entrance to the punishment block. The moment he heard the shots, Pak Choy would start to lay down his 80 mm salvo. With the door guards taken out, Manning and his two partners would make for the punishment-block entrance. Dar Tan would use his launcher to blow the doors of the block, giving Manning and Hung the opportunity to get inside. Tan would remain outside, defend the parked vehicles and watch the main gates.

They reached the final cover in front of the cleared section of ground approaching the base. Manning dropped to one knee, laying down his weapons, and made a final check of the rifle. He was hoping it had been sighted in. He wasn't going to get too many chances. He clicked off the safety and brought the heavy rifle to his shoulder, peering into the scope. He had to use the knurled ring to focus it. It didn't have the best optical clarification he would have liked, but he had to work with what he had.

The big Canadian took his time sighting in on the first guard, marking the center of the man's chest, which at least gave him a little error on either side. His finger slid against the trigger and he began to ease against the poundage. The moment his target turned full-on, Manning drew a breath, held it, and took the trigger all the way. He felt the solid slam of the wood stock against his shoulder and felt the muzzle rise as the shot went off. Still on the scope, he saw the bullet strike slightly left of center, which was only a fraction out. It was close enough for the 7.62 mm projectile to core into the target's heart. He saw a small puff of dust blossom from the hit. The crack of the shot was still in Manning's ears as he moved the rifle to the second target.

The remaining guard had seen his partner go down and was reacting, turning in toward the doors and the box-mounted telephone fixed to the wall. Manning's second shot hit him high in the left shoulder, erupting through the front in a spurt of black flecks. The impact pushed the guard against the wall and Manning hit him with bullet number three, placing this one between his shoulders. The Chinese bounced off the wall and fell away, slumping to his knees.

A momentary flash erupted from behind Manning as Choy fired the first of the 80 mm rockets. It streaked across the sky trailing white vapor and impacted against the wall of the site. The explosion tore a ragged hole in the wall, sending debris spinning into the darkening sky.

"Let's go," Manning urged.

He dropped the rifle and snatched up his P-90. With Hung and Tan close by, he broke cover and began to sprint toward the punishment block.

Tan waited until he was in range, then dropped to one knee, the launcher on his shoulder. He released the missile and it streaked by Manning and Hung, detonating when it struck the double doors. The explosion ripped both doors off their supports and demolished a section of the front wall.

Regular explosions ripped the air. To Manning's

right he saw flaming bursts beyond the outer wall as Choy dropped his missiles inside the perimeter. His strikes had to have targeted something flammable as a heavy fireball suddenly gushed into the twilight, rising to a considerable height before spreading and sending billowing smoke in a thick cloud.

"Watch out," Hung yelled from somewhere in the gloom close by.

Manning saw armed men in Chinese military uniforms emerge from the smoke around the shattered entrance to the punishment block. They were a little dazed from the explosion, and that gave Manning and Hung some advantage. They opened fire, raking the figures with sustained bursts, taking down a number of enemy guns with their initial firing. The others reacted, spreading apart and returned fire. Manning fished out a grenade. He yanked the pin and hurled the bomb at the advancing Chinese. The solid detonation spread the grenade's deadly contents and bodies were hit and thrown aside by the burst.

Hung paused to throw one of his own grenades, eliminating the last of the Chinese. With the current opposition cleared Manning made directly for the entrance, Hung covering him and Tan turning aside to go for the parked vehicles and watch the main gates.

Reaching the entrance to the block, Manning stepped over the scattered debris, peered into the dimly lit interior and moved on.

THE EXPLOSIONS ALERTED the imprisoned Phoenix Force team. The high barred window made it impossible for them to see what was happening, but they were able to hear.

"I don't know who it is, but let's hope they keep this up," McCarter said.

When the rocket took out the main doors of the block the whole structure shuddered, concrete dust showering the captives. The single fluorescent light, recessed in the ceiling behind metal mesh, flickered and faded. Then it went out completely before coming back on.

The detonations went on, followed by heavier explosions. From the other side of the thick cell door came the rattle of autofire and the spiteful crack of grenades. Men were yelling in Chinese. There seemed to be a great deal of confusion.

Another rocket struck the perimeter wall. Shock waves caused concrete to crack, spilling jagged chunks into the cell. Where the wall joined the ceiling, a gap appeared, showing a strip of the evening sky. The occupants of the cell moved to the far side.

James and Encizo moved to check the door. They were disappointed to find it was still secure.

"Only way we're getting out of here is if someone opens it from the other side," James said.

McCarter had to agree with that. There was nothing on their side that would allow the door to be opened. All the controls were on the exterior. The feeling that there was nothing they could do annoyed the Briton. He hated being left helpless, unable to contribute to whatever was going on outside the cell. He wanted to be in the action himself, not relegated to being a bystander.

There was more autofire, the crackling echo of sound seeming to be closer to their cell. The hard sound of the door's locking slides being activated caught their attention. The door was pushed open, swinging slowly to expose the passage outside, smoke curling around the armed figure standing there.

"This is the one," a familiar voice yelled. "They're here."

It was Gary Manning.

He looked a mess. His combat gear was torn and filthy. His face was bruised and bloody. He was cradling his P-90 under his right arm, and he was gesturing with his free hand.

"Come on, you lazy bastards. I didn't do all this for you guys to stand around staring. Let's move it."

McCarter grabbed Anna's hand and hauled her alongside as he made for the door, pausing to exchange a brief word with Manning.

"Talk about making an entrance."

Manning grinned.

PAK CHOY HAD LEFT his distant position to join the fight inside the compound. He had the launcher slung over his back and was using his assault rifle to drive back the Chinese gunners as they emerged from the smoke and debris—most of which he had created himself by his rocket salvoes. Now the stocky Uygur was pushing deeper into the complex, his taut features illuminated by the swirling glow of the numerous fires his missiles had started.

The men of Phoenix Force had armed themselves with weapons taken from downed guards, taking extra assault rifles and any magazines they found. Even Anna had found herself a pistol. They took McCarter's lead, pushing their way across the inner compound in the direction of the research block.

"Vehicle coming," Hung yelled above the rattle of gunfire.

A 4x4 FAV came in their direction, weaving in and out of the swirl of smoke and flame. It was picking up speed as it moved along the concrete apron running the length of the site.

Choy put down his assault rifle and dragged his launcher into play. He fed a missile into the tube and raced forward, dropping the weapon across his shoulder. He braced his legs apart, swinging the muzzle to bear on the speeding truck. There was a rattling crackle of heavy autofire from the Type 89 machine gun mounted on a swivel in the open back of the oncoming truck and Choy's body was ripped open by the 12.7 mm burst. He went down hard, the launcher draped across his bloody corpse.

Encizo turned back without hesitation. He ran across to where Choy's shattered body lay and snatched up the launcher. With the weapon in place the Cuban twisted around so he was facing the truck, leveled the launcher and pulled the trigger. The missile leaped from the tube, swooping in at the truck. The driver made an attempt to get out of its path, but his maneuver was too late and too little. The 80 mm missile hit straight-on, the ensuing blast ripping the truck and its occupants apart in a burst of flame and smoke. The stricken vehicle was lifted off the ground and became a blazing object of extreme menace. Its forward motion hardly seemed to have been affected and Encizo dropped flat, hugging the ground as the wreck arced over him. It hit the ground only yards beyond him, disintegrating in a burst of flame and smoke, leaving shattered pieces of debris raining across the area.

Encizo rolled to his feet, pausing to check out Choy's motionless form. The Uygur had taken the full impact of the machine gun's burst. There was nothing anyone could do for him now. The Cuban kept the launcher and picked up the canvas bag holding the missiles. As he moved away, he grabbed up the discarded assault rifle.

Coming face-to-face with Hung, he shook his head. "Sorry, Hung, he didn't make it."

The Chinese nodded. "We should go," he said briefly.

Rejoining the others, they formed a loose skirmish line as they crossed the site, closing in on the research block.

"Rafe," McCarter said, indicating the entrance doors.

"Those doors are steel," Manning stated.

"And those rockets are designated armor-piercing," Hung said.

"Let's see if they qualify," Encizo suggested.

He fed a missile into the launcher, swung the readied weapon to his shoulder and lined up on the doors. His finger eased back on the trigger, sending the 80 mm rocket at the target. It curved in at the doors, trailing a mist of smoke, impacting with a thump of sound, throwing up a ball of fire and smoke as it shattered the doors and blew them off their hinges. Debris fanned out across the frontage, pattering to the ground in a dark shower.

"You see," Hung said.

"Cover us," McCarter said to Manning and James. "Rafe, bring that bloody tank-buster. We might need it."

Hung passed Manning the small satchel he carried with the extra grenades.

"Make good use of them."

Manning and James took up defensive positions near the breached doors.

McCarter, Anna and Hung made for the entrance, Encizo following after he had reloaded the rocket launcher. Smoke hung around the entrance, moving where the internal air-extractors dragged it away.

"The stairs are over there," Hung said, indicating the way.

They moved to the foot of the stairs, but stayed to one side when McCarter waved them back. He had spotted movement on the upper landing, heard subdued voices and the rattle of weapons being cocked.

Their presence had been noticed and the sharp crackle of autofire echoed through the area. A volley of 7.62 mm slugs chewed at the wood stair rails and the floor at the base of the steps. Sharp commands were heard, followed by the thump of boots descending.

McCarter let the advance party reach the halfway point, then leaned out, tracking his assault rifle on the enemy gunners. His finger stroked the trigger, the weapon steady in his grip as he laid down a deadly volley. His initial burst took out the men in the lead, blasting them back against the risers. One slid down the stairs, falling on his face at the base. McCarter heard boots retreating up the stairs and he took the advantage, stepping farther out and firing a second burst at the fleeing soldiers.

Hung stepped alongside McCarter, a single grenade in his fist, the pin already out. He released the lever and waited a long moment before he threw the missile. It curved up and struck the landing, bouncing and rolling, scattering the armed men assembled there. The detonation was hard, ringing metallically off the concrete walls of the research block. A shower of dust and plaster fragments rained down the stairs. A brief cry was heard, quickly lost in the general noise of the explosion.

"Go," McCarter yelled, taking the lead up the stairs.

He reached the upper landing. The grenade had done its job. Three bodies lay on the floor, clothing tattered and bloody. A fourth man was slumped against the blackened wall, rubbing blood from his eyes with a grimed hand. He still held his assault rifle and as he heard McCarter's approach the Chinese swung his rifle around.

There was a flurry of movement beside the Briton and the crack of a pistol shot. The Chinese soldier twisted away from McCarter, the impact of the round sliding him across the wall. Mei Anna touched McCarter's arm and when he turned he saw the automatic pistol in her hand.

"Come on," she said urgently.

The others had joined them, Hung pointing the way along the bare corridor that angled to the right.

"The place we want is at the end of this passage. It's where all the data is stored and the designs held in computer banks."

As they neared the access to the research facility, McCarter could see that the doors were solid steel. A flashing light sequence above the doors indicated that the sealed unit was active.

"Well?" Anna said. "That looks as if it could present a problem."

"Rafe?"

Encizo studied the doors. "No way of knowing how they're secured. Could be solid steel rods that slide from one to the other. May be an electronic lock."

"Only one way to find out," McCarter said. "Discussing it won't get us far."

"Back off," Encizo said.

They all retreated, giving Encizo the space he needed. Hung turned and moved to where he could observe the stairs and the entrance area.

"Fire in the hole," Encizo said, triggering the launcher.

The rocket hit the doors where they met. Encizo had tried for that spot, deciding it would be the weakest point of the doors. The detonation blew a spout of flame and smoke back along the corridor. As the smoke cleared, the Cuban saw that although he hadn't breached the doors the explosion had damaged them. There was a definite bow in the steel and deep striations marked the metal. He reloaded, yelled his warning and hit the doors a second time. When they were able to see again, the steel doors had been breached, leaving a smoking gap wide enough for them to step through.

"Hung, put a grenade through there," McCarter said.

The Chinese tossed the grenade through the gap. The bomb hit the hard floor inside, bounced once then detonated with a harsh sound.

"Let's move, people," McCarter said.

He led the way inside the unit, his assault rifle cradled against his hip, searching for a target. Through the swirl of smoke he saw soldiers moving in the direction of the doors. Others were sprawled on the debris-littered floor.

"Keep your eyes open," he called over his shoulder.

An enemy gunner rushed in his direction, rifle stuttering as the man fired without checking his target. McCarter dropped to one knee, swinging his own weapon into play and laid a short burst into the advancing figure. The man stumbled back, the muzzle of his weapon sagging floorward. His finger was still on the trigger and his magazine expended itself into nothing. The Briton fired again, driving the wounded man off his feet.

A concentrated rush of movement warned of more defenders. McCarter and his team scattered before the Chinese soldiers were clear of the smoke, then hit them from different directions. The fierce rattle of autoweapons died almost as quickly as it had started.

"No more buggering around," McCarter snapped. "Hung, get those explosives planted."

The Chinese nodded and moved with Encizo to assess the best locations for the explosives.

McCarter bent over one of the dead Chinese and helped himself to a fresh magazine for his rifle. He discarded the empty one and reloaded. He took another, loaded it and handed it to Anna.

"Now isn't that thoughtful," she said. "Any girl can get flowers. I get an assault rifle."

Anna moved deeper into the room, keeping her eyes on the breached door. She backed into a recess formed by heavy iron support pillars. From her position she could see clearly across the room to the entrance.

McCarter watched as Hung and Encizo placed their charges. They were concentrating on the rows of computers and data storage banks.

"Take a look through that observation window over there," Hung said.

McCarter looked down on a brilliantly lit workshop where long workbenches held electronic instruments and assembly stations. Long, shelved racks were full of items of hardware. There were no personnel in the place.

"Is that where they put the units together?"

Hung nodded.

"Can we get down there?"

"There should be an access door at the far end of this unit," Hung said without looking up from his work.

"Can you manage if we go down there?"

"Yes. As long as I don't get interrupted."

"Rafe, you're with me. Bring some of those packs. Anna, you cover that door."

He led the way to the door at the far side of the room and pushed through, with Encizo close behind. A metal stairway led down to the workshop. McCarter stood watch as Encizo spread his packages around the workshop. The storage racks held an array of completed electronic units and circuit boards. He made sure one of the explosive packs was planted near the racks. He set the detonators and activated the switches one by one as he returned to where McCarter stood.

"They're all set for eight minutes and the clock is ticking," the Cuban said.

"So why are we standing here talking about it?"

They climbed up the stairs and back to where Hung was just completing his own settings.

"Set them for six minutes," Encizo suggested. "That should bring them close to the ones I set down there."

"Time to get the hell out of here, then," McCarter said.

They moved out of the room.

"Loy, is there anything else we should concentrate on?" Anna asked.

"Our inside man said the main targets should be the ones we just dealt with. There are other storage bays for raw materials, but back there is where the completed equipment is held."

"Let's hope so," McCarter said.

They reached the stairs and went down quickly, pausing at the entrance doors.

Manning and James were still exchanging sporadic fire with unseen resistance out in the darkness.

"We're coming out," McCarter called.

"Okay," James yelled. "Just keep you heads down. We have more company."

From outside the main gates the sound of a rocket launcher cut through the rattle of autofire. The missile exploded and detonated something that preceded a secondary blast. Dar Tan was still at his post.

"Rafe, you got any missiles left in that bag?" McCarter asked.

"Three."

"See where the concentrated fire is coming from? Drop one in the middle of that. Should scatter the opposition long enough for us to make a run back to the cell block. If we can reach cover, it should give us a chance to reach those parked vehicles."

Encizo loaded his launcher. He leaned his left shoulder against the corner of the research block's wall to steady his aim. The launched rocket streaked in the direction of the muzzle-flashes and exploded with a searing thump. The firing ceased as the gathered Chinese were hit by the blast.

"Go," McCarter yelled, and they broke into a wild

run across the first stretch of open ground. "Use anything you can see for cover."

There was scant resistance as they covered the distance to the punishment block. Smoke was still filtering out of the shattered building. As the others ran inside, Encizo paused, turning back to pinpoint the pair of missiles on their cradles. He loaded the rocket launcher, sighted on the missiles and pulled the trigger. He saw the missile streak across the smoke-filled site. It hit the closer missile at its center. The detonation was followed by an even larger, louder, destructive blast that expanded to take in both missiles and turn them into a fiery maelstrom. A roiling ball of blistering fire reached into the night sky, illuminating the entire site.

DR. LIN CHEUNG STEPPED back from the thick safety glass of his office window as the huge explosion rocked the research block. He had been in his office when the attack had begun, and when the invaders had reached the block he had activated the security locking system, sealing his protective doors. Even through the thick walls he had been able to hear the firefight that had taken place. There had been a lull, then more weapons fire outside the building. He was uncertain what was happening because he had found the telephone system was no longer working.

Damn Kang, he thought.

Where was the man at a time like this? Away on his flight of fancy, searching for the people who had taken the stolen circuit board from the downed missile. Kang should have been on site to defend the facility. The way things were going it might not matter any longer. The series of heavy explosions assured Cheung that serious damage had been done to the site. So serious none of them might survive.

When the pair of cradled missiles was destroyed, the massive explosions throwing fire and destruction across the site, it simply confirmed what Cheung had imagined. The facility wasn't going to survive.

Something else crossed his mind and the thought chilled him.

Had the invaders planted explosive devices within the research block itself?

He felt the floor beneath his feet shake and the walls vibrate, and he saw cracks appear. As the multiple explosions ripped through the research block, Cheung stumbled as the floor tilted, then split wide open. The thick window glass shattered. Debris pelted him and his ears were filled by the thunder of the blasts. Flame and smoke erupted from the splintered floor, which opened beneath his feet. Cheung felt himself fall. When his terrified gaze took in the fiery scene he was falling into, he had time for only a short, frenzied scream before it engulfed him completely.

AFTER THE PAIR of missiles blew, the planted explosives detonated and ripped the research block apart.

Rafael Encizo felt the pressure from the blast push him back against the punishment block wall. The heat touched his skin. As debris began to pound at him, Encizo turned and ducked inside the block, heading for where the rest of the team had gathered briefly. As they made their way through the building, crossing the abandoned guards' area, they saw their own equipment scattered across a wide table.

"Kit yourselves up," McCarter said, grabbing his belt and holstered Browning. He picked up a combat harness and pulled it on, took one of the P-90s and moved to cover the door as the others loaded up. "Move out."

The rest followed suit, grabbing weapons and combat harnesses. James picked up his M-16/M-203 combo.

Behind them came the raised voices of the Chinese, the rattle of weapons as some of the Guang Lor garrison got themselves together and began to infiltrate the punishment block.

McCarter hung back, with Encizo at his side.

"Anything left for that thing?" he asked.

The Cuban smiled. "Just the one."

He loaded the missile and moved to where he was able to aim the launcher in the direction of the rear of the building.

"Do it, Rafe."

Encizo fired the rocket. As it sizzled into the shadows, the Cuban discarded the launcher and followed McCarter toward the front exit. The explosion behind them echoed loudly. Smoke billowed and they were able to hear the crash of falling debris.

The others were already commandeering a couple of the multipurpose vehicles. Hung, Dar Tan and James took one, with the Phoenix Force commando taking charge of the swivel-mounted 12.7 mm machine gun. Manning was in the rear of the second vehicle, Encizo on the machine gun, with McCarter behind the wheel and Anna beside him.

"Hung, we need to reach that rendezvous point in the Wakhjir Pass," Manning called across to the Chinese.

"I know. Follow my lead," Hung said.

Dar Tan had placed his remaining missile in the launcher he carried. He turned and leaned out of his seat, firing the missile at the other parked vehicles. It struck one of the larger trucks, spewing flame and debris. The resultant explosion engulfed the other parked trucks.

"That might slow them down a little," James said.

As the two powerful engines burst into life, Hung rolled his vehicle in a tight circle, McCarter close behind. They used the final light of day to guide them to the dusty, rutted trail that served as a road, cutting across country.

Behind them the orange glow rising from Guang Lor was overhung by a heavy cloud of smoke that started to drift in the breeze that had risen.

"Will we make it?" Anna asked.

McCarter's teeth gleamed white against his smoke-streaked face.

"We have so far, love," he said. "All you need is faith."

And a truckload of good bloody luck, he added silently.

CHAPTER SEVEN

Major Kang stared at the microphone in disbelief. Rage, fear, a need for retribution and a sick sensation threatened to overwhelm and choke him. A cocktail of emotions rendered Kang speechless. He slumped back in his seat, unseeing eyes fixed at some distant point on the other side of the Plexiglas canopy of the helicopter.

Guang Lor had been devastated, the prisoners gone.

Lin Cheung was dead somewhere in the wreckage of the destroyed research block.

Kang lowered his gaze, focusing on the images of his dead squad members, still laid out in the ruins of the now deserted village. Not one had survived. He knew who was responsible. The signs were clear. The damned Uygur rebels had killed his men, slitting their throats as a final humiliation.

He caught movement. The six-man squad he had brought with him from Guang Lor were still searching, actually going through the motions because there was nothing else they could do. The Uygur had moved on.

A search of the demolished village had come up empty. Hung and his companion had gone. Kang tried to work out exactly what had happened.

The Uygur had to have returned after he'd left with the prisoners and surprised his squad. They had killed them, stripped them of weapons and had to have located Hung. He had also noticed that both the EQ2050 vehicles were missing. One of his scouts had checked tracks. One had moved off to the west, while the other seemed to have traveled back in the direction of Guang Lor. A rescue mission to free the prisoners? If so, it seemed to have succeeded. Assuming, then, that the Americans were free, Hung with them, where would they go?

Even that came with an answer. The information he had received from Guang Lor, coming in snatches over a poor connection, told Kang that vehicles had been taken from the pool, and they appeared to be heading in a westerly direction.

West? To where?

Kang had considered that and provided his own logical conclusion.

The Americans had to have entered Xinjiang Province from the Afghanistan border. It was close, and there were American bases in that country. That would be their destination. Kang sat upright, almost smiling. He might yet be able to salvage something from this mess. He called to his second in command and told him to get the squad back inside the helicopter. As soon as they were on board, Kang told his pilot to get them in the air.

"We have some fugitives to catch," he said.

And some pride to reclaim.

Kang would never admit to anyone that he felt guilty of committing a grave error of judgment. He had been so elated at capturing the American team and Mei Anna that he had allowed his judgment to slip. He knew now that he should have remained with his squad and ensured that Loy Hung was apprehended while he had the opportunity. As a sop to his own conscience he did allow that if he had stayed, then he would most probably be dead as well as his men. He realized that this was no excuse. Beijing would only consider the fact that he had abandoned, albeit temporarily, his prime mission. Walking away from capturing Loy Hung would be indefensible in Beijing's eyes. Kang's salvation lay in completing his mission by delivering Loy Hung and the missing circuit board. The destruction of Guang Lor was another matter. Whatever the outcome of that, Kang *had* imprisoned the American team but they had escaped and struck at the facility.

His future looked bleak.

Kang might soon become a demoted major. He was well aware of the severity of punishment for failure. Beijing didn't show a great deal of mercy in such cases. His only option was to attempt to lessen his error by delivering Hung, the board and, if possible, recapturing the Americans and Mei Anna. In itself a major task, he admitted, but he had little choice. His life could depend on achieving success.

Kang stared out through the canopy of the helicopter, seeing little except a bleak time ahead if he failed. Fate was a capricious mistress. Only a few hours ago he had accomplished a great deal. Just as swiftly his victory had been snatched from beneath his nose. If Kang had been a religious man, he might have prayed for celestial guidance. Reality, however, had taken a different stance. Now he had been left to stand or fall alone. No one would help him. His future lay in his own hands.

"IF WE CAN KEEP THIS pace we should reach the pass by first light," McCarter said.

"Makes me uneasy when you begin every sentence with 'if,'" Anna remarked.

"I like to hedge my bets."

"Tell me about it."

Ahead of them Hung's lead vehicle was throwing up clouds of dust. McCarter had to ease off the gas pedal and drop back a few yards. He noticed the slight buffeting of a rising wind slapping against the sides of the vehicle.

"You feel that?" he asked.

"You should try being up here," Encizo called.

He had felt the gradual increase in wind velocity himself in his exposed position in the open back of the truck. He lowered himself to a sitting position, his back against the canvas flap, hands pushed into the folds of his combat jacket. Encizo felt the beginnings of a dust storm. If one blew in, their progress would be hampered. Night driving over this kind of terrain was difficult enough. The addition of dust clouds rolling across the landscape would minimize their ability to see clearly. The only good thing about it, it would have a similar effect on anyone out looking for them.

"KEEP THEM COMING," Kang said. "I need those reinforcements if I am to prevent enemies of the state reaching the border. You have my coordinates." He ended the transmission and lowered the handset.

"Major," his pilot said urgently.

"Yes?"

The pilot pointed, and Kang saw curling dark shapes materialize from the night sky.

"What is it?"

"A dust storm, Major Kang. It looks as if it is moving into our area."

Kang shook his head. He felt he could scream in pure frustration. A dust storm. Could he have anything else go wrong for him? Somehow he didn't think so.

"Will we still be able to fly?"

"Unless it becomes too intense. Then I will have to land. The air intakes can suck dust into the engine. If that happens they will shut down and we crash."

Momentarily, Kang was defeated. He simply nodded in response to the pilot. Peering out through the canopy into the darkness, he wondered if the anticipated dust storm would affect the fugitives, as well.

LESS THAN A HALF HOUR later the storm struck full-on. The wind, slicing down from the north, brought with it gritty dust that hammered the sides of their vehicles like buckshot. As visibility almost reached zero, Mc-Carter lost sight of Hung's taillights a number of times, and when Hung halted his vehicle the Briton almost tailgated him. Swinging out of his seat, McCarter made his way to speak to the Chinese, Anna close behind.

"How long will this last?" McCarter asked.

"These storms have been known to blow for days," Hung said. "But this time of year they run out after a few hours."

"Great. That's all we need."

"If we can't see, neither can Kang's soldiers," Anna said.

"Any place we can take shelter?" McCarter asked.

Loy Hung shrugged. "If it was a clear day I could find somewhere easily." He gestured in defeat. "In this I might run us into a hole, or worse."

McCarter accepted the man's reasoning. Urgent or not, there was little they could do.

"Okay. We'll stay put for now. The minute this clears enough for us to see, we move out. Let's stay awake in case Kang's men stumble onto us."

They grouped beside the vehicles, using them as cover and turned their backs to the wind, weapons cradled in their arms in case they were needed.

The storm increased in intensity, the sheer power of the wind rocking the vehicles. At one point the wheels of one of the vehicles left the ground for long seconds. The quick thinking of those sheltering beside it, reaching up to put their combined weight against the vehicle, prevented the vehicle from tipping over.

BY MCCARTER'S WATCH three hours had passed when the wind began to ease. He leaned across and tapped Hung on the shoulder. The Chinese raised his head.

"What do you think?" McCarter asked.

Hung pushed away from the vehicle and checked the velocity.

"I think it may be weakening. Moving away from us. Let's get these vehicles started and get out of here. If it clears for us, it will be the same for Kang."

THE MAJOR WAS ROUSED out of his semisleep by the sound of the helicopter powering up. Kang sat upright, peering through the canopy. Not only had the dust storm receded but the day was brightening around them.

"Is it safe?" he asked.

The pilot nodded, concentrating on getting the helicopter back in the air. As it rose, swinging back on course, the radio crackled into life.

"Yes?" Kang asked.

The reply he received lifted his spirits. Two helicopters were coming to rendezvous with him. They were troop-carrying transport helicopters, each with a complement of soldiers from the main base. As they had been coming from a distance beyond even Guang Lor, they hadn't encountered the dust storm until its final phase, so they hadn't lost as much time as Kang had expected they might.

"I am going on," Kang said. "Get to my location as soon as you can. We need to control the area and pin these dissidents down. Remember that if we engage I want to try to take them alive if possible. Wound them if need be, but do your best to recapture them."

HUNG'S VEHICLE REFUSED to fire up when he hit the start button. The engine turned over, but the ignition refused to catch. McCarter left his idling vehicle and hurried to Hung's. He freed the hood and raised it, reaching inside to inspect the engine.

"Try her again," he said.

The response was the same. The engine wouldn't start, and it soon became apparent the battery wasn't going to give them endless power to keep trying.

"What is it?" Anna asked.

"Can't prove it without stripping the bloody thing

down, but I think she sucked dust in through the air filter and it's clogged up."

"Nothing we can do?" Manning asked.

McCarter shook his head. "Needs time and equipment. We're short on both. We leave this one. It's going to be a squeeze, but we'll have to make do with what we have left."

They moved off minutes later, McCarter at the wheel, with Hung guiding him. As the dust storm abated enough to allow them a clear view of the way ahead, Hung was able guide them with a little more certainty, and McCarter used his skill behind the wheel to keep the vehicle moving at a steady pace.

The first pale streaks of dawn began to show as the storm faded behind them. Hung called a halt so he could establish their current position.

"We've drifted north a few miles," he said. "We need to get back on our path. That way."

McCarter upped the pace. Now that they were able to make out the terrain they were crossing, travel was easier.

"If the fuel holds out," the Briton said, "I think we might just do it."

"Hey, you want to rethink that?" James called.

They all followed his finger and saw the military helicopter swooping down out of the cleared sky. The moment it was in range, the 12.7 mm machine guns it carried opened up, sending lines of shells toward the vehicle.

"What was it you were saying about making it?" Encizo asked.

The Cuban hauled himself up behind the swivel-mounted machine in the rear of the vehicle and returned fire as the helicopter burned overhead, the rotor wash rocking the bouncing vehicle.

"Son of a bitch," McCarter yelled, jamming his foot on the gas pedal, sending the vehicle roaring forward. "As they say in the best circles, ladies, hang on to your hats. This might get a little bumpy."

The helicopter made a wide sweep, then angled in again, its weapons firing as it came. McCarter saw the earth-spouting bullet hits and swung the wheel hard, taking the vehicle out of the line of fire. Everyone was forced to grab hold of something to prevent being thrown out of the bouncing, bucking vehicle as it cut a wild track across the uneven terrain. Even Encizo, trying to handle his machine gun and return fire, was forced to abandon the idea while he clung on to the weapon.

"To the right," Hung yelled. "That will take us to the border. The pass is beyond those ridges."

McCarter wrestled with the steering wheel, gripping it hard as the vehicle crabbed from left to right, the spinning wheels jumped over the harsh ground. Out the corner of his eye he saw the fleeting shape of the pursuing helicopter as it came in for yet another attack, dropping even lower. The hard rattle of the machine gun sounded. Bullets struck only feet away. McCarter heard the rattle of splintered rock as the burst moved in closer. He wished he could give Encizo a better chance to fire back, but he knew that if he stopped, or even slowed, it would simply present the helicopter with an easier target.

Machine-gun fire raked the side of the vehicle, whining off the metal panels. McCarter felt the vehicle shudder.

Too bloody close, he thought. The bugger is getting his range now.

He stamped down hard on the gas pedal, working the gears, and felt the vehicle surge forward. In the pale dawn light he was able to see his way easier. Or so he thought, until someone yelled a warning. McCarter responded quickly, but he felt the vehicle hit a hidden ridge. It seemed to rise in slow motion before plunging over the ridge and dropping into a shallow ravine. The vehicle hung suspended for what felt like an eternity before it actually dropped. The rear wheels spun as they lost traction. Clouds of dirt and loose stones flew into the air as the truck bounced down the side of the fissure, swaying from side to side. The creak and squeal of tortured metal mingled with the roar of the heavy engine.

McCarter hung grimly on to the wheel, trying to keep the vehicle on a direct line as the base of the slope rushed toward them. He ignored the brake. There was no point even trying to halt the truck's motion. Momentum and the sheer bulk of the vehicle kept it moving. One side of the windshield cracked with a loud sound.

"Hang on," McCarter yelled above the din. "We're—"

He didn't get the chance to complete his warning as the front of the vehicle plowed into the base of the ravine, throwing a roiling cloud of dust up and over the hood. The truck lurched, almost stopped, then traveled a few more feet before it came to a complete halt, the engine stalling. A hiss of steam rose from the radiator.

McCarter pushed himself away from the steering wheel. The impact had slammed him bodily into the wheel, and he could feel a burning ache across his left side. He grabbed his P-90 and kicked open the door, almost falling from the vehicle. He climbed to his feet and saw the rest of the team disembarking.

He took some dirty looks as they stumbled to the ground.

"Is this the way you test those sports cars?" Manning asked. "I thought you were an *expert* driver?"

"Bloody hell," McCarter said, unable to hold back a grin. "This isn't exactly a thoroughbred. It's a Chinese military truck."

Further discussion was abandoned when James warned of approaching hostiles. He had climbed to the lip of the ravine and had seen Kang's helicopter disgorge a six-man armed squad.

He spotted something else—a second military helicopter fast approaching the same coordinates.

"Looks like Kang called in help," James said as he slid down to join the others.

McCarter indicated the snaking course of the ravine. "Let's move. Right now there are too many, too bloody close. Move back then hold."

He led the way, the rest falling in behind, distancing themselves from the crash site.

The sound of shouted orders reached Phoenix Force as they scattered, using the truck's bulk while they pulled back, looking for better cover. As they headed along the boulder-strewed base of the ravine Manning, spotting movement above them, yelled his warning. "Incoming."

One of the Chinese soldiers had appeared on the rim, dropping to one knee and shouldering the launcher he carried. He pressed the trigger and the missile burst from the rocket tube, streaking for the truck. It sailed beneath the tailgate and impacted against the steel chassis cross members. The dull boom of sound became a sucking roar as the fuel tank blew, engulfing the stricken vehicle in a ball of flame and smoke. Debris flew in every direction, smoke trails in its wake. The fireball and smoke obscured the view of both groups. As it dissipated, Phoenix Force took the offensive, moving to firing positions and raking the oncoming Chinese with steady, accurate fire. Two of Kang's men went down in the first few seconds, another stumbled, his shoulder torn and bloody.

There was a lull before the squad from the second chopper appeared, swarming over the rim, firing as they came. Another half dozen soldiers came into view, rushing to join up with the remainder of the first group. Within seconds they came streaming down the slope toward the blazing remains of the truck and Phoenix Force, who had pulled back again during the break in hostilities. As the first line entered the ravine, additional soldiers appeared to reinforce their ranks.

"What the hell they got out there?" James asked. "The First Beijing Brigade?"

"Hey, don't ask for something you don't really want," Encizo warned.

They backed along the ravine, firing as they moved, using every piece of cover they could find.

James fed an HE round into his M-203 launcher, sending the explosive shell into the bunched Chinese on his flank. The detonation put three down and wounded a couple more. The action held the others back long enough for James to load a second HE round and send it in the direction of the advancing squad. This one scattered the troops and they stayed out of range.

"Time we got out of here," McCarter yelled above the crackle of autofire.

Crouching beside him, Hung nodded. "Wisest thing you said since we fell in this hole."

"Anna, you move Hung and Tan up the far side. Rafe, give them cover fire. Gary, far side. Watch for any movement up there."

He caught James's eye. "You're with me."

"THEY WILL NEVER GIVE IN," the sergeant from the relief troops said. "As long as we fire only to wound, they are going to keep killing us, Major."

Kang watched as more men from the two reinforcement helicopters moved in the direction of the spot where the truck had crashed. Smoke was still rising from the vehicle. He knew the sergeant was right. The Americans and their allies were offering strong resistance and already had taken out a number of the soldiers. Their determination had not slackened. If they continued fighting back, they would deplete his force even more and additional reinforcements were unlikely in the short term.

His desire to capture the enemy alive might not happen. Kang wanted it desperately, but the situation was not working in his favor. It appeared he might yet have to deliver his prize to Beijing in body bags rather than in chains.

"Pass the order," he said. "If capturing them alive can't be done, take them dead. But at least achieve that, Sergeant."

HUNG HAD ALMOST REACHED the top of the slope when Dar Tan and Anna were distracted when one of the advancing soldiers, coming down the far side, opened up with his assault rifle. The burst of 5.56 mm fire peppered the rocks around them.

Tan swung his own weapon on line and returned fire, his shots way off target. They spit chipped stone against the soldier's legs, distracting him for a moment. Seeing this, Dar Tan advanced against Anna's warning, losing target acquisition in the process. By the time he realized his error, the soldier had taken advantage.

Dar Tan's rising muzzle trailed behind the soldier's. His weapon crackled harshly, the short burst catching Tan in the right side, in his lower ribs. Tan gave a startled cry, his face rigid with the shock of being hit. He stumbled to his knees, sucking panicky breaths into his lungs.

Anna had moved quickly to cover the soldier, her P-90 coming on track. She triggered a burst that punched into the man's chest a split second after he had fired on Tan and knocked him off his feet.

"Are you badly hit?" Anna asked.

Tan stared at her, his gaze vacant.

"Dar," she yelled. "On your feet."

He stared a few seconds longer as her harsh words penetrated, then blinked, and when his eyes focused again Anna could see a gleam of coherence in his gaze.

"I… Mei Anna?"

He didn't finish the sentence. A figure appeared at his side, gripping his upper arm.

"Come. Let us go quickly."

It was Loy Hung. He had returned to assist Anna and between them they pushed Tan up the slope and over the far rim, where they lay in the dust, hearing the firefight raging around them.

Anna bent over Dar Tan, her hands pressed over the bloody wounds in his side. She could feel the warm liquid oozing between her fingers. She felt helpless, knowing there was little she could do for him. Without medical attention he might simply bleed to death.

"Loy, how far to the pass from here?"

Hung glanced over his shoulder, then back to stare at her.

"Maybe a half mile," he said. "Why? We can't move Tan ourselves."

"I wasn't thinking of that."

"Then what?"

"Going for help. Bringing that helicopter here to us. It could fend off Kang's people easily and we could airlift Dan out, too."

"Anna?"

"I can do it," she said.

Hung watched as she discarded her combat harness. She thrust the P-90 into his hands. All she retained was her holstered 9 mm Beretta with a couple of extra magazines.

"This is foolish," Hung protested.

"No one ever told me I was being wise joining the Pro-Democracy group, either," Anna said, smiling briefly. "Loy, Kang has too many men out there. I can't just sit here and let you and my friends die for nothing. I have to at least try to help them."

"That's what I was told about breaking you out of Guang Lor. What is it about these Americans that they refuse to abandon one another?"

"It's the way they are." She touched his arm. "Looks as if it's catching, too."

Before Hung could say another word Anna pushed

to her feet and moved off. He watched as she cut off across country, marking the distant ridges as her destination. She broke into a gentle trot, then increased to a steady run, moving in an easy, rhythmic stride.

Behind Hung came a rattle of sound. The Chinese turned, bringing up his weapon as David McCarter hauled himself over the rim and lay flat on the ground. He took in the picture, searching for Mei Anna.

"Hung, where is she?"

"Gone for help. To the pass."

"That crazy…"

McCarter twisted and brought his P-90 into play, raking the slope below to drive back a rush from some of the Chinese troops. His covering fire helped the rest of Phoenix Force to clear the rim of the ravine, bullets smacking into the slopes around them. There was a break in the firing as the Chinese realized they were exposing themselves too readily if they continued to try to breach the ravine with the enemy strung out along the opposite rim.

"Hung?"

"Tan got hit. He's going to need medical help soon. Anna just decided. She was gone before I could do a thing."

"Sounds like our girl," James said, moving to Tan's side. "There's not a lot I can do, either. Those mothers took my first-aid pack when they detained us and I didn't get it back."

Hung freed the backpack he had around his shoulder. It held the circuit board and digital camera. There were some folded cloths he had used for protection. Hung unwrapped the board and handed the cloths to James.

"I might be able to fashion a pressure bandage," James said.

He bent over Tan and began to open the man's clothing.

THE BINOCULARS TOLD Kang all he needed to know. He saw Mei Anna and Loy Hung assist the wounded Dar Tan over the rim of the ravine. The sight of the Chinese woman roused his anger to a high level. He was unable to ignore the image of her bloody, battered face and those defiant eyes daring him to hurt her more.

Damn you, Kang, you should have killed her when you had the opportunity, he thought.

He was regretting that more with each passing second.

Then he was rewarded by the sight of Mei Anna discarding her equipment. She was talking to Loy hung, making some point. And then she rose to her feet and began to move, breaking into a run as she turned in the direction of—the border.

She was going for help. Of course, he realized. The Americans had to have some transport waiting on the Afghani side of the border, there to pick them up on completion of their mission.

"Sergeant, take command. Don't pull back. I want those men dealt with."

"Where are you going, Major?"

"One of them is trying to escape. If she reaches the border we could lose her, and she might bring reinforcements."

Kang turned back to his waiting helicopter, indicating to the pilot to start the engine.

This time Mei Anna had made an error. Out there

in the open there was no way she could run a helicopter. He flung himself inside, closing the door.

"Go," he yelled. "The other side. The woman is trying to reach the border. This time she will not make another of her famous escapes."

The chopper rose, hovered, then swooped forward, over the ravine in pursuit of Mei Anna.

CHAPTER EIGHT

"Just go," Manning said. "Sitting there making faces isn't helping anyone. On your feet and go get her."

"Do it, hombre," Encizo said.

"Get the hell out of here," was all James said, without looking up from ministering to Tan.

McCarter pushed to his feet and set off after Anna.

The others turned back to the ravine, eyeing the Chinese on the far side.

"It's going to come to them that all they have to do is fly over in those choppers," Manning commented.

"I was hoping no one would mention that," Encizo said.

On cue Kang's helicopter rose into the air. It gained height and flew over the ravine, ignoring the men on the ground and settling on a course that followed Mei Anna's tracks.

"That isn't going to make the boss's day," Manning muttered.

"Responsibilities of command," James said.

"Talking of responsibility," Encizo said, "maybe

we should take it on board and get the hell out of here, too."

"You mean, retreat?" Manning asked.

"Strategic withdrawal?" Encizo suggested.

Loy Hung clicked in a fresh magazine and cocked his assault rifle. "Sounds good to me."

"Let's see if we can beat the boss to that border," James said. "Sitting here we get cut off."

"I'll take Tan," Manning said.

The burly Canadian hauled the wounded man to his feet and with James's help swung the dissident over his shoulders.

"You okay?" James asked.

Manning nodded. "I've hauled deer heavier than this guy."

James fed one of his two remaining HE grenades into the M-203 grenade launcher as they moved out. Whichever way this fell, Phoenix Force was not going to go down quietly.

THEY HAD COVERED no more than three hundred yards before the beat of rotors reached their ears and one of the Chinese helicopters rose above the far side of the ravine. It swooped in low, casting around the former position Phoenix Force had occupied before turning and heading in their direction.

"Spread," Manning yelled. "Give them a hard target."

The four running figures veered apart, aware that the speeding aircraft would reach them easily. The heavy pulse of the helicopter's engines increased as it bore down on them, even with the beat of the power plants, the crackle of machine-gun fire could be heard, and the chopping thud of bullets hitting the ground was unmistakable. And then it was hanging over the area.

Encizo was the first to return fire, ignoring the hovering presence of the Mi-171. The rotor wash kicked up thick dust, almost obscuring him as the Cuban went to one knee, his P-90 jammed to his shoulder. He raked the underbelly with a hard burst, seeing his fire chew into the aluminum panels.

Alerted by the hits, the Chinese pilot worked the controls to pull the helicopter back, yelling for the door gunner to respond. He received a reply that told him the gunner couldn't see the enemy because of the dust.

JAMES HAD NO SUCH difficulty. The dark bulk of the chopper hovering overhead showed clearly to the Phoenix Force warrior. He was flat on the ground, concealed in a shallow dip, and from his prone position James could make out the detailed camouflage pattern painted onto the machine's fuselage. That was intended to hide the helicopter when it was on the ground, not when it was framed against the open sky.

He responded quickly, knowing full well that the Chinese helicopter wasn't going to stay motionless for long. He picked up the rattle of shots from Rafael Encizo, heard the metallic sound as they struck, and decided if he was going to make his shot it had to be now.

James judged angle and distance, raising the M-16 and locating his window of opportunity, which in this case was the open side hatch where the door gunner peered over the sights of his weapon. James used the hazy outline as his target acquisition point and eased back on the M-203's trigger.

The HE grenade launched with a dull thump, curved up in an almost lazy arc and sailed in through the open hatch.

THE HELICOPTER PILOT heard a frenzied cry from the door gunner over the communication line. A moment later the HE grenade exploded and the blast expanded to engulf the crew compartment. The surge of heat and the concussion hit the pilot. Razor-sharp pieces of shrapnel blew into the flight deck, slicing into the pilot's back and arms. He attempted to stay in control, but the controls had gone heavy and failed to respond. Fighting the stabbing pains engulfing his body, he struggled to keep the chopper in the air, but a secondary explosion weakened the aircraft's infrastructure and it began to come apart. Searing flame rushed into the flight deck. The barely conscious pilot saw the ground seeming to rise up in front of his eyes before the impact crumpled the nose section and he was crushed still strapped in his seat.

MEI ANNA HAD COVERED HALF the distance to the border point when she heard the thwack of rotors and the hard beat of the engines. A glance over her shoulder showed Kang's helicopter as it dropped to within a few feet of the ground. Anna felt the slap of hot air and shielded her eyes against the raised dust.

"Throw down your weapon," Kang's amplified voice demanded.

The helicopter turned sideways so Anna was able to see the 12.7 mm machine gun aimed directly at her. A short burst into the ground at her feet emphasized the threat.

"Your choice, Mei Anna."

Reluctantly she accepted there was no other choice. It was a simple equation. Surrender or die. That was Kang's unspoken ultimatum. With death she was of no use to anyone. As long as there was still life in her, so there was hope.

Anna discarded her pistol and raised her hands.

"Inside," Kang ordered as the chopper touched down, and she could almost sense his triumph.

He watched her approach the open hatch where the door gunner held his weapon on target. The moment she climbed into the crew compartment Kang ordered his pilot into the air.

MCCARTER SAW IT ALL take place. Even though he was too far away to do anything, he broke into a hard run, bringing the P-90 on line. He lowered the weapon almost immediately because he knew there wasn't a thing he could do. Any aggressive action on his part might conceivably harm Anna, and he wasn't about to do that.

He was forced to stand by and watch Kang's helicopter gain altitude before it turned and soared away. His attention was totally fixed on the retreating aircraft. So much that he failed to even acknowledge the heavy blast behind him when the transport helicopter crashed to earth, the explosion heard only as a distant, peripheral distraction.

KANG'S PILOT WAS FORCED to bank violently as the downed chopper blew, sending a backwash of fire and smoke into the air. The helicopter lurched as the shock wave caught it.

"Your American friends persist in their resistance,"

Kang said, turning in his seat to smile at Mei Anna as the door gunner held her at pistol point.

"Like me, they don't give up," she said. "Send all the men you like, Kang, you won't stop them."

"I'll still beat them. This time they will do what *I* demand."

"Why so sure, Kang?"

"I have something they want, Mei Anna." He jabbed a gloved finger at her. "I have you."

THE RUMBLE OF THE explosion faded, replaced by the powerful whine of twin turbines. The sound penetrated McCarter's dulled senses and he glanced up to see the familiar shape of *Dragon Slayer* streaking toward him. McCarter turned to signal the others and they started toward the hovering combat chopper. The moment it touched down the side hatch hissed open. McCarter scrambled inside, almost stumbling. Grimaldi met him in the crew compartment, reaching out to grab him by the shoulders.

"Let's go," McCarter said, his voice taut, ice-cold. "Now, Jack. Get this thing in the air now."

"Hey, easy there, buddy."

McCarter gave an angry snarl and manhandled the Stony Man pilot aside, moving to the forward compartment.

"David, what the hell is going on?"

McCarter had sagged against the rear of one of the body-form couches. His resistance was waning rapidly as the effort of the past few days caught up with him.

"Jack, you don't understand. The bastard took her. I let him snatch her right from under my nose."

Behind Grimaldi the rest of the team appeared,

climbing into the crew compartment. The moment they were all inside Manning lowered Dar Tan to the deck and turned to hit the hatch button, closing and securing it. James headed for the medical compartment, reaching inside to extract what he needed to tend to Dar Tan's wounds.

"Somebody tell me what's going on?" Grimaldi snapped.

"That chopper you saw take off had Mei Anna in it. The guy in charge, Major Kang, has taken her."

Grimaldi shot a look at McCarter's slumped form.

McCarter raised his grimy face, fixing his eyes on Grimaldi. "That's why I acted like a bleedin' wanker, Jack. Sorry, mate, I lost it there. No excuse to take it out on you."

"Forget it, pal. I'd have done the same." Grimaldi paused, checking out the weary, battered faces of the men who had just boarded *Dragon Slayer.* "It may be a stupid question, but why has this Kang grabbed Anna?"

"I can tell you that," Loy Hung said. He raised the backpack he had been carrying for what now seemed an eternity. "Because he knows we have this, and he wants it back." He held up the stolen circuit board.

Grimaldi studied it for a moment. "Jesus, is that what this has all been about?"

"Part of it, mate," McCarter said. "But right at this minute we have a pressing problem that needs sorting out before we do another damn thing."

Grimaldi turned to look where McCarter was indicating and saw the menacing outline of a Chinese helicopter hovering over the downed transport chopper, taking its squad of troops back on board, prior to heading in the direction of *Dragon Slayer.*

"Where the hell did that come from?" James asked.

"Kang must have pulled in some heavy favors," Encizo said.

"Excuse me, ladies, I have a guest to welcome," Grimaldi said, easing past McCarter to slide into his seat. "Buckle up, people, we may be in for a bumpy ride. My, oh, my, just look at that big-assed baby. Come on, honey, let's boogie."

"How IRONIC," Kang said. "I have you, and I also have the means to destroy your interfering American friends and also that circuit board. If I can't take it back, the second option is to destroy it. Then the Americans will have nothing to accuse us over."

"Kang, you can't."

"Of course I can. That is an American helicopter on Chinese soil. It holds an American strike team that has already caused a great deal of damage and killed many loyal soldiers of the State. They are criminal invaders. Isn't it my job to defend my country?" Kang smiled.

"Yes, it is."

He picked up his handset and contacted the commander of the Mi-17V5/6.

"If they refuse to negotiate a surrender, I want that machine totally destroyed. Completely wiped out. Nothing left. You understand?"

"Understood, Major."

Kang leaned forward to observe. "This should be interesting."

Mei Anna said nothing. It was plain that Kang knew nothing about *Dragon Slayer,* or its capabilities. If he had, he wouldn't have been so complacent.

GRIMALDI POWERED UP the twin turbines, easing
Dragon Slayer into the air. He quickly reached altitude,
arming the weapons system and locking in on his helmet's visor display. The visor readout allowed him to
aim and target by simple head movements. Grimaldi
had spent many hours fine-tuning his abilities with the
slave system, and combined with *Dragon Slayer*'s sophisticated computer feedback that was linked to the
missile pods and multibarrel chain gun, he had at his
control an awesome set of ordnance.

As he brought the combat chopper on a direct heading, Grimaldi studied the bulky configuration of the
Chinese helicopter. He recognized it as an Mi-17V5/6.
China had previously purchased a number of them from
the former Soviet Union during the cooperative years.
The Mi wasn't a dedicated combat machine, it was more
of a support, but it had been said that the Chinese had
adapted some to carry weapons. Flicking through his
internal database Grimaldi recalled that this armed version of the Mi had machine-gun pods and was capable
of launching unguided rockets from its weapon cluster.

The Mi-17V powered forward, its nose dropping
slightly as the pilot took manual aim, releasing one of his
missiles in an attempt to force the confrontation and
make a fast strike. The missile curved in toward *Dragon
Slayer,* slower than even Grimaldi had anticipated. He
touched the controls and rolled the combat chopper aside,
the missile streaking past harmlessly. Having been able
to assess the other aircraft's potential, Grimaldi eased
back and took *Dragon Slayer* in a swift climb, then leveled off. He brought the chopper around to bring the Mi
ahead, and there was no hesitation in his actions when
he locked on and launched a pair of heat-seeking missiles.

They streaked across the intervening space, sourcing the Mi-17V's heat output and hit midway along the fuselage. The chopper was severely damaged by the explosions. With flame and smoke trailing its descent, the Chinese helicopter fell nose-down to impact with the ground. At the point of impact the structure collapsed along its length, flame erupting in a swirling fireball. Thick smoke began to burn off the wreckage and the crackle of exploding munitions was accompanied by arcing lines of bright sparks leaping from the burning mass.

Grimaldi leveled off and turned the chopper toward the downed troop transport, bringing the chain gun on line.

"Is it true these things can't fly without rotors?" Grimaldi asked.

McCarter nodded. "So I heard."

Grimaldi flew in close and opened fire, raking the rotor assembly with cannon fire. The concentrated burst from the six-barrel rotary weapon tore the housing and linkages apart, leaving the transport ship crippled in the ravine, rotors drooping limply.

"Kang," McCarter said.

Grimaldi turned *Dragon Slayer* and they searched for Kang's helicopter.

It had vanished.

"He can't have disappeared just like that," McCarter exploded. "Come on, Jack, we can find him."

"He will have headed in-country," Loy Hung said. "Back to Guang Lor, and he will call for more backup."

"Where we can't go," Grimaldi said evenly. "Much as I'd like to. Look, this close to the border, we've already pushed our luck to the limit."

He let his words hang in the silence, gently easing

Dragon Slayer onto a course that would take them back into Afghanistan.

"And I need to get Tan to Bagram ASAP," James said. "He needs intensive medical care."

McCarter's shoulders slumped in resignation. "I know. Take us home, Jack."

Grimaldi opened a channel and relayed a message to Bagram, using the U.S. Military ComNet, informing them he was en route. As soon as he received acknowledgment, he switched to the satellite link that would patch him through to Stony Man. He made contact with Huntington Wethers.

"I still have you on satellite," Wethers said. "Got you heading for the Afghan border. Nice image. Saw that run-in with the Chinese gunship."

"Did you pick up the third bird that fled the scene?"

"Yes."

"How long will you be able to track him?"

"I have a lock with the Slingshot satellite system. That and Zero station should allow me an overlap scan. Two, maybe three hours. Why?"

"We need to know where that chopper ends up and where the occupants go after that."

"I'll get what I can. So, hey, Jack, Phoenix come through?"

"I guess it's Phoenix on board. They're a sorry-looking bunch. They need sleep, food, patching up and a change of clothing, but I think I can recognize them."

"They all got back, huh?"

"Except for Anna?"

"She isn't...?"

"She's alive, Hunt, but she's one of the passengers on that chopper we need you to track."

"Understood."

"Unless we hear sooner, we'll contact when we touch down at Bagram. Over and out."

Computer Room, Stony Man Farm, Virginia

HUNTINGTON WETHERS RAN a hand across his forehead. He could feel a slight headache starting. He leaned back, closing his eyes for a few seconds. The extra time he had spent staring at monitors for the past few hours was beginning to tell. Wethers kept his feelings to himself. He was no worse off than the rest of the cyberteam. They were all drawing long shifts at present. The ongoing mission, broken effectively into three operations, was commanding the entire facility.

While he was tracking the movements of the man he knew as Major Kang, Aaron Kurtzman was working on the data from Oliver Townsend's computer. The team's youngest member, Akira Tokaido, was assisting Kurtzman. Carmen Delahunt had the task of delving into the background of Townsend's associate, CIA Agent Pete Tilman.

It was dedicated work, with little time for relaxing, but the cyberteam kept going. The lives of their people out in the field depended on Stony Man's responses, and they had never been let down. The SOG worked seamlessly, with the backup personnel as much a part of the ongoing missions as the men facing the physical dangers. It was an unspoken bond.

A flashing alert caught Wethers's attention. He scanned his monitors, checking the satellite images and the text data that accompanied them. The hard drive log was recording every piece of information that came in, ready for access when required. One of his peripheral monitors was a permanent listing of scans and data, allowing for speedy recall. Each section was assigned a code number, and all it took was a keystroke for Wethers to go back to a particular data stream.

He flicked to his large review monitor and tapped in a sequence. The screen flashed up the data he had asked for. Wethers studied it for a while, a slow smile crossing his face as he digested the information. It was just what he had been searching for. The answer Phoenix was waiting for.

Wethers reached for the satellite phone that would connect him with *Dragon Slayer* in Afghanistan.

The wheels sometimes turned slowly—but they did turn.

CHAPTER NINE

Bagram Air Base

Grimaldi made his way to the hut Phoenix Force had been assigned by the Air Force, basic barracks style, with few amenities apart from the double row of military-issue cots. As far as the Phoenix Force was concerned it was the best they had ever had the privilege to flop onto. Pausing at the door, Grimaldi had a guilty moment when he knew he was going to have to wake at least McCarter. With the news he was about to deliver he felt safe from harm.

The Briton opened his eyes and glared up at Grimaldi for a moment, then cleared his murderous thoughts when the Stony Man pilot told him what he had. He sat up and took the printed sheets Grimaldi held out.

McCarter read the data and examined the satellite camera images. "This for real?"

"I guess so. Hunt isn't one to pass out lame-ass data."

"Okay. So why is Kang holed up in some out-of-the-way place with Anna in tow? Why not head for home?"

"My guess? He's waiting for us to respond. The man must know we have the best tracking money can buy. He'll figure, one way or the other, that we'll spot where they are and come looking for Anna. Didn't we already show him we don't leave our people behind? He's got Anna for bait and wants to use her to get his damned hardware back."

"You think so?"

"David, you trashed his facility and kicked ass with his security squads. The circuit board was his responsibility. Something the Chinese still want because it allows them a big jump in technology. Kang let it slip away. You guys made him look like an idiot. Now I'm just a dumb flyboy, but I can see where he's coming from."

"Kang won't be a popular bloke at the moment. If he doesn't get a result, he'll end up sweeping the streets of Beijing. Or worse."

"So he's going to sit out there, wait for you to come for Anna and try to make a trade."

McCarter stood, easing the kinks out of his lean frame. He made no comment when he handed the data sheet back to Grimaldi, just let the silence stretch until the Stony Man pilot let go a long sigh.

"Just stop looking at me with those sad eyes. You remember what I said about not being able to invade Chinese airspace?"

"Yes."

"I was lying."

McCarter grinned. "Jack, we do this, the hammer will fall bloody hard. It's unsanctioned. Against every rule. Hal will have steam coming out of his ears and I daresay even the President will do backflips if he hears. We might all end up out of a job."

"You just gave me every good reason why we have to go for this," Grimaldi said.

"Does this mean I will owe you big-time?"

"For the rest of your extremely long life, mate."

"Jesus, what have I done."

"Times that by three," someone said.

McCarter turned to see the rest of his team sitting up and smiling broadly.

"You all crazy?"

"If you have to invade China," James said, "even *you* need a little backup. You don't think we'll let you go in on your own?"

"Anna is one of us, hombre," Encizo said. "That lady earned her stripes big-time."

McCarter still had the photo image in his hand.

"I'll be right back," he said. "There's somebody I need to talk to."

McCARTER WENT LOOKING for Loy Hung and located him coming out of the base medical facility. The Chinese smiled when he saw the Briton.

"Tan will be fine," he said. "Your people have operated and he is comfortable. We both owe you a great deal."

"Works both ways, Loy. If it hadn't been for your group we wouldn't have that piece of hardware, or the photographs."

"But we may have lost Mei Anna."

McCarter shook his head. "Not likely," he said. "That's why I was looking for you. Our base back in the U.S. got a satellite lock on Kang's chopper. We know where he is. And we're going in to bring Anna home."

"Which is what Kang will be expecting."

"Then I wouldn't want to disappoint him."

"It will be a trap."

"Loy, don't worry about us. I just need some help."

"Anything."

McCarter showed him the print taken from the satellite camera. "This is where Kang is holed up. Does it mean anything to you."

Hung studied the image. "It is a lookout position. The military built a number of them in the country close to borders. They are simple redoubts, built to withstand attack but basic inside. Thick walls. No windows. Just gun slots. Roving patrols could use them for replenishing supplies. Usually no more than four-man teams are stationed there. They have radios for contact with their main base and to keep up with the vehicle patrols."

"Are they still in regular use?"

"Some were allowed to fall into disrepair because of personnel problems, but others were maintained."

Hung examined the image again.

"That's Kang's helicopter you can see," McCarter told him.

"All this from a satellite orbiting the planet? Remarkable."

"Not smart enough to actually rescue Anna. That's still down to us."

"I will come with you if you wish."

"Hung, you've earned your break. This is our job, but thanks. Anyway, you'll have enough on your hands briefing our people all about Guang Lor. And somebody needs to keep their hands on that stuff we brought out with us."

Hung indicated the backpack he still carried. "This is not leaving my sight until I hand it over to your people."

"If you can fix it, I'd like you to get a message to Shin Tek. Tell him we are grateful for his help, and we hope the Uygur get what they want."

"I will tell him."

THEY TOOK OFF AT NOON, planning to wait at the Wakhjir Pass border crossing until nightfall. Grimaldi had plotted their course and fed in all the topographical data Wethers had sent via the computer link. He had allowed four hours for the flight in. The operation would take place in the dark. Staying at a low altitude, Grimaldi would use the terrain configuration to keep them from being picked up too readily if there was any kind of radar in the area. According to available U.S. intelligence, the Chinese didn't have systems that were sophisticated enough to cover the vast expanses of isolated terrain they would be covering. The landmass they would be flying over was mountainous, undulating and would provide some natural cover for *Dragon Slayer.* Staying below any possible surveillance was their best window of opportunity. Either way, they were going to have to risk the chance of being spotted in case the Intel had it wrong.

From *Dragon Slayer*'s lockers they outfitted themselves with black clothing and equipment, using black face paint to darken their hands and faces. This as always provoked a knowing smirk from Calvin James as he observed his partners.

"Put on all you want, brothers. It still won't make you as good lookin' as me."

"Next mission, I swear, will be in the Arctic," McCarter said.

They all wore lightweight com-links, and each man pocketed a compact signal device they could use to call in *Dragon Slayer* if an urgent need arose.

Grimaldi always made sure his weapon's lockers were outfitted with ordnance to cover every conceivable event to cover whatever Phoenix Force might need. Before shipping out from the U.S., he had included a selection of weapons and backup. Ordnance for this return into Xinjiang was selected on the basis they needed reduced noise for their initial assault. The P-90s were exchanged for Heckler & Koch MP-5 SDs, a version of the standard MP-5 fitted with an integral suppressor and 30-round 9 mm magazines. Available handguns were the Browning Hi-Power for McCarter and 9 mm Berettas 92-Fs for the rest of the team. Every weapon was coated in a nonreflective matt-black finish. They took a selection of stun and fragmentation grenades, and each Phoenix Force commando had a sheathed knife strapped to his leg.

Gary Manning also chose a Barnett crossbow and half a dozen of the cyanide-filled hardwood bolts, nestling in a foam-protected carrying case. In addition there was a Barnett crossbow scope fitted to the bow. It was a programmed five-point, multireticle crosshair system that would allow for fast target acquisition. The combination was exactly suited for the conditions Phoenix Force would encounter at Kang's stronghold.

Once they were in the air, heading for the Wakhjir Pass, McCarter went up front, settling in his couch beside Grimaldi. Using the monitor screen on his side of the flight deck, he tapped up the satellite overview of Kang's redoubt. Wethers had managed some overhead and angled shots of the structure, and from these he had also created an extrapolated image. It allowed Mc-Carter a thorough impression of the building, and with the topographical detail he was able to formulate their plan of attack. He sat studying the on-screen data, constantly flicking from image to image as he devised and rejected various schematics. Grimaldi, aware of the man's concentration, kept quiet.

The inevitable call from Stony Man came after they had been in flight for more than an hour. It was Hal Brognola. There was no mistaking the gruff undertone in his voice when he asked to speak to McCarter.

"Hi, boss," McCarter said casually.

"I just received word you guys took off from Bagram again in that damned chopper."

"That right?"

"That's right," Brognola snapped back. "So none of your bullshit. You're supposed to be on your way back to the U.S. I won't even bother to ask what the hell you're doing. We both know."

"Looks like we're both as smart as each other, then, boss."

"I don't have time to waste swapping jokes here. Your mission is supposed to be over, and you should be on that plane heading for home."

"Uh-uh, Hal, this mission isn't over. Not until the whole team comes out."

"You realize what this damn jaunt could cost?"

"Take it out of my wages, Hal."

"I'm not talking money and you know it. I'm talking about the political cost to the White House if you screw up and get caught."

"I understand that. It was convenient for the President to forget when it was a matter of getting his electronic gizmo back, but not when it's a human life. Well, we did that, Hal. Snatched back his bloody board and even took pictures to back up his claim the Chinese stole it. This trip we're going to retrieve something else that belongs to us. Same deal, Hal. It comes with the package."

There was a long, deep sigh on the other end of the connection. McCarter could almost sense the tension at Stony Man. He waited, allowing Brognola to make his next move.

"Hell, David, I know how you guys feel about Anna. She's as much family to the rest of us as she is to Phoenix."

"So we don't abandon her. We'll take the flak when we get back. Drum us out of the service if you want, but this is still mission time for us. If the Man doesn't like it, bugger him, Hal."

"You want me to quote you on that?"

"Bloody hell, yes. What can he do? Have me shot?"

"Probably."

"He'll have to get in line then. Anytime now we could have the Chinese army after us, so the President is liable to have a long wait."

"I'm gonna chew your ass for this when you get back. The same for the rest of that damn crew of yours."

"I'll pass that along."

"And I'll ground that Grimaldi, too."

"I heard that," Grimaldi said.

"You still going for it?"

"Yes, Hal."

There was another protracted silence.

"Just try not to piss off the whole Chinese nation. Promise?"

"Thanks, boss."

"Yeah…be safe, guys."

There was brief silence, then Barbara Price came on the line.

"Do what you have to. Make sure that lady comes home, too. We'll update you with anything that comes in on your situation."

"Thanks, Barb. Listen, make sure Hal is okay. Buy him a coffee. Send out for a box of those cigars he likes to chew. Put it on my tab."

Price chuckled. "I might just do that."

McCarter signed off.

"That went well," Grimaldi said.

"Yes. Better than I expected," McCarter said, "That's the part that worries me."

THE COMBAT HELICOPTER, running in silent mode, touched down two miles south of the redoubt. With Phoenix Force gone EVA, Jack Grimaldi activated the chopper's sleeper mode and settled back to wait. He was able to pick up body signatures from the external IR scanners until the team moved beyond range.

Rafael Encizo took point, utilizing both his own skills and the electronic assistance of the compact GPS unit from the helicopter. Before they left Grimaldi had downloaded the satellite specs for the area and the position of Kang's redoubt.

As Encizo moved ahead at a steady pace, the rest of Phoenix spaced out, with James bringing up the rear.

They became aware of the inhospitable temperature within minutes of leaving the sheltered and temperature-controlled helicopter. The terrain, hot and dry during daylight hours, had turned cold, the chill factor encouraged by the wind drifting down from the high peaks off to the north. Grimaldi had advised of the climate change after reading the data provided by *Dragon Slayer*'s outer probes, and Phoenix Force had dressed accordingly. Despite this, any exposed skin was still subjected to the chill night air.

As they moved east they encountered adverse changes in the landscape, having to negotiate a series of razorback ridges. The ground underfoot was loose and dry, the only vegetation they encountered brittle grass that clung to any spot of soil it could find. A few times they had to move off track due to some obstacle they were unable to go over. The GPS unit allowed them to get back on the correct heading without problems.

"TARGET IN SIGHT," Encizo transmitted.

Phoenix Force moved in on Kang's redoubt, forming a tight group as the men hunkered down behind a spill of ragged boulders.

McCarter pulled out his night-vision binoculars and scanned the target. The green cast image allowed him to check out perimeter and stationed sentries. As his full pan moved to the extreme left he picked out the bulk of Kang's helicopter standing some distance from the redoubt. There was an armed sentry close by the aircraft.

"Listen up. One by the chopper. Four roving sentries I could see. There might be others on the blind side. And there are two on the roof manning a 12.7, belt-fed machine gun. Anyone tell me what's wrong with that count?"

"Seven plus Kang, his pilot and Anna," Manning said. "More than his chopper could carry."

"The sneaky mother has pulled in a few extra reinforcements," James said. "Question is, how many?"

"I hate it when people do this," McCarter grumbled. "Screws up the logistical parameters."

"Yeah?" James said. "Fucks up the odds, as well."

"Comic asides do not help," the Briton said.

Manning had been quietly preparing his Barnett crossbow. He eased into a position that allowed him an unobstructed firing line.

"You people going to sit around all night, or are we going to get this done?" he asked.

"Rafe, around to the rear. Call in when you're in position. Cal, the guy guarding the chopper. If we can do it quietly we take out all the exterior personnel first."

Encizo and James donned their night-vision goggles before they faded into the darkness, leaving McCarter and Manning to wait until they were in position.

"This could take some time," Manning said.

The Canadian quietly unzipped the case that held the cyanide-filled bolts for the crossbow. McCarter watched in quiet fascination as Manning took one and loaded it into the crossbow.

"A lot more humane than a bullet," Manning said, aware of the Briton's scrutiny. "Get hit with one of these, and the cyanide is in your bloodstream so fast you're dead before you can take a breath."

"I believe you. Not much fun for the poor bugger who catches the shot."

"There's no nice way to kill, David. Only more efficient ways." Manning tapped the hardwood bolt. "And this is efficient."

"I suppose. When it comes down to it, we are in a bloody business. Deciding to take other men's lives at a moment's notice. No prior consultation. Just our judgment. I'm glad I'm not a religious man, Gary, otherwise I might have to start moralizing."

"You want to wait until this is all over?"

McCarter grinned. "Passing thought is all."

He made another check, scanning the area with his night-vision glasses. The sentries made their rounds. On the roof, the machine-gun crew sat in stoic silence, watching and waiting.

The lone man guarding Kang's helicopter suddenly vanished from sight. As McCarter focused in on the sentry, he saw a shadow flicker behind the guy, then the Chinese simply fell out of sight into the deeper shadows.

"Helicopter secure," came James's voice over the com-link. "Sentry down. Going to disable chopper."

Manning glanced at McCarter. "Game on."

The Briton nodded.

In the next couple of minutes Encizo called to say he was in position, too. He had seen one sentry at the rear of the redoubt.

"Moving in now. Go when you guys are ready."

Manning heard and positioned himself at his firing point. He extracted a second bolt from the case and laid it on a flat surface close by. He used the crossbow's scope sight and spent a little time selecting his first target. He chose the machine gunner. The moment the man's head was turned away from the gunner, Manning locked on his primary target, squeezed the trigger and released the bolt. All McCarter heard was a soft hiss of sound as the bolt winged its way toward its target. He had his glasses on the guy and saw the Chinese stiffen as the bolt struck, driving in just below his jawline. He didn't even have time to raise a hand to the shaft buried in his throat. McCarter saw him sag forward over the machine gun.

The moment he fired, Manning cocked the crossbow again and slid the second bolt into place. This time he barely seemed to aim, simply raising the bow to his shoulder, picking up the figure of the loader as the man turned back to his partner. He saw the gunner slumped over the weapon, paused a second as he took in the sight, but before he could do or say anything, Manning's finger released the second shot. It slammed into the man's chest. He looked down at the stub end of the shaft sticking out of his body, then toppled back across the roof.

"Clear here," Encizo reported. "Moving to rear of building."

"Cal, commandeer the roof. Man that machine gun and maintain a clear field around the building."

"Affirmative."

"Gary, with me, let's go."

McCarter, his night-vision goggles in place, swung his MP-5 into position and broke cover, staying low as he approached the redoubt's frontage. He moved as fast as he was able, trusting his way was clear underfoot while he concentrated on the closest of the ground sentries.

The lean Chinese, taller than average, was doing something with his assault rifle, head down. He glanced up, checking the area without warning, and looked directly at McCarter.

And then he began to yell. McCarter understood the warning, even though he couldn't catch the words.

The Chinese swung his assault rifle up, turning it in McCarter's direction.

"Talk about bloody bad timing," the Briton muttered, the MP-5 chopping out its suppressed sound. The volley of 9 mm rounds ripped into the target's chest and spun him to the ground. "Everybody go," McCarter snapped into his com-link.

There was moment of silence, then McCarter heard the feedback from the rest of Phoenix Force's weapons.

A darting figure off the Brit's Phoenix Force leader's changed direction and slammed into the redoubt's stone wall before he slumped to the ground, one of Manning's crossbow bolts protruding from the back of his neck. The big Canadian, moving in to cover McCarter's back, had used his loaded crossbow to deal with the Chinese. Now he slung the weapon and exchanged it for his MP-5 as he closed the distance between himself and the Briton.

The full-on crackle of a Chinese assault rifle broke the silence, broadcasting the news that the redoubt was now under attack.

MAJOR KANG SNAPPED his head up at the sound of gunfire. He stared around him for a moment, gathering his thoughts, then pushed up off his seat. The rattle of weapons came as a distant, muffled sound, blanked by the thick walls of the structure, but it was gunfire.

The American team?

How had they got so close, so quickly? He dismissed that line of thought. No matter. They were here and engaging his men. He snatched up the assault rifle he had propped against the wall and turned to go.

And heard a soft, taunting laugh from the other side of the room.

Kang turned.

"You were supposed to catch *them* unaware, Major Kang. How many times now have they surprised *you?*"

He stared across at Mei Anna. Not for the first time was she mocking him. Despite the bruising and discoloration, her beautiful face still defied him. Her eyes held his gaze. The turn of her lips showed her contempt.

He aimed the assault rifle in her direction, snapping back the bolt to cock it, and his finger trembled against the trigger.

Oh, how he wanted to kill her. To see his bullets tear the sneer from her face and wrench the life from her body.

Never in his life had Kang wanted to see someone die as much as he wanted her to die. The urge was so great it took a sheer act of willpower to stay his finger from the trigger.

He had to keep her alive. She was his saving grace, the one thing that might save him from Director Han's and Beijing's wrath. Kang told himself again that he would be held ultimately responsible for what happened at Guang Lor. He alternated between righteous anger and panic. He was trapped, alone as the already judged perpetrator of this complex and undeserving accusation. Whichever way he turned, the pointing fingers were there. The whispers that condemned him for the entire catalog of errors that had seemed to spin beyond control. First the rogue missile crashing and the Pro-Democracy group snatching the offending circuit board from under his nose. Then the initial capture of not only the American invaders, but also Mei Anna. That victory had turned sour when the Americans had broken out of captivity and turned their destructive talents on Guang Lor, virtually laying the facility to waste. Kang's pursuit had become a near rout.

In fact the only victory had been the recapture of Mei Anna.

And now the Americans had come back into China to make their final attempt to free her.

Kang had no intention of making a trade. He simply wanted the Americans back so he could wipe them off the face of the Earth. If any of them survived they would accompany Mei Anna to Beijing. If they died, so much the better. The thought crossed his mind as to whether they had brought the offending circuit board with them as a last-resort bargaining ploy. He hoped they had, because returning that item would show his resourcefulness. If he was honest, he doubted the item had made the return journey. The Americans might prize Mei Anna's life highly and they would battle to the last to save her life, but the thought of using the circuit board to pay for that freedom wouldn't have entered into their plans. Kang dismissed the thought. Right now the important matter was the destruction of the Americans. Other considerations faded to the back of his mind.

"Why don't you just pull the trigger, Kang? Kill me like you want to. Oh, wait, you can't because I'm important to you as long as I'm alive."

Mei Anna, hands tied behind her back, had struggled into a sitting position on the low cot so she could face her tormentor.

Her words were bitter in his ears. Kang knew she would have sacrificed herself simply to render herself useless to his cause. Delivering her dead body to Beijing would be a pale victory against what the State could gain from her alive and on public trial. Mei Anna shown to the nation, denounced as a dissenting voice of unreason, was worth a dozen corpses. Beijing's moral victory gained from humiliating and deriding her in a show of strength and nationalistic pride would gain far more.

"I may yet see you die," he said. "But I expect it to be at your public execution, Mei Anna."

Kang crossed the room and picked up the communications handset. He keyed the transmit button.

"This is Major Kang. All units move in. I want no mistakes this time."

He turned quickly and exited the room. Outside he slammed the heavy wooden door and closed the bolts.

Even in the basement of the redoubt he could hear the rattle of gunfire. A surge of excitement raced through his body as he ran up the stone steps. This would be the final confrontation. One way or another matters would be settled here tonight, and he, Kang, would see his future settled irrevocably.

Stony Man Farm, Virginia

"Jack, you read me?"

Huntington Wethers waited impatiently, his gaze flicking back to his main monitor and the satellite image feed he had just picked up.

"Jack? Come in."

"…hear you."

"Listen up. I just acquired satellite imagery again. I lost it after downtime. I have Phoenix's position on monitor now and there's a set of images moving on them from the south. Looks like Kang had some people he kept in reserve. I see a chopper on the ground."

"How long?"

"Minutes."

"Thanks, Hunt. There goes my time out."

WHILE DRAGON SLAYER fired up, Grimaldi opened his communications link with Phoenix Force.

"Heads up, ladies. You should be expecting company moving in from the south. Just got the word."

"And?" came McCarter's reply.

"I'm on my way. Fight the good fight, guys, and I'll keep the party crashers off your back."

THEY HAD BEEN ABLE to get imagery of the redoubt's exterior. The inside of the squat stone structure was another matter entirely. McCarter and Manning, taking a direct route to the building, saw the open entrance. What they would find inside was unknown to them.

The Phoenix Force pair moved in unison, each handling the threat coming from their particular direction, the suppressed MP-5's seeking armed figures looming out of the darkness. The night-vision goggles they wore gave them an advantage, allowing them to spot their opponents emerging from the misty green images seconds before the Chinese were able to see them.

The 9 mm gunfire cut into the enemy gunners, pitching them to the ground, while McCarter and Manning kept up their forward motion.

Above their heads the sudden thunder of the machine gun on the roof told them that Calvin James had gained his position. The flickering bursts of flame from the weapon lit the darkness, the brassy clinking of shell casings littering the roof.

As they broached the entrance McCarter flattened against the wall, ejecting his spent magazine and locking in a fresh one. As he snapped the bolt back, cocking the weapon, Manning took an M-67 grenade from his harness, yanked the pin and released the lever. He counted off two of the four-second delay before tossing the grenade inside. The high explosive detonated, throwing deadly fragments cascade along the interior passage. Smoke billowed out through the open entrance.

McCarter allowed for the debris to fall before he ducked inside, his night-vision goggles letting him see along the smoky passage. There were two Chinese down, bodies bloody and still smoking from the blast. He heard Manning behind him. The Canadian kept an eye on the entrance to take on anyone coming up on their rear.

Pale light from fluorescent tubes suspended from the low ceiling allowed them to drop their goggles. Somewhere a generator rumbled, providing the power that charged the lights. The sound vibrated from beneath their feet.

The interior of the redoubt was crude and Spartan. Ahead of them, they could hear autofire and the harsh yell of angry voices. Then came the suppressed stutter of an MP-5.

"Rafe," Manning said.

"We're inside," McCarter said into his com-link.

An acknowledgment came in the sudden blast of a grenade.

HAVING DISPOSED OF THE two guards he had spotted at the rear of the redoubt, Rafael Encizo pushed on to the rear entrance. It was nothing more than a wooden door, and even via his night-vision goggles the Cuban could see it was both weathered and flimsy. He took a moment to make certain his MP-5 was cocked and ready before turning and slamming a booted foot against the door. As it crashed inward Encizo twisted against the wall, hard against the rough stone. He heard the click of weapons and then the crackling burst of autofire as someone on the inside raked the exposed entrance.

He waited a few seconds, then crouched, leaned around the open frame and triggered his own weapon, sweeping the muzzle back and forth. He heard the 9 mm slugs hitting the inner walls, then caught the soft grunt as they scored a hit on human flesh.

The hard bursts from James's machine gun followed as he ducked inside and scanned the passage ahead. The stamp of booted feet reached his ears and Encizo plucked a grenade from his harness.

He picked up McCarter's terse affirmation that he was inside at the front of the redoubt.

Pulling the pin, Encizo rolled the grenade along the passage as he saw gunners emerge from the depths of the building.

KANG HEARD THE COMMOTION overhead as he raced up the stone steps leading from the basement—autofire, the steady crackle of the machine gun on the roof, and then coming close on each other, two grenade bursts. The detonations shook the walls of the redoubt, dust cascading from the ceiling.

He paused, glancing back over his shoulder at the locked basement door. More firing filled the redoubt.

The door at the top of the steps burst open and three of his soldiers crowded through, firing as they retreated.

"Too many, Major," one of the men yelled. "They are inside."

Bullets struck the frame of the open door, splinters of wood flying from the post. The soldiers backed down the stairs, firing as they went, hoping to delay whoever was beyond the door.

Kang returned to the basement, his mind working frantically. It was going wrong again.

Damn those Americans. Each time he thought he had them outfoxed, they simply charged his defenses and just kept coming.

He keyed his handset. "Sergeant Lim? Can you hear me?"

There was nothing from the handset except static.

"Lim. I order you to answer."

The line crackled and a disjointed voice leaped from the speaker.

"…order? Order what? We are under attack from a helicopter."

"I need you here now," Kang yelled, losing his composure and his desire for maintaining control. "No more of your excuses, Lim. You will do as I—"

Lim's reply came in the form of heavy cannon fire. Some kind of powerful machine gun. Mingled with it were the yells and screams of injured men.

"Major Kang," Lim screamed, "I don't care what you want. My men are dying, so you can go to—"

Lim's voice was cut off in midsentence, the handset emitting a final cacophony of jumbled sounds before falling completely silent.

"Major."

Kang looked up and saw two black-clad figures at the top of the steps, their suppressed SMGs firing, punctured bodies tumbling back down the steps, bloody and torn. In the frenzied moment before he turned away Kang recognized the tall, grim-faced man from the American team, followed by a second broad-shouldered figure.

He turned and raced along the passage for the basement door. Kang slammed the bolts free and hauled the door open. He stepped inside, looking in the direction of the cot.

It was empty.

He lifted the assault rifle and swept the bare room. Only at the last moment did he sense someone moving in from his left side. He turned, a smile edging his lips.

Mei Anna, still with her hands bound behind her, took a couple of fast steps before launching herself at Kang, executing a high kick that slammed in under his jaw. The blow snapped his head back. Kang felt his teeth crunch together from the impact. Something broke and he tasted warm blood in his mouth. The kick sent him reeling, stumbling back across the room. He fought to take control, but his head was spinning and he found it hard to maintain his balance.

Landing on her feet, Mei Anna gathered herself to strike a second time. She could see that Kang was attempting to recover, and the sight of the assault rifle in his hands spurred her into a swift response. She ran across the hard floor, launching a full body slam that hit Kang chest-high. The impact threw him across the room and he fell, half rolling until the wall halted him. He lay panting, his body aching from the severe impact. He realized he had dropped his weapon and looked around for it. The weapon lay only feet away. Kang reached out and closed his finger over the rifle, dragging it to him. He sucked in deep breaths and pushed himself up off the floor.

When Anna impacted against Kang she lost her balance and crashed to the floor herself, the breath driven from her body. The side of her head struck the hard slabs and the blow made her black out for a few seconds. As she struggled to clear the fog from her brain, she tried to gain her feet. It was hard, with her bound hands and her sudden lack of strength.

She twisted around to find Kang and saw him using the wall at his back to support him as he pushed upright, his assault rifle back in his hands.

For a brief span their eyes met and held.

"If I lose, then so do you," he said.

There was an odd blend of regret and envy in his tone, as if whatever else they might have against each other there was a sliver of respect. Kang stood for everything Mei Anna hated—repression and the overwhelming desire to deny the Chinese people their true destiny. Kang and his kind were reluctant to allow China to emerge from the gray shadows of the past into what could be a brighter future. The country had the will and the strength to become something far better than it was if only it shook off the trappings of the old ways. It had shown those things could happen, but there were still too many in power who defied every move to turn full circle. Kang represented that old philosophy. He believed in it because it was all he had been taught. He knew nothing different and refused to bend—yet he saw the same determination in Mei Anna's resolve and in that respect they were the same.

"It would have been interesting to have this out with you. But now it has come to this…"

Anna saw the assault rifle dip as he aimed it at her.

Kang licked at his bleeding mouth, almost smiling, but then she saw his eyes darken and he jerked his head toward the door.

"Kang."

The tall foreigner stood in the doorway, his weapon trained on Kang.

Major Tchi Chuy Kang, who only a few days earlier had been on a rising career curve, stared into the black maw of inevitable destruction. He managed to finally rise to his feet, then deliberately turned the muzzle of his rifle on the man. At the back of his mind he had already accepted defeat. This time, no matter how he connived, or planned, or tried to negotiate, there was no way out. So he chose the only path left open for him and died in a burst from McCarter's MP-5 that left him a bleeding, broken corpse on the basement floor of his final refuge.

"Gary, call Jack to see if he's free for a fast pickup," McCarter said as he crossed to help Mei Anna to her feet before using his knife to free her hands.

"This could become a habit," Anna said.

"Don't knock it," McCarter said. "Now let's get the hell out of here before the rest of the PLA turns up."

He snatched up the assault rifle Kang had dropped and handed it to her. Anna checked it, then nodded, following him and Manning out of the room.

"PICK UP ON THE ROOF," Grimaldi said into his comlink. "I'm swinging around now. Just tell that trigger-happy guy up there I'm on your side."

"Just don't sneak up on me," James responded.

"How's it look out there?" McCarter asked.

"The opposition has pulled back," Grimaldi advised. "I don't know whether it's for good, or just so they can regroup and maybe wait for backup. But I don't feel inclined to hang around to find out."

"We're on our way. We have our package safe and sound, and we're not meeting much resistance down here."

THEY MADE THE RETURN flight back to the Afghan border in under three hours. Grimaldi had the throttles wide open all the way, running low and dodging the terrain contours as he flew. If they were picked up by any Chinese surveillance, nothing came of it.

Phoenix Force slept most of the way, only Gary Manning rousing himself when he felt *Dragon Slayer* accelerating down. Pale light was spreading over the landscape as Grimaldi swooped down into the Wakhjir Pass and on to Bagram air base.

Manning dropped into the seat beside Grimaldi.

"Busy few days," the Stony Man pilot said.

"I've had less stressful ones."

"Job done?"

Manning gave a worn smile. "Not until we've faced the wrath of Brognola," he said.

"Ouch, I'd forgotten about that."

"Don't worry, Jack. He'll remind you soon enough."

Grimaldi pulled a face. "Hey, Gary, you want me to double back and we'll go harass Beijing? Got to be less of a choice."

"Jack, don't tempt me."

CHAPTER TEN

Shanghai, China

Director Su Han replaced the telephone receiver and leaned back in his leather padded executive chair, reflecting with an almost amused feeling that life had a strange way of turning matters upside down.

He had just spoken with one of his trusted aides and had been informed of the news coming through from Xinjiang.

Guang Lor was in ruins. Dr. Lin Cheung was one of the casualties of the armed strike against the facility. His body had been located in the demolished research building where work had been carried out developing technology for the proposed range of missiles. The destruction of the building had resulted in the loss of all the hardware, including the American originals and the computer data files holding development schematics and test results. The final piece of information had referred to another matter, though it was just as damning.

Major Tchi Chuy Kang was also dead. His final attempt at righting the whole miserable affair had resulted in his force being confronted by the American commando team he had been pursuing across country. Kang's capture, for the second time, of the Pro-Democracy dissident Mei Anna had again been thwarted. Survivors of Kang's force had told of Kang being killed, the woman liberated and the Americans leaving the scene of the battle in a powerful, unidentifiable helicopter. Last reported sightings had been of the helicopter heading south toward the border with Afghanistan. It was also assumed, and Han was in no doubt that it was true, that Mei Anna's accomplice Loy Hung—had also escaped with the American circuit board from the downed C26-V missile.

The aide's final words had been in the form of a question.

"What do we now, Director Han?"

Han had told the man not to worry and had then broken the connection.

What to do indeed, he thought as he stared out the window of the apartment overlooking Shanghai's Huangpu River. The river snaked through and divided the city into two parts, east and west. Han found the view, day or night, beautiful. Great modern skyscrapers vied for place with the older buildings in different architectural styles that made Shanghai a vibrant and cosmopolitan place.

This was his place, his refuge when the responsibilities of his position became overbearing. He had bought the apartment on a whim, after being invited to a similar residence owned by one of his superiors. The man had made no pretence of hiding his acquisition.

Members of the ruling party were allowed these dispensations, Han was informed. What was the point of power if it couldn't benefit those who held it? At the time it had seemed a logical reason, which held little comfort for Han now. He crossed to the far end of the living room where he had created a work environment, complete with a large desk made from pale ash, and a leather executive-style chair, pausing to fill a thick tumbler with a generous amount of smooth malt whiskey from his private stock before seating himself. At one corner of the expansive desk sat a high-tech computer, complete with high-resolution flat-screen monitor. The director was extremely proud of his desk. It afforded him great satisfaction to sit behind it and conduct official business. Even hold audience with lesser individuals.

Now, alone and not a little concerned over his future, Director Han felt *himself* a lesser individual. He recalled his recent telephone conversation with the unfortunate Lin Cheung, how they had conspired to make certain the now late Major Kang be made the scapegoat for the sequence of events at Guang Lor.

With Cheung and Kang dead, only Han remained to shoulder responsibility for what had happened. The thought rested heavily on him. He sat for some time formulating his coming moves, taking into account how his superiors would be assessing his performance.

The fact that he had a high-ranking position within the administration meant nothing. Mistakes were viewed with great seriousness in Beijing, because any flaws within the ruling enclave reflected on everyone. From bitter experience Han had only to look back on others, some he had called friends, who had fallen out of favor. A minor infraction meant either death or a long sentence in a labor camp. The latter was simply another death sentence. The only difference was that it took longer to die. In either situation the guilty ones—in the eyes of the Party—would simply vanish and never be seen again. Han's long service, his unblemished record, would count for nothing if he was found guilty of mismanagement. He decided he was being too optimistic and changed "if" to "when." The day of his judgment was coming. So Han decided it was in his own interest to stay one step ahead of his fate.

He reached for the cell phone on his desk. It was a private phone, purchased independently and paid for in cash. The service provider was based in Taiwan. Han paid for the contract out of his own substantial accounts. As loyal as he had been to the Party, Director Su Han had always looked to the future and his own survival. In his position there had always been access to substantial funds. It went with his job. Han had been putting aside regular amounts for years, placing the money in secret accounts. When the connection with Shadow came along, the greater amounts he had to play with meant the ability to siphon off even larger amounts. With his rank came other privileges, such as the ability to manage covert operations. With that in mind, Han had people and his own network, reaching across Asia and the Pacific Rim, even to Europe and the U.S.A. The acquisition of a secure and private means of communication had been a simple matter, and now he was about to use it to secure his future survival.

He tapped in a number from memory and waited for the triband phone to connect.

"Oliver, may I now call you that?"

"I believe our relationship has developed to that point, Director Han."

"Ever the diplomat. Please call me Su."

"How can I help?"

"I assume you are aware of the unfortunate turn of events in Xinjiang?"

"News has filtered through up to a point. Perhaps you can give me more details?"

Han described the events in detail. "I think we need to meet, Oliver. To talk in private. On neutral ground perhaps, where we can discuss our dealings for the future."

"I'm intrigued. It presents no problems as far as I'm concerned. If you give me a little time I'll work something out and send you an email with the details. Is that satisfactory?"

"Extremely. I will wait for your message."

Han broke contact and laid the cell phone on the desk. He remained seated for a while, swiveling his chair so he could gaze out the panoramic window and watch where Shanghai's lights were coming on against the deepening shadows. He was going to miss his apartment, the views, his position in the Second Department, Intelligence. He consoled himself with the irredeemable fact that life wasn't a constant. It evolved, it changed. As fluid as water, it ebbed and flowed and eventually found its own level. It seemed, due to circumstances beyond Han's control that his life was about to do just that. He had known for a long time that the Party had a rigid stance. Its members demanded only success and frowned on anyone who failed to maintain the status quo. Knowing them as he did, Su Han saw himself as having done just that.

So the time had come for him to move on. And quickly before his superiors chose to remove him. The full facts concerning Guang Lor had yet to be presented to those who would condemn him, so Han had a small window of opportunity. Contacting Townsend had been Han's opening play.

Turning again he studied the apartment. This had been his retreat for almost two years. He wasn't a man who gathered many personal belongings so there was little he needed to take with him. There was a case in his bedroom always packed and ready for quick trips. This time the trip would be for himself and not the department. He opened a drawer in the desk and took out a leather wallet. Inside was his passport and personal documents, as well as a substantial amount of cash in U.S. dollars—always welcome currency. There were credit and cash cards. He placed all these items in a slim attaché case. Han reached back inside the desk drawer and took out his personal firearm, a powerful 9 mm SIG-Sauer pistol. He considered the option of taking the weapon with him, but decided against it. He might be able to get it through internal Chinese checkpoints, but once he reached foreign soil it could easily arouse suspicion and even panic.

Reluctantly he placed the pistol back in the drawer. He would be able to get a weapon from Townsend once he reached his destination. Closing the drawer, he reached for his whiskey glass, draining it. He tapped the space bar on his computer keyboard and brought the machine out of standby. Checking that he was still logged into the department database, Han took a couple of USB flash drives and inserted the first into the port. Tapping in instructions, he initiated a download that would transfer all his data from the department mainframe into the storage unit. While this was working, Han went to the bedroom and collected his packed case and brought it back into the living room. Then he returned and changed into comfortable clothes for traveling. He checked the computer and saw that he had incoming mail. Opening the file he saw it was from Townsend. He read the brief message and smiled. As usual Townsend was proving to be consistently efficient. Han sent a quick acknowledgment, then erased the message.

Townsend had advised that Han join him at Jack Regan's Santa Lorca residence.

Han saw that the flash drive had completed its transfer. He extracted the slim unit and placed a second one in the port, tapping in more instructions. This time the data he was extracting were his own, personal files, encrypted, and detailing bank accounts, global contacts and the names of people who not only owed him favors, but also those he could coerce into providing assistance due to the incriminating material Han had amassed on them.

Using his cell phone he called Shanghai Pudong International Airport and booked a domestic flight that would take him to Hong Kong. He used one of his credit cards to pay for the ticket and was told his flight would leave in two hours. His official standing allowed him priority treatment. Han had to smile at that, wondering how much longer that would last. How soon would officialdom strip away his power? If it could be forestalled for a few hours longer, he might yet make it out of the country. He made another call, this time to Hong Kong International Airport, and booked a flight that would take off only an hour after he arrived, again using his official authority to gain privilege status.

Han saw that his second flash drive had completed its download. He extracted the stick and placed both of them in an inner, zipped pocket of his jacket.

He was about to delete his database on the computer when he saw a small warning indicator in the top right of his monitor. It told him that his computer was being accessed by an outside source. The safety protocol was something that had been installed some time ago by Han himself. It meant someone was attempting to get into his files. Han realized that he was being monitored, an indication that his position within the department *was* being investigated. He did nothing, because he had also embedded within his system a device that would, the moment someone hacked into it, wipe the entire memory of his hard drive. He experienced a momentary pang of regret that his years of devotion to the Party could be so quickly wiped away. Trust being dismissed so easily. It seemed that previous achievements meant nothing to the people in control.

Han gathered his travel items, pocketed his wallet, took a last tumbler of whiskey and watched as the hacker broke into his system. There was a pause, then Han's computer activated the installed program and began the swift and irreversible erasure of everything contained within its electronic heart. Han raised his glass in farewell and drained its contents.

He left the apartment and made his way to the express elevator that would take him to the basement car park. When the doors opened Han walked quickly to his parking bay and unlocked his Mercedes. He stowed his luggage and started the car, leaving by the exit ramp. He swung around the apartment building and headed for the road that would take him to Pudong International.

Traffic was light, so it wasn't hard for Han to check whether he was being followed or not. His work over the years had given him experience in such practices, so he understood the signs to look out for. He saw nothing.

Perhaps there was no need to panic yet. The computer intrusion proved that he was under observation, but he had no problem with that. It would be the first step in any checking into his affairs. The Party, whatever else, followed the rules. There would be a certain protocol to follow before anything else happened, and it was that rigid adherence to the rules that might allow him the time to clear the country.

He reached the airport in plenty of time, leaving his car in a far corner of the parking lot and walking to the departure lounge where he picked up his ticket. When he reached the gate he showed his department credentials and was ushered through with little fuss as soon as his case had been checked in. He had twenty minutes to wait before the flight call and despite his outer show of calm, Han was inwardly admitting to some nervousness. His fears were unfounded and he made it on to the plane without any incidents. A genuine feeling of relief washed over him when the jet finally hauled itself off the ground for its flight to HKIA.

Han realized that no matter what happened now there wasn't a thing he could do about it, so he tilted his seat back and closed his eyes.

HONG KONG INTERNATIONAL Airport was teeming with people. Those arriving and those waiting to leave came together in surging waves. Han approached the check-in desk for his flight, first checking the surrounding area in case there were any security personnel waiting to jump on him the moment he showed his face. The young woman at the desk was fully accommodating, especially when she realized who he was. It was, Han thought, interesting to be able to see how people reacting coming face-to-face with someone as important as Director Su Han.

Not for much longer, Han admitted.

"Have a pleasant flight, Director Han," the woman said.

His final hurdle was passport control. As he stood in line, Han watched the close scrutiny of the officials at the desk. They were being thorough, as usual, so he saw nothing to be alarmed about. By the time it came to his turn Han was in full control, acting as he always did when confronted by any form of lesser officialdom.

He passed his documents to the customs officer and saw the raised eyebrows as the man read Han's passport. Han placed his case on the belt and allowed it to go through the detector. "Is there a problem?" Han demanded brusquely. "Is my passport out of date?"

"No, Director Han," the officer said. "Everything appears to be in order."

"So it should be," Han snapped. "If the director of the Second Department, Intelligence, has out-of-date documents, then we are in trouble. Yes?"

"Exactly so, Director."

"Do you wish to check my luggage?"

"I do not think so," the officer said hastily, glancing at his superior, who stood a little way off.

His superior stepped forward.

"There are rules about this," he said.

Ah, Han thought, here we have the one. Self-important and following the regulations.

"You are?"

"Captain Tien…" The man became aware of Han's immobile expression, his expectancy of a completion of the address as he read the passport and absorbed the details. "Director Han."

Han beckoned the man to step away from the other passengers who were becoming interested in the moment of intrigue.

"Captain, I appreciate the difficulty of your position. However, allow me to explain something. If I do not board this aircraft, an individual who has already passed through your section and who is waiting to leave may be lost to us."

"Someone wanted for a crime?"

"In the process of committing a security breach. He is involved in passing state secrets. This flight will take him to a meeting with his contact. I am in the process of following him so I can apprehend him when he meets his buyer at the other end."

Tien absorbed the information. "Perhaps I should inform *my* superiors."

"To what purpose? They will not have any knowledge of this operation, Captain Tien. It is highly classified. If you contact them, there could be a reaction that would delay the flight and raise suspicion in my suspect. If that happens, he will avoid making contact and all my department's work will have been wasted.

If you believe you should make that call, please do so. But if my suspect is lost, Captain Tien, there will be questions asked. The first and most important will demand the identity of the person who interrupted an operation in progress."

Han paused, allowing the implicit threat to hang in the air, and could have laughed at the sudden jolt of panic that filled Tien's eyes. He would be the one who caused the problem. He, Tien, would be the one to carry the burden of guilt. Han felt a moment of pity for the man, because he was in the same position. His pity only lasted a microsecond.

"Captain Tien?"

Tien cleared his throat. "There will be no problem here, Director Han."

Han nodded. "Your cooperation in this matter will be highlighted in my report, Captain Tien. It is heartening to deal with a professional,"

Minutes later Han was seated in the departure lounge, breathing a little easier as he waited for the flight that would take him to Central America, where he would be met and flown for the final leg of his trip to Santa Lorca and his meeting with Oliver Townsend.

TOWNSEND'S DECISION was made quickly, and once he had made that decision he acted on it.

"Ralph, in here," he called as Chomski walked into view.

Chomski joined him, sensing immediately that something was about to happen.

"Somebody start World War III?"

Townsend smiled. "I believe our friends in China might look at it that way."

"Tell me?"

"Guang Lor has been taken down. Blown to hell in a hand basket. Cheung is dead. So is Kang, the guy who ran the military setup there. This strike force we've been hearing about has been running riot in Xinjiang. It looks like they recovered the stolen circuit board and it's on its way back Stateside. I got this directly from Director Su Han a short time ago."

Chomski perched on the corner of Townsend's desk. He stared out the window, across the dusty yard and watched T. J. Hawkins making his way to the bunkhouse. He experienced that uneasy feeling he always got when he saw the newcomer, but kept it to himself. Townsend had enough on his plate right now. The last thing he wanted to hear was gossip.

"Have the plane readied."

"Vacation time?"

"Not exactly. We need time to assess the situation. Somewhere the hard hand of the law isn't going to fall on our shoulders."

"You think this mess in China might hit us?"

"Ralph, we skinned ourselves out of that CIA setup because Tilman did us a favor. It might not happen next time. Kibble could have exposed us. Security has been stepped up on all our potential sources. We've got that here on our home ground. Now the Chinese business might, and I say might, lead back to us. Let's face it, we're in a high-risk enterprise. I need some clear time to sit down and figure out how we work our way around it."

"Okay. Where're we going?"

"Santa Lorca. Regan's place. Me, you, Rik and Hawkins. Joseph, too."

"The crew?" Chomski queried.

"Keep a skeleton crew. Send the rest home on a paid break."

"I'll call for the chopper to pick us up and take us to the field. How soon?" Chomski asked.

"Soon as you get your butt off my desk and do it?"

Chomski grinned. He left the room and located Brandt, explaining what was happening.

"I'll go and tell the guys."

"Rik, Hawkins doesn't hear about this until I give the word. Understand?"

Brandt frowned but nodded.

"Whatever you say, Ralph."

TWO HOURS LATER the ranch was nearly deserted. All the men had left, except for three, plus Vic Lerner, who was still confined to his bed. Hawkins had no idea what was going on. The departing crew members were strangely silent, simply throwing packed bags into vehicles and driving away.

Crossing in the direction of the bunkhouse, Hawkins spotted Chomski standing at the entrance. He had an odd smile on his face, as if he were hoarding a big secret.

"What's going on, Ralph?"

"Go pack a bag, Hawkins. You're on special detachment. A little trip down south."

"South as in over the border?"

"Sharp as ever, T.J., now get a move on. We don't have all day to stand around gabbin'."

Hawkins went inside the bunkhouse and threw his stuff in his duffel. On his way out he passed Lerner's room.

"Hey, buddy," Lerner called.

"How you feeling?"

"Stiff and sore." Lerner put down the magazine he was reading. "So you get to go on a trip?"

Hawkins shrugged. "Mystery tour down south is all I heard."

"Santa Lorca. Our pal Jack Regan has a big hacienda there. Outside the big city of Port Cristobal."

"You been before?"

Lerner nodded. "Couple times."

"See you when we get back."

Lerner grinned. "I'll be here."

As HAWKINS STEPPED outside the bunkhouse he heard the sound of a helicopter coming down for a landing. Townsend. Chomski, Brandt and Joseph Riotta emerged from the house. All carried bags. Hawkins didn't hesitate. He couldn't afford to show any signs of not wanting to join the group at this stage. Whatever was going on in Santa Lorca might prove both interesting and informative, even if he had no idea what it might be at this moment in time.

As he made his way across the yard he found himself wondering about his backup team. Able would be nearby, maybe even watching what was happening. He hoped they were. Depending what went on once he was in Santa Lorca, he might need the special talents of Carl Lyons and company.

"WELL?"

Lyons's demanding tone made Blancanales subdue any casual comments he might have been considering.

"T.J. was on board," he said.

"Fuck." Lyons spoke the word very softly, without emphasis, and it sounded all the more threatening than if he had bellowed it out.

Blancanales listed the people who had boarded the helicopter.

"Townsend's top line. Something important is going on and we lose them."

"Only three left at the ranch as far as I could see. Rest of the crew has been shipping out over the last couple of hours."

Lyons turned suddenly and climbed into the SUV. Blancanales followed, tossing the powerful binoculars he'd been using onto the rear seat. He was slammed back in the seat as Lyons floored the gas pedal, turning the 4x4 in a tight circle, dust billowing from beneath the heavy tires.

"You want to let me know where we're going before we hit Warp Factor 7?"

"The ranch," Lyons snapped testily. "Townsend left some of his crew behind. They can tell us where he's gone. I'm tired of creeping around like an old woman. Time for some direct diplomacy."

Blancanales muttered something too low for Lyons to pick up.

"Say what?"

"I was just thinking I wish I'd never asked."

The 4x4 bounced as it left the dirt track and hit the blacktop. The tires squealed in protest as Lyons fought the wheel and brought it back under control, pushing the vehicle hard as he went looking for the entrance to the Townsend property.

"Isn't this going to hang us out to dry?" Blancanales asked. "Show our hand?"

"You think I give a shit? We just lost our guy. The one we were supposed to keep safe. He's gone off into the blue yonder and we haven't a clue where. I don't like being jerked around."

"You want me to update Stony Man?"

Lyons uttered an affirmative grunt.

"You're going where?" was Barbara Price's comment after Blancanales explained what was happening.

"The Townsend spread. I see this as an exercise in pushing luck to the limit."

"Just don't start another OK Corral."

"That was Tombstone. Arizona. This is Texas."

"Don't split states with me. Just do what you have to."

Lyons drove without letup, swinging off the main road and onto the long, dusty dirt road that brought them into the Townsend ranch proper. He braked in a cloud of dust outside the main house and was out of the SUV before Blancanales could stop him.

A figure appeared from the main house, dressed in work clothes. He stood on the wide steps and watched as Lyons approached.

"Do something for you?" he asked.

Lyons held up his left hand and let the man see the Justice Department shield.

"See that? Know what it means?"

"Means you got a shiny badge."

Lyons smiled. It was almost a pleasant smile. Blancanales caught it as he joined his partner.

"You're looking at something rare," Lyons said. "A real stand-up comedian."

"I feel privileged," Blancanales said.

"What is it you want?"

"It's like this," Lyons said. "We were hoping to see

Mr. Townsend, but it appears we just missed him." He waved his free arm in the air. "He just flew off in that fancy chopper of his. Right?"

"You say so," the man said. He came down the steps to face the Able Team pair. "Looks like you wasted a trip."

"No. We've got *you*, so it isn't all bad."

"Hell, I just work here. I don't know a thing."

"Strange thing to say when you haven't a clue why we're here," Blancanales pointed out. "Makes me start to think maybe you have something to hide."

"The hell you say. Fuck this, you can't stroll in and accuse people of—"

"That's another mistake," Lyons cut in. "First you don't know anything. A classic sign of guilt. And now you get defensive when we haven't accused you of a thing."

"All we were going to ask was, where has Townsend gone?"

"I don't know."

"There you go again," Lyons said. "I knew Texas was short on talk but you're taking advantage."

"I'm not from around here."

"Maybe we should take this guy in," Blancanales suggested. "At least we'll have an arrest on our file."

Lyons nodded.

The man glanced around, looking for somewhere to vanish. There was nowhere he could go, except back inside the house.

"You carrying a gun?" Blancanales asked out of the blue, his voice harsh.

The man's reaction was sudden, not unexpected, and broke all the rules of common sense. Instead of denial, or admitting he had a weapon, he simply reached behind him for the pistol jammed down the back of his jeans.

As he went for the weapon Lyons erupted into movement, stepping right up to the man and executing a savage head butt that crunched against the other's nose. The appendage broke and the man swayed back, stunned, oblivious to the sudden gush of blood that washed down his face and splattered his shirt. Following through, Lyons stepped around the man, grabbing the hand that was reaching for the gun. Lyons arced around behind the guy, twisting the arm up his back and took possession of the pistol himself.

"Bad choice, pal," Lyons whispered, jamming the muzzle of the pistol against the side of the man's head. "Now make sure the next thing you say is the correct thing. Unless you want the top of you head and the brains under it on the ground by your feet. Think about, sucker. It's your choice."

The man swayed, shaking his head, blood still dribbling heavily from his nose.

"I—I…" The guy was having problems forming coherent sentences. "Fuck, man, it hurts."

"It's supposed to hurt. Gets your attention. Now tell me what I need to know. Where the fuck has Townsend and his buddies gone? And don't give me any shit about the local Wal-Mart."

Blancanales spotted movement across the dusty yard, where a figure had appeared in the door of a long building he took as the bunkhouse. It might have been cowboy country, but there was nothing Western about the weapon the guy was carrying. It was a very modern M-16 A-1.

"Gun," Blancanales yelled at his partner. "Behind you."

Blancanales hauled his Beretta from the hip holster

under his jacket and moved to cover behind the bulk of the 4x4.

Lyons hefted the bulky pistol he had taken from Broken Nose. He spun suddenly, clouting the guy across the skull with the heavy weapon. The struck man grunted and went flat down on the ground. By that time Lyons was moving to join Blancanales. He was a few steps short when the guy with the M-16 A-1 opened up. The ground exploded in dusty spouts where the 5.56 mm slugs dug in. Lyons last steps turned into a hurried dive that took him behind the 4x4.

The rifle man ran in the direction of the vehicle, raising the assault rifle as he closed in.

Lyons rolled to his feet, spitting dry dust from his mouth.

"Okay, now the hard way."

He dropped the pistol and moved the length of the 4x4, walking around the rear, and when he stepped out he had the Colt Python in his hands. The rifle man caught a glimpse of Lyons an instant before the Able Team commando opened fire and laid a trio of Magnum slugs in his chest. The force picked him off his feet and he twisted violently before he hit the ground, raising a cloud of pale dust.

There was movement just inside the bunkhouse door, followed by the staccato rattle of autofire. One of the 4x4s window blew out.

Blancanales leaned across the hood of the vehicle and sighted along the barrel of his 9 mm Beretta. He made out the dark outline in the bunkhouse door's shadow, then stroked the trigger. His shot hit the man's shoulder. The guy slumped forward, exposing more of his upper body. Blancanales fired again, twice, and saw his bullets punch into the target's chest and put the man down hard.

Blancanales picked up the pistol Lyons had dropped and tucked it in his belt. He jogged to the guy Lyons had slugged and hauled the groggy man to his feet.

"Let's go, hombre."

The man was too dazed to protest.

Lyons had reloaded his Colt with some loose shells from his pocket. He was heading directly for the bunkhouse, checking for further movement. When he reached the man he'd put down, he cleared the M-16, then checked for further weapons. Not that it mattered. The man was dead.

The man Blancanales had fired at was dead, too. One 9 mm round had cored through his right shoulder, two more directly into his heart.

Blancanales pushed his prisoner against the bunkhouse wall.

"Now I'm sure you realize the error in not cooperating," he said.

The man stared at the pair with obvious terror in his eyes and decided that a broken nose and a crack on the skull was preferable to being dead.

"Jesus, you win. What the hell, I didn't sign on for a fuckin' war with the crazies."

"Any more around?" Lyons asked, making sure his Python remained in full view.

"Only one inside. He's confined to bed. Took a slug in the shoulder a few days ago."

"Lead the way," Lyons said, prodding the man with the tip of the Python's muzzle.

They entered the bunkhouse and moved through the living area to the individual rooms.

"Hear that?" Blancanales asked.

Lyons nodded. He had heard the sounds, too. Someone was moving around, awkward, stumbling. A man was cursing to himself.

"What's this guy called?" Lyons asked Broken Nose.

"Lerner. Vic Lerner."

Lyons glanced at Blancanales. "Just had to be him."

"Hawkins's old Army buddy?"

Lerner appeared then, leaning around the door frame to peer along the passage at the group heading his way. He wore light pants, no top. His left shoulder and upper arm were heavily bandaged and in a sling. He held a Beretta pistol in his right hand. It took him a few seconds before he recognized Lyons.

"What the hell are you doing here?"

"Just put the gun down, Lerner, unless you want a matching right shoulder," Lyons said, his Python already lined up for a shot.

"Vic, do it," Broken Nose said. "They already took down Norris and Davies."

"Good advice, Vic," Blancanales said, stepping out from behind Broken Nose to show his own weapon.

Lerner saw sense quickly enough. He secured the Beretta and lowered it to the floor, kicking it clear. Blancanales stepped forward and took possession of the pistol.

"Now let's get across to the house," Lyons said.

As they retraced their steps to the main house, Lerner kept stealing quiet glances at Lyons. Just before they entered he stopped and turned to face him.

"T.J. is a plant? That deal in the bar was to set me up?"

"He's smart," Lyons said.

"Son of a bitch," Lerner said. "Got to hand it to T.J. He fooled the whole bunch. Son of a bitch, he always was a canny old dog." He hesitated. "Chomski is going to be mad as hell when he finds out."

Inside the house Broken Nose and Lerner were seated where Blancanales could keep an eye on them while Lyons called Stony Man to apprise them of the situation. He found himself talking to Brognola.

"Ranch is secure. Nobody left here except a few guys house-watching. What…? Some resistance. We took care of it…. What do you mean, *how?* Hal, I went in with a white flag and appealed to their patriotic side. Expand it…? Okay, we had to shoot the shit out of them. That make you feel better…? Two things. Be advisable for you to get people in here. This place needs checking out from floor to attic. And Townsend's storm troopers need dealing with. Second, and more important, we need travel arrangements made to get us down to Santa Lorca. I want to be there for T.J. I let him slip away. Talk to the President. He promised any help we needed, didn't he? Your words. So make him cough up. Divert the Pacific Fleet if he needs to. Just get us a ride down there and the Navy can drop us on Santa Lorca without the locals hearing about it…. Thanks, Hal, I'll wait for your call. Hey, don't forget our relief. We got two live ones here and I don't want them getting any chance to find a phone and tipping Townsend off. Sure, Hal… Trust me, I was trained for this."

Lyons was smiling when he put the phone down. He returned to where Blancanales was watching the prisoners.

"All sorted," he said. "You guys will be in the care of a special task force before you know it."

Broken Nose peered over the top of the bloody towel he was holding to his face.

"They friends of yours?"

"Yeah," Lyons said. "Just like me, too. Caring and dedicated to their work."

"Gives me a lot to be thankful for," Broken Nose said in a totally unconvinced tone.

Santa Lorca, Central America

TOWNSEND REALIZED Han was tired from his long flight from Shanghai to Santa Lorca. Picking him up from the local airport, which was for minor flights, Townsend drove the Chinese to Jack Regan's hacienda fifteen miles up country from Santa Lorca's capital city, Port Cristobal. Han said very little during the drive. The strain of his flight was only part of the reason for his mood.

His long hours in the air had allowed Han to consider his future and attempt to dispense with the baggage of his past. He regretted having to leave China. The circumstances left him little choice. Remaining in the country would have simply been the end of his existence. Han accepted that being a living exile was preferable to a dead martyr. It made him aware of the inflexible attitude of the country's leaders. Their obsession with maintaining China's political stance had seemed an admirable thing to Han in his younger days, but the dogged refusal of the ruling class to emerge from the dusty shadows of the Marxist ideology was harming China more than it was helping.

The country had proved it could adapt and become as one with the West. Manufacturing processes were already bringing in financial security, and the future had seemed bright. New construction in many areas was improving the living standards, though there was still much poverty in other environments. Rural China still existed as it had for centuries. But the obsession with military might, on a par, or better, than the West, was one of the drawbacks in China's thinking. The panic when Russia had declared its intention to update its missile systems had created a state of fear and panic within the Party. In a state of extreme paranoia, their vowed declaration to draw level with America and Russia had kick-started the Guang Lor projects. The decision to enter into industrial espionage and steal American technology had been hailed as a brilliant concept. And it had been progressing well until the unfortunate crash of the Guang Lor missile. Bad enough in itself, the incident had been compounded by the appearance of the Pro-Democracy team. Their judicious snatching of the American-made circuit board from under the nose of Major Kang had been embarrassing. But the added interference of the American strike team had only increased the problems.

What galled Su Han was his implication in the final result. After doing his duty to the state he was now being forced into exile by the very people he had served. It was trial without jury, a guilty verdict brought down on him simply because a fall guy, as the Americans would have put it, was needed. The realization hurt. It burned within him and made Han even more determined not to let the matter destroy him.

He slept from sheer exhaustion that afternoon and woke feeling refreshed in the evening. Regan's sprawling home was well appointed. Each bedroom suite was self contained, even down to private bathroom. Han took a long shower, shaved and dressed in lightweight clothing before making his way to the dining area. The meal was already under way, and as Han appeared Jack Regan waved him toward an empty chair.

"Help yourself, Han," Regan said.

Han took some salad and fruit, poured himself a glass of orange juice, checking out the others as he did.

He knew Townsend and Regan, Ralph Chomski and Joseph Riotta. There were two more men he failed to recognize. Townsend introduced them.

"These are a couple of my guys, Su. The big one is Rik Brandt and the younger feller is one of my new associates, T. J. Hawkins."

Han shook hands with the two, then resumed his meal. The food on the planes had been typical fare. Nothing to make a fuss over and not very filling. Now his appetite was returning.

"We may be joined in the morning by a couple more guests," Townsend said, "Our CIA friend Tilman and someone from your part of the country."

Han looked up sharply at that. "Who?"

"Hey, don't sweat, bubba," Regan said. "Just your pal from the firm. Chen Low."

Sammo Chen Low.

"I don't understand," Han said.

"He was out of the country the last few days," Townsend explained. "He got the word about the Guang Lor fuck-up and saw the writing on the wall. Got to give it to the guy. He didn't mess around. Figured it might not be safe calling home, so he phoned me. I told him what little I knew and suggested he get his ass over here pronto. Wasn't long after you'd spoken to me."

Just like Chen Low, Han thought. He was as shrewd in personal matters as he was sharp in business. He would have kept himself informed about the ongoing Guang Lor incident, assessing the way it was going, and the moment everything came crashing down, Chen Low would have looked ahead to the inevitable damage limitation exercise Beijing would put in motion. Chen was closely associated with Su Han, part of his immediate unit, so he would catch much of the fallout. Chen Low, being a financier, had his own agenda bubbling away in the background. Being the official paymaster for Han's deals he had been responsible for considerably-large amounts of hard cash as well as the electronic transfers. Han had been privy to Chen Low's accounting. He understand creative accounting, and he knew Sammo Chen Low.

So Low was saving himself, too. Han had to give the man credit. He could see a creative partnership in the future for them both.

"Are you happy to talk in front of everyone here?" Townsend asked after a decent interval.

"I have no secrets from any of you."

"Okay," Townsend said.

Su Han told the unfolding story from the moment the missile from Guang Lor went out of control and crashed, up to an including his own final hours in his Shanghai apartment. He concluded with the details of his leave-taking from China.

A subdued silence descended over the table as the events and their implications were absorbed. The first to break the silence was the younger man called Hawkins.

"Mr. Han, was there any indication who these Americans might be?"

"What the hell kind of a question is that?" Chomski asked.

Townsend leaned forward, raising a hand to calm Chomski.

"What's your thinking, Hawkins?"

"Were they regular military? A mercenary team? A covert incursion by a group from the intelligence community?"

"As in CIA?" Townsend queried.

Hawkins glanced at him. "Just a thought, boss," he said. "It's clear as day the Agency isn't going to sit on its butt after what happened to those three agents. Maybe they've been working on the quiet and uncovered a connection to your dealing here with Mr. Han. Followed it through and came up with a full hand. All I'm saying is they might be sniffing around, just trying to tie up loose ends. Pays to be cautious."

"Your young man is very perceptive," Han said. "To answer your question directly, I had no contact with these people, but from what I managed to learn via reports they were professional and extremely adaptable. They outwitted Major Kang at every turn, taking on whatever he put in their way. Despite everything, I have to admire their resourcefulness and their dedication when it came to retrieving lost comrades."

"Maybe we should recommend them for a fuckin' medal," Chomski said bitterly.

Han glanced across the table. "Mr. Chomski, they may be the enemy, but it is not a sign of weakness to acknowledge their qualities. Understanding your adversary is an important lesson in the battle to overcome him."

"Fortune cookie philosophy?"

"No, Mr. Chomski, plain common sense. The art of war is far more than simply pulling a trigger."

Chomski fell silent, knowing he was on a loser. He flopped back in his seat, but managed to cast a dark scowl in Hawkins's direction.

"T.J., you might have something there," Townsend said. "Take one of the cars and run into Port Cristobal. Have a quiet look around. See if there are any fresh faces in town. Hell, you'll know what to look for. You're new to the team so you can look around without being picked out. We've all been tagged one way or another by the Agency so they'll know our faces."

"Whatever you want, boss. If you're happy for me to go."

"Joseph, give him some cash. Our locals are happy to talk for a few dollar bills. You might pick up something. Worth a try."

Hawkins stood, taking his time. Riotta had left the table, returning a short time later to hand Hawkins a thick roll of money.

"You want receipts, Mr. Riotta?"

Townsend laughed. "I like this guy. He's funny."

"Yeah. He cracks me up," Chomski said.

"And he knows big words, too." Brandt grunted.

"Education is a wonderful thing," Hawkins said.

He turned to Townsend. "Is there a number I can call here, boss? In case I need to contact you fast?"

Regan scribbled a number on a card he took from his pocket. "Here you go, bubba."

Hawkins pocketed the cash and the card, turning to leave.

"Hey," Chomski called, "watch your back. It's a bad world out there."

Hawkins smiled at the man as he passed Chomski's chair.

"Knowing you care, Ralphie, just makes me warm all over."

"You keep that in mind."

When Hawkins had gone, Chomski stood and gestured to Brandt.

"Just something I need to talk over with you, Rik."

He glanced at Townsend. "Be back shortly."

Townsend barely acknowledged him. He was deep in conversation with Su Han.

CHAPTER ELEVEN

Pete Tilman had been working a day shift. He was close to quitting when the TV monitor in the main office picked up a newsflash from CNN. Although official denial followed the report, the details that came over the broadcast told about the arrest of a RossJacklin employee named Raymond Dupont. Dupont had been apprehended trying to leave the Dayton research building with a classified piece of electronic software. When challenged, Dupont had made an abortive attempt at fleeing the scene but had been caught by company security. Although the incident had supposedly been blacked out by the authorities, someone had managed to leak details to CNN and they had included the report in their midafternoon program.

"Same company who lost that other stuff," Tilman heard someone say.

"That guy killed in Dayton worked for RossJacklin. Mark Kibble."

"That's right. Weird stuff."

Back in his office Tilman slid into his seat behind

his desk and stared at his blank monitor screen, trying to make some sense of what was happening.

The graph curve was dropping with rapid speed. Too much too quickly. And none of it encouraging. One minute life was running smooth, turn around and it was raining crap. Bad enough Kibble had started to run scared and had to be taken out. Now the reports Townsend had been getting from China were just as depressing. The Guang Lor business was reaching out to swallow them all in Tilman's mind. The missing circuit board—one piece of technology—might come back to haunt them all. If its theft was traced back to Shadow, then it might also sting Tilman himself. He'd heard of guilt by association. He couldn't argue the semantics on that. He *was* guilty and there *was* association. Sooner or later someone would fit all the tiny pieces together and they would spell, among other things, the name of Pete Tilman.

From his association with Shadow it wouldn't be a gigantic leap to connect him to the slaying of three CIA agents. And the day that happened he could kiss goodbye to his Agency pension.

His cell phone rang. Tilman picked it up and recognized the soft drawl in the voice immediately.

"Don't talk. Listen. I need to speak to you. Pay phone. You got my number. Do it now."

The phone went dead. Tilman stood and pulled on his jacket. He left the office and made his way downstairs and out of the building. He walked along the sidewalk until he spotted a pay phone. He used one of the prepaid phone cards the Agency supplied to access the line, tapped in the number and waited until the connection was made.

"Jack?"

"Hey, bubba, listen up and don't interrupt."

"So?"

"Don't make the trip down here. Something is brewing and it isn't smelling too good. We might have been compromised. Caught with the goods and identified as being in the loop. You know we got Su Han here? He had to skip the old country 'cause his deal with Shadow has been busted right down the middle. Han got the hell out before his lords and masters decided to give him a Beijing haircut. You know, from the neck up? It wouldn't be wise you coming down here."

"In other words, I'm fucked, Jack."

"Hey, *we* be fucked. Seems Su Han's people let the circuit board we sold him get snatched by some group called Pro-Democracy who passed it to a covert American force. This whole thing runs like a season of *24*. Bottom line is, the dots are being joined up. You understand? Do not come down here. You want my advice? Take your money and be gone."

"What about you?"

"Hey, bubba, I been around too long to get my balls caught in a bear trap. Don't worry about me."

Tilman stared around him for a moment. "Thanks for the warning, Jack."

"What're friends for? We'll talk again. Hell, we walked out of El Salvador, bubba. It's all a picnic in the park after that. Don't you forget it."

The phone clicked and Regan was gone.

MINUTES LATER, back in his office, Tilman did the hardest thinking in his life. Through the glass partition he watched the routine of the field office, the coming and going of his colleagues. Those same colleagues would soon change their view of him if details of his attachment to Shadow were exposed. More so if it came out he had been responsible for killing three of their buddies. He opened desk drawers and slid out items he wanted to take with him. There were also a number of floppy disks he wasn't about to leave behind. The items went into his attaché case. Tilman added his service weapon and extra magazines. He carried out these maneuvers calmly, even though he was eager to leave the department as quickly as possible. Closing his case, Tilman slipped into his jacket, shut down his computer and stood.

Beyond the partition no one was taking any notice of him.

He walked out of the office and through the department, nodding to people on his way. No rush, just an agent on his way to a meeting maybe, heading for a rendezvous. On assignment.

Next the basement garage, where he picked up his car and drove to the exit. He had a brief word with the guard in the booth, watched the barrier raise, drove up the ramp and swung around the building to pick up the main drag that would take him to his apartment.

It was a pleasant enough Washington day, warm, a slight breeze drifting in through the open window of his car door. Tilman fished out the cell phone in his jacket pocket and hit the speed-dial number he wanted. Listened to it hum and click, then connect and start to ring.

The sound of her voice, as always, brushed away the tension.

"Hi," he said.

"Pete? Is something wrong?"

"Does it sound like there is?"

"Yes."

"Toni, I need to get away for a while," Tilman said.

"Away? As in skip town? Walk out?"

"As in vanish."

"We need to talk. Where are you?"

"Driving home." He told her.

"I'll meet you there." A slight pause. "Don't make hasty choices."

HER NAME WAS Toni Hendrick. She was twenty-eight years old, a striking beauty that gave her an advantage when it came to her dedication to her profession. Hendrick was tall, with hazel eyes, natural thick chestnut hair cut in a short style. A lithe, toned body that carried greater strength and agility than she allowed to show. She also possessed a keen, inquisitive mind that seldom remained idle.

Now, as she replaced the receiver, following her brief but illuminating talk with Tilman, she was already defining her upcoming actions.

Reaching across the desk, she opened a drawer and removed a disposable cell phone. She tapped out a number and as soon as it was answered she spoke.

"He's just been on the line. What we discussed yesterday seems to have reached him."

Hendrick reported what Tilman had said. The man on the other end of the connection sighed.

"A nuisance but these things happen. My sources have just updated me. It does appear that Su Han has fled China because his superiors need to hold him accountable for what happened at Guang Lor. A great shame. The Shadow operation was progressing nicely. Our friend Townsend had negotiated some lucrative deals with the Chinese."

"I doubt they'll give up. Once the Han matter is settled, they'll be on the lookout for another supplier surely?"

"I have no doubt. But it's not going to be as easy second time around. The President has already ordered tighter security at government contractors. Look at RossJacklin. They have intercepted the man trying to pick up where Mark Kibble left off."

"So what do we do about Tilman?"

"Need you ask, my dear? Tilman was useful. His Agency involvement had advantages but they could also work against us, so he is a luxury we can no longer afford. The moment the web starts to unravel, certain players become dispensable. Tilman has already shown signs of panic by telling you he wants to get away. Does he still believe you are the love of his life?"

"Of course." It was said without any kind of exaggeration. "He hangs on every word I utter."

"Then use that. Get him out of Washington. Use the team. We need damage control. See to it. Just ensure it can't be traced back to us. And once he has been dealt with, make sure he didn't have any incriminating data with him. I'll arrange to have his apartment searched."

"Understood."

Hendricks shut down the cell phone and slipped it into her pocket. She crossed the apartment to her bedroom where she picked up two packed travel bags. She took them with her and left the apartment, taking the stairs to the basement garage where she then walked out by the side exit, went to the street and hailed a cab.

"Union Station first," she said.

TILMAN STARED AT the monitor of his laptop. He had tried to log in to his offshore account, but the bank kept rejecting his password. He tried his local bank and got the same rejection. He didn't understand what was going on until he called the bank and asked them to check his account status. The answer came back that he had changed his password and his ATM card number the day before. He spent long minutes arguing with the bank that he hadn't changed his details. The bank was adamant he had changed his details, and he could sort it out if he called in personally. In the end he slammed down the phone, angry and starting to become a little concerned. Something was going on beyond his control, and Tilman found the whole process alarming. What he didn't like was not knowing who was behind the problems.

The Agency?

Or the people who had engineered the operations in China?

And if they were, how had they gotten control of his financial details?

The more he thought about it, he realized he was doing the wise thing by getting out.

Tilman opened the attaché case, checking what he had brought from the office. He crossed the room, opened the wall safe concealed behind a small painting and took out items he would be able to use in the future: a stack of computer disks, a leather-bound day planner. He placed them in the attaché case.

He heard the apartment door chime and crossed the room.

"Who is it?"

"Christ, Pete, it's me. Toni. Let me in."

He opened the door and she was standing there with a couple of travel bags. She pushed by him, dropping the bags and turning to face him as he closed the door. And locked it. Then tried the handle.

She put her arms around him, pressing herself to him, kissing him. Her touch was, as usual, able to ease away some of his tension.

"Hey, relax, honey," she said. "My God, you look so tense."

"That about sums it up," he said, then proceeded to tell her about his bank accounts. "I can't even get my hands on a penny of my own money."

"What about your Agency account? You once said you had, what was it—seed money to finance operations."

"Beautiful *and* smart."

He returned to his laptop and accessed the account. This time there was no problem. The account still had a high balance. Tilman took out his wallet and checked he still had the ATM card for that account. He switched off the laptop and placed it in the attaché case, closing the lid.

"See, one problem solved," Hendrick said.

"I already packed my bags," he said. "We can leave anytime."

"So let's do it," she said.

"When we spoke before you said don't be too hasty. Now you bring your luggage with you and say let's go. What changed your mind?"

Hendrick smiled.

"A woman's choice. And I got to thinking maybe you had it right all along. You need time to work things out away from this town. We need to find you somewhere quiet and out of the way."

"Where?"

She pulled a slim envelope from her jacket and waved it under his nose.

"Two tickets for the Capitol Limited. Leaves Union Station at 5:30. That gives us plenty of time. Washington to Chicago, then on to Denver. Hire a car in Denver and drive on through to Aspen. We can find ourselves a cabin up in the mountains and you can figure things out. Could you stand being cooped up in cabin for a couple of weeks? Just the two of us."

"I can think of worse things."

HERMANN SCHWARZ WATCHED as Tilman and the young woman left his apartment building and climbed into the cab that had just pulled up. They were both carrying travel bags, and Tilman had an attaché case with him. He started the Blazer's engine and pulled into the line of traffic, keeping a couple of vehicles between himself and the cab.

As he drove, Gadgets tapped in a speed-dial number and heard Barbara Price on the other end.

"What's up, Sherlock?"

"Now everyone's a comic."

"I take it your buddy Tilman is on the move?"

"Him and his ladyfriend. Very pretty young ladyfriend. They just picked up a cab, heading across town. They both have travel bags with them."

"He's found out his accounts are blocked. Aaron registered him trying to log in a while ago."

"Don't ever let the Bear find my bank account."

"Any idea where Tilman is heading? The airport?"

"Wrong direction." Schwarz checked his location. "I think they're making for Union Station. It's ahead of us."

"What're you going to do?"

"Stay with them for the moment. See where they're heading."

"Watch your back, Gadgets. The way things are going, Shadow and its associates are under pressure. Sounds like Tilman is starting to run scared and frightened people do weird things."

"If he gets scared enough he might decide to talk."

THEY HAD PLENTY OF TIME before their train. Hendrick dawdled at a newsstand, buying papers and magazines. There was no such ease for Tilman. He wasn't about to relax fully until they were on board and the train was rolling. He did manage to locate an ATM machine and withdraw cash from the Agency seed account. He took three thousand dollars, aware that the account might be canceled if he finally became compromised. Until then he could keep withdrawing. The Agency had no limit on how much could be withdrawn at any time until the limit was reached. Tilman pocketed the cash and put away his card.

He had spent his life in these kinds of situations, where life could tilt either way and he might end up victorious, or at worst dead. He had worked missions in Central America, in jungles and urban dead zones. Killing had been his stock-in-trade for a number of years, so why was he feeling the way he did? He couldn't pin it down. Was his time ebbing away? His long-buried conscience finally betraying him? There didn't seem to be any logic to the mood swings he was experiencing. He turned and watched Toni as she deliberated over magazines and she glanced his way, her face brightening when she caught his eye. Perhaps she was the reason. His relationship with her, fraught at the outset because she had targeted him deliberately, pulling him into the dangerous game of treachery that had finally brought him to this point. But the relationship that had blossomed on the unsure foundations of their beginnings, had grown in strength, sucking them both in deep. As far as Tilman was concerned, she was all that mattered now. He didn't give a damn about the others. If they wanted to carry on with their game, let them. He was moving on, moving out, and this time there was no going back.

SCHWARZ COULDN'T PUT his finger on the problem, but he was certain something wasn't right. Or perhaps he was becoming too much of a cynic, trusting no one and nothing. Stony Man operated in a world of deceit and mistrust. With every mission they embarked on, the combat teams faced every facet of human betrayal. It programmed them to the point they could almost smell it. And if not they could certainly sense it.

Which was exactly what Schwarz was experiencing at the moment.

Tilman he knew. The background data on the man had him as an experienced and battle-hardened agent. His theater of operations had taken him down some dark paths, leaving him with a back history of covert missions, wetwork and the ability to turn his apparent loyalties at the flip of a coin. Tilman was no beginner. He knew his game, played it for all he was worth, and from his psych profiles the man appeared to lack any kind of remorse for the deeds he had done on behalf of his country—or himself. But circumstances could change an individual's outlook, and perhaps that had happened in Tilman's case.

The woman was something different. Attractive. Desirable. No argument there. She appeared to be paying devoted attention to Tilman. From where Schwarz was standing, close enough to observe, her manner was less that genuine. The moment Tilman turned away from her, the smile vanished and she watched him with a detached, clinical expression that reminded Schwarz of a praying mantis sizing up its next meal. And wasn't it that insect that devoured its partner after mating? There was that feeling about her that cautioned Schwarz against getting too close to her.

THEY BOARDED THE TRAIN and made their way along the corridor until they reached their booked compartment. Tilman pushed open the door and let the woman pass him. He entered and the door closed behind them. Schwarz, following at a discreet distance, made a note of the number and kept the door in sight until the train had rolled out of Union Station.

Schwarz located the conductor and showed his Justice Department badge, explaining he was on board following a suspect. He gave the man the telephone number that would connect him to Stony Man Farm, where his cover story would be verified. Then he made his way to the lounge car and took a seat in a quiet section. He took out his satellite phone and called Stony Man. He spoke to Carmen Delahunt.

"I need to know who the woman is with Tilman. They're in compartment 4B on the Capitol Limited. It's making the run from Washington to Chicago. Left Union Station at 5:30. See if you can get me anything. If you do ID her, run the name through the system."

"Why the woman, Gadgets?"

"There's something about her. To be honest, Carmen, she gives me a bad feeling just watching her."

"I'll call you back soon as."

THE CALL CAME FASTER than Schwarz had anticipated. He opened his phone and listened as Delahunt gave him the rundown on Tilman's female companion.

"Looks like she bought the tickets. They're booked right through to Denver. Change at Chicago for the California Zephyr. They get in at 8:25 with a four-and-half-hour stopover. Zephyr leaves at 1:50. The woman's name is Toni Hendrick. We ran a computer check on her. And came up with some odd connections we're still following though. Twenty-nine years old. Five-nine. According to her profile she works for a PR company based in Washington. Seems to have a lot of contacts within political-industrial figures. Can't get much on her origins. I'll call you back if we find anything else."

"That's fine."

"Hey, Gadgets, you like riding trains? Hope so because you're in for a long haul."

"I really needed to hear that."

Cuyahoga County Airport, Cleveland

A CAR WAITED TO MEET the two men when they disembarked from the Learjet. A black Crown Victoria LX, with tinted windows, sat on the tarmac, a pale trickle of vapor seeping from the exhaust.

Conklin and Freeland deplaned and made their way to the car, opened one of the rear doors and climbed in. The moment they were settled, the Crown Victoria eased away from the landing area and cruised unhurriedly toward the exit, then picked up the route that would deliver them east ten miles to the rail station on the Cleveland Memorial Shoreway. They were in plenty of time to meet the Capitol Limited outward bound from Washington.

Their itinerary was fixed and precise. They would leave the train at South Bend after carrying out their mission. A car would be waiting to take them to South Bend's Regional Airport Corporate Wing, off Lathrop Street where the Lear would be waiting. It would return them to Washington, and by that time Pete Tilman would no longer be any kind of threat to their employer.

It was all worked out. Nothing could go wrong. Conklin and Freeland were pros. They left nothing to chance. All the bases were covered

Except for one thing.

They had no idea that Tilman and Hendrick had been followed from his apartment, or that the man who had trailed them was also on the train.

SCHWARZ FELT THE TRAIN slowing as it approached Cleveland. He glanced out the window at the rain slanting from the dark sky. Pushing to his feet, the Able Team commando stretched, easing the kinks from his muscles. He turned and retraced his steps to the coach where Tilman's compartment was located. He stood at the end of the coach, watching the door to 4B. He wasn't sure why, maybe just a feeling. Instinct? His suspicious nature?

As the train came to a stop, Schwarz peered out the window. The platform was empty except for two men who were dressed in dark suits. One of them carried a slim attaché case, and they looked out of place on the deserted platform. He didn't know why he felt that. Maybe it was the assured manner the two men handled themselves. They didn't seem like a pair of weary businessmen picking up a ride. This pair looked too alert. Too confident.

Out of the corner of his eye, Schwarz sensed movement. It was Toni Hendrick, leaving the compartment and making her way to the far end of the coach. He watched her vanish through the door. Turning back, he looked at the two men, saw them acknowledge someone and step toward the train. Schwarz eased back into the shadows and waited.

He saw Hendricks appear, followed by the two men. They moved along the coach to 4B. Hendricks opened the door and the three went in.

"YOU GET THE COFFEE…"

Pete Tilman glanced up as Hendrick stepped inside the compartment and the question faded when he saw the two men accompanying her. The last man in closed and secured the door, standing with his back to it.

"No time for coffee," Conklin said. "It's the end of the ride for you, Tilman."

Tilman looked across at Hendrick. The young woman had moved aside, leaving Conklin to dominate the scene. Her hard gaze held Tilman's, and there was not a trace of emotion in her eyes.

"Toni?"

"Don't talk to her," Conklin said. "Right now I'm the most important person in your life. Nobody else matters."

Tilman felt a powerful surge of mixed emotions rise within him—anger, betrayal, fear.

And a growing sense of loss, because he knew without a shadow of a doubt that he was dead.

"Bastards…"

He reached for the pistol holstered on his hip, pushing up off the seat as he did.

Conklin reacted swiftly. His right fist, clenched tight, swung around and delivered a full-on punch that slammed against Tilman's jaw. The blow was expertly judged. It spun Tilman's head around, blood spraying from mashed lips, and there was the distinct crack of bone. The agent fell backward, hitting the seat, senses out of kilter. His gun hand missed the mark and he was too dazed to try again. He felt Conklin snatch the gun away and step back, an amused smile on his lips.

"You wanted this?" he said almost conversationally, then lashed out with the gun and hit Tilman across the side of his skull. "How's that?"

Tilman sprawled awkwardly over the seat. The compartment had gone out of focus. His head hurt, pain pounding within in his skull. He didn't dare move his jaw because the first punch had done something to it. It felt locked.

"He won't give us any more trouble," Conklin said.

"Not after what you did to his jaw," Freeland said.

"When are you planning to leave the train?" Hendricks queried.

"Tired of our company already?" Conklin asked.

"After all the times we've worked together, Conklin?" she asked. "You should know better than that."

"Should I leave the room?" Freeland asked.

Hendrick smiled. "I'll try to control myself."

"I'll leave at South Bend with our buddy here," Conklin said. "Freeland stays behind with you all the way to Denver as Tilman. Once you're there, arrangements will be in place to let you move on. By then Mr. Tilman will be the dearly departed."

The train jerked as it began to pull out of Cleveland.

Hendrick sat across from Tilman, observing him with a detached air. It was as if she had never seen him before that moment, and watching her through hazed eyes Tilman realized he didn't know *her* at all.

It had been a setup from day one. A simple means of keeping her eye on him for her employer. The feigned love she had shown him, the tender moments and even the sex, had all been phony, planned to keep him under observation. Pete Tilman, the man who had spent so many years fooling others, had been hoodwinked by a pretty face and a prettier body. The experienced CIA agent with a background in double-dealing and trickery had been put through the wringer and taken for a damned fool. He had to give her credit. She had been good.

He listened to their discussion, understanding what they were going to do—take him off the train as one of them, leaving behind a decoy who would ride all the way to Denver, by which time he would have vanished for good. Smart. Well organized. A neat plan to cover their tracks and dispose of someone who had become a risk.

He waited awhile, allowing himself a chance to regain at least some strength. If he was going to die, he wasn't going to just sit back and let it happen without a fight.

He hadn't been expecting the sway of the coach as

the train hit a curve, but it made the opening he needed. And he took it...

Tilman gathered himself, using his pain as the catalyst that powered him off the seat. He slammed into Conklin, catching the man off guard enough to catapult him across the compartment. They crashed against the far wall, Conklin grunting as the breath was driven from his lungs. Tilman slammed his right knee up into his adversary's testicles, dragging a roar of pain from the man. Jamming his right forearm under Conklin's chin Tilman shoved hard, squeezing tight against the man's windpipe. He applied all the pressure he could and felt something crunch with a soft sound. Conklin coughed harshly. Hands clamped down across Tilman's shoulders, fingers digging in deep, and he felt himself being dragged away from Conklin. It was Freeman. He hauled at the CIA man, pulling him off Conklin. As the agent let go, he dug his heels into the carpet and pushed hard. The pair backpedaled...

SCHWARZ HAD BEEN at the compartment door when he heard Conklin's pained yell. The scuffle that followed told the Able Team warrior that something was going down on the other side of the door, and the sounds were far from friendly. He pulled his Beretta, thumbing off the safety, and decided that discretion was not the best policy right now. He raised his right foot and drove it at the door just beneath the handle.

The door swung open, slamming against Freeman as he and Tilman stumbled back.

Schwarz ducked low as he went through, his Beretta tracking ahead as he took in the scene.

The man he assumed to be Conklin struggled for breath, reaching for his pistol.

Tilman was in a half clinch with Freeman, pushing at the man's right arm to divert the pistol his adversary was trying to bring on line.

The woman, Hendrick, turned from a bag lying on one of the seats, the dull gleam of a pistol in her hands. She kept up the movement, swung the pistol in Tilman's direction and pulled the trigger. The sound of the shot was loud in the confines of the compartment. The slug went wide, ripping through the wall.

Tilman smashed his elbow back into Freeman's face as the man slid sideways around the CIA man's body. Freeman grunted, blood spurting from his crushed nose, and Tilman snatched the pistol from his fingers, twisted and jammed the muzzle into his opponent's body. He triggered three fast shots. As he began to turn, Hendrick fired again. This time she hit Tilman in the left shoulder.

Schwarz saw Conklin raise his pistol, the muzzle zeroing in on Tilman.

The CIA agent came face-to-face with Hendrick and began to pull the trigger of Freeman's pistol, the heavy weapon jacking out rapid shots. Two hit the woman, slamming her back against the compartment's window, the rest of the volley plowing into wall and glass. The window blew out, and rain swept into the compartment. The woman went down with a shocked expression on her face.

Conklin hit Tilman with point-blank shots that cored into his chest.

From his kneeling position on the floor, Schwarz angled his Beretta up and put half a clip into Conklin, pinning him to the compartment wall for long seconds before he dropped.

The rattle of the train came in through the broken window. As Schwarz pushed to his feet, his Beretta tracking the compartment, he felt the cold slap of the rain blowing inside. He could hear distant shouts as passengers reacted to the shooting. He took a slow look at the bodies on the compartment floor. There seemed to be a great deal of blood.

"Jesus…"

Schwarz glanced at the sound of the voice.

The uniformed conductor was standing at the compartment door, his face pale, eyes wide with shock.

Reaching inside his jacket, Schwarz pulled out his Justice Department badge and showed it to the man. He had introduced himself previously, but the man seemed paralyzed and needed to be prodded into action.

"Special Agent Rinelli," he said harshly. "Snap out of it. You'd better call ahead to the next stop. We may need medical aid. At least the medical examiner."

"Yes, sir, Agent Rinelli. What happened—"

"Just call ahead. Keep everyone away and close the door."

The conductor took one look at the pistol in Schwarz's hand and fell silent. He backed out, pulling the door shut.

Schwarz moved around the compartment checking the bodies. The only one showing signs of life was Pete Tilman. He had been hit hard. He stared up at Schwarz.

"I'm not even going to ask who the fuck you are," he said. He had to talk slowly because of his damaged jaw.

"I'm not with them," Schwarz told him.

Tilman shook his head. "They all screwed me." He raised a hand and pointed to a slim attaché case lying on the seat. "You want the prize? Take that. Bring the mothers down."

That was all he said before he died.

Schwarz took out his cell phone and called Stony Man.

"Hey, Barb, is the boss home?"

She put Brognola on the line.

"Yeah?"

"Did somebody once say rail travel was the safest and most peaceful way to travel?"

"I think I've heard something like that, why?"

"Don't you believe a word of it."

CHAPTER TWELVE

"Just do it, Rik."

Brandt recognized the hard shine in Chomski's eyes and knew this was no time to argue.

"Okay. I'm gone."

"Hawkins will take the main road. You go the back way into town. You can be there well ahead of him."

"What am I supposed to be looking for?"

"Guys in blue, riding horses and calling themselves the fucking U.S. cavalry. Jesus, Rik, think."

"If he does link up with anyone?"

"Just observe. Make notes but don't spoil his surprise."

Brandt walked away, leaving the bright lights of the house, and climbed into one of the parked SUVs. He moved off, and Chomski watched the taillights disappear into the gloom.

"From that touching little scene I take it you don't entirely trust our Mr. Hawkins?"

Chomski didn't need to look around to know it was Riotta who had spoken.

"I would expect someone like you to understand the concept of insurance, Joseph."

Riotta stood beside him, dragging on a long sweet-smelling cigar.

"I understand completely."

"I could be wrong. If I am, no harm done. But I'd rather have it pinned to the wall than get caught napping. This Hawkins came on the scene pretty close to when things started to get frayed around the edges. Now, that might have slipped by Oliver, but I'm not such a trusting soul. Okay, he hasn't done anything I can put my finger on, and the guy did good work on that turnaround we pulled on Calvera. But he gets to me. He's too sharp to be the loser he makes out. There's more there than just a smart mouth. He's got it up top, and that worries me."

"Fine. The way things have been happening, you might be right. Do what you have to but keep it between us for now. Oliver has enough to deal with."

"Where is he?"

"Closeted very privately with our Chinese compatriot."

"Honest opinion, Joseph. What's going on?"

"I believe Han is finished back home. If he goes back he'll end up in prison, or he'll find himself very dead one morning. I have an idea he's about to make a deal with Oliver."

"What kind of a deal?"

"Consider his background, Ralph. Mr. Han has been responsible for working deals on behalf of the Chinese government. Seeking suppliers and arranging the purchase of items. In the course of that dealing he will have built up a long list of contacts. He'll be in the know concerning people who want to buy and sell. And what is the nature of *our* business?"

Chomski smiled. "Son of a bitch," he said softly. "Goodbye Chairman Mao, hello Uncle Sam."

HAN PLACED THE PAIR of flash drives on the table that stood between the two recliners. He picked up the tall flute of chilled white wine and took a sip.

"As a gesture of my intentions, I would like to offer you the chance to examine some of the files I have stored there," he said.

"Downloaded before you said farewell to Mother China?"

"Exactly. I realized there was little chance Beijing would offer me an early pension plan, so I awarded myself a bonus."

"Su, you do realize that because of what happened at Guang Lor, the U.S. government may find a link between us both? If they do, we'll have all manner of aggravation. People are going to be very upset. Vengeful. Countries do tend to suffer from righteous anger when their secrets are stolen and passed to hostile administrations."

"You were a soldier, Oliver. I also served in the military before I moved into government work, and then immersed myself in industrial espionage and deceitful practices. I have been aware of risk and personal danger for many years, and never once did that prevent me from carrying on. Why should it now? What am I supposed to do? Take my money and scurry off into some quiet corner of the world and raise rare orchids? No, my friend, I think not. The boredom would destroy my soul. I would rather take my chances with someone like you. If we combine our talents and our knowledge, I am sure we could create a thriving enterprise."

Townsend raised his glass. "I'll take a look at those files, Su. I'm sure I'll like what I see." He thought of something else and leaned over to pick something up from beside his recliner, handing Han the heavy package. "You wanted this."

Inside was a SIG-Sauer P-226 pistol and a couple of additional magazines. Han examined the weapon, smiling in gratitude.

"Thank you, my friend. I assure you I feel safe in your company but I am also aware that certain factions in Beijing, once they discover I have gone, will not feel so well inclined toward me."

"Su, I know exactly what you mean."

Port Cristobal

HAWKINS PARKED OUTSIDE one of the many bars in Port Cristobal. From his previous visit he remembered the place as having a frontier town atmosphere. Port Cristobal had once been a Spanish settlement, and many of its buildings reflected the influence of the occupation. In contrast there were an equal number of timber structures merging with the white-painted stone buildings. Neon signs battered the humid night air, throwing garish light across the streets.

It was close to eight o'clock, and Port Cristobal was warming up. There was a burgeoning oil industry in Santa Lorca, and the town welcomed the income the field crews brought in. A sprinkling of Americans was in evidence from the U.S. oil companies. Hawkins sat behind the wheel of the SUV studying the crowds. He was going to have to fake this visit and report back to Townsend he hadn't spotted any suspicious characters. A wry smile edged his lips as he scanned the crowd. In truth there were any number of suspicious faces out there. Not that it indicated the presence of any threat.

Hawkins climbed out of the vehicle, locked it and made his way through the pedestrians filling the street. He chose the first substantial bar he found and made his way inside. He elbowed his way to the bar and ordered himself a beer. When it came he found it was a familiar American brand, well chilled. He leaned against the bar and surveyed the customers. He spent a slow ten minutes drinking the beer, then wandered back outside and made a steady tour of the town.

He was solicited a couple of times, had an offer of *genuine* Rolex watches, shares in an oil well, and after a long half hour found himself close to Port Cristobal's dockside.

The waterfront was quieter. The last time Hawkins had been here was during the Phoenix Force mission that had first brought them into contact with Jack Regan. The confrontation had ended in a bloody firefight, a fiery explosion and a frantic flight from the country.

He paused in shrouding gloom, staring out across the water, and decided that when he returned to the main street, he would use the chance to call Stony Man to give them the lowdown on the situation.

Hawkins turned and came face-to-face with the last person he had expected to see in Santa Lorca.

RIK BRANDT HAD PICKED UP Hawkins with minutes of his arrival in Port Cristobal. Brandt had been in town for a quarter hour before the SUV showed. Hawkins parked outside a bar and sat for a while studying the area before climbing out and entering one of the bars.

When Hawkins left the bar, wandering the streets for a time before going in the direction of the docks, Brandt fell in behind him. He stayed out of sight, but close enough to observe Hawkins.

And then Brandt got the break he'd been hoping for as a figure moved out from an ally to confront Hawkins. The two men stood talking. It was clear they knew each other and when the newcomer stepped into the light from a window Brandt realized he knew the man's face.

The last time he had seen it had been inside the gun shop at Landry Flats when Hawkins had gone to collect Townsend's shotgun.

"Ralph, you are going to love this," Brandt muttered as he pulled his cell phone from his pocket and made the call.

RALPH CHOMSKI PUT his phone away and turned to find Townsend. The man had completed his talk with Su Han, and the pair was back with the others, seated in the living room. Chomski recalled what Riotta had said about leaving Townsend out of the loop. That was canceled now. He made his way across the room, catching Townsend's eye and jerking his head. Townsend, relaxed and enjoying the company, frowned, then reluctantly stood and joined Chomski.

"What's got you smiling, Ralph?"

"You know how it is when it all comes together."

"Don't do enigmatic," Townsend said. "You got a fur ball, spit it out."

"Your current buddy, T.J., is screwing us, Oliver. I just had the call from Rik."

Townsend stepped back mentally, taking a moment to absorb what Chomski had announced.

"You sent Brandt after him? Without telling me?"

"Because if I'd suggested it, you would have had a hissy fit, Oliver. So I did it behind your back and we hit pay dirt. Bawl me out later, but listen to what I have to say first."

A muscle in Townsend's cheek tensed, bunching beneath the skin. He took a long swallow from the glass in his hand, then stared into Chomski's eyes.

"This had better be good."

"Hawkins went to town. Didn't do anything except go in a bar and wander around. Then he went to the docks and met this guy. Rik says it's plain they know each other, and more important, Rik recognized the guy. Last time he saw him was in Landry Flats in the gun shop the day Hawkins picked up your shotgun."

"Brandt's sure?"

"Rik isn't the sharpest but he doesn't make mistakes like this. He says the guy knows Hawkins. They were talking like best buds."

Townsend considered the facts. He didn't say anything, but when he turned to look at Chomski his face was set. Without warning he hurled his tumbler against the wall and it shattered into glittering fragments.

Every head in the room turned at the sound.

"Hey, bubba, something wrong?" Regan asked.

"Nothing we can't put right," Townsend said. "Nothing at all."

"How did you track me here?" Hawkins asked.

"We hit Townsend's ranch after you left," Blancanales said. "Had it out with his crew and found out what we needed to know. Even met your old buddy Lerner."

"Vic? He okay?"

"By now he'll be answering questions, or staring at the walls of his cell."

Hawkins shrugged. "He made his choices."

They were in the hotel room Lyons and Blancanales had taken and were using as their base.

"We were caught off guard when you left in that chopper," Lyons said.

"Kind of had me worried, too," Hawkins admitted. "I had no idea at the time what it was all about."

"You do now?"

"We're at Jack Regan's place a few miles out of town. Big gathering. Townsend and his people. And now this Chinese guy, Su Han, shows up, the one who bought all the stolen technology from Shadow. It appears Han was forced to jump ship. His people in Beijing need a patsy for the mess at Guang Lor and Han's the last in line. I guess he didn't want to take the fall so, he got the hell out before the ax man came to call. The way I figure it, he's here to join forces with Townsend and combine their talents."

"So we have all the eggs in one big basket," Blancanales said.

"Not exactly," Hawkins replied. "They're waiting for a couple more. Another Chinese called Sammo Chen Low. He was Han's financial adviser. Seems he got the word and legged it, too."

"Who else?" Lyons asked.

"Pete Tilman, the CIA guy."

"Gadgets is watching him," Lyons explained. "If

the word's out, he might not chance coming all the way down here."

Hawkins perched on the edge of one of the beds and ran his hands through his hair.

"Man, I'd rather be in the middle of a damn firefight than this covert stuff."

"You had enough?" Blancanales asked.

Hawkins grinned. "No, I'm fine."

He glanced at Lyons. "What's the plan?"

"Right now you need to get back there and monitor the setup. Once we get them all together, we can move in."

"And?"

Lyons had his Colt Python in his hand, thumbing loads into the chambers. "We'll handle that when it happens."

"That's what I'm afraid of," Blancanales said.

"You do have the U.S. Fleet anchored offshore to pick us up when the war starts?"

Lyons gave a wolf's grin. "How do you think we got down here so fast?"

"He kidding?" Hawkins asked

"We hitched a ride on a couple of Navy jets. They winged it across the Gulf and down here. Landed us on a Navy carrier in the area. They choppered us inland and dropped us on a strip of desert a few miles along the coast."

"T.J.," Lyons said, "take this."

Hawkins accepted a small black disk that was no larger than a quarter.

"When you want the cavalry to come in just squeeze it hard. That'll activate the signal sender. We'll tail you back to the house and wait outside. If we pick up that signal, we'll be all over the place before you take your finger off the button."

"I have your word on that," Hawkins asked lightly.

"Would I lie to a friend of Mad Dog McCarter?"

Hawkins grinned. "Not a wise thing to even think about."

JACK REGAN FINISHED his call and replaced the receiver on the cradle. He turned and crossed the room, peering out across the ground fronting the hacienda. Bright curves of light from the numerous security lights spread across the lawns and as far as the thick foliage that surrounded the property.

Regan wasn't one to panic, but he did veer on the side of caution. It had served him well over the years, during his early days and his dealings with the CIA in Central America. Those had been heady, dangerous days but they were full of good memories. Regan's association with the Agency had been fruitful. Not only had he made good money he had also made solid contacts that had, for the most part, stayed with him. He was still supplying clients who had started with him, and many of them were now powerful men in their own right, having come in from obscurity as rebels, to positions of authority. And in the volatile climate of Central America there was still a need for weapons. Jack Regan, with his global contacts, was able to supply most anything.

His dealings with Shadow and Townsend had brought Regan bigger paychecks, had expanded his customer base across the Pacific and had brought him closer to China, North Korea and a number of struggling groups eager to pay good money for top-class weapons. That was one of the reasons for Regan's success. He never sold his customers inferior goods. It wasn't good practice. Sell poor guns, you were liable to get your clients killed. And if they survived they wouldn't forget the individual who delivered those defective weapons. The type of people Regan dealt with tended to have long memories and were somewhat dedicated when it came to settling grudges. Deliver excellent weapons, on time, and at the agreed price and the customer would always call on you if and when the need arose again. In Regan's business word of mouth meant a great deal. It wasn't as if he could go around advertising on television.

Regan's association with Pete Tilman went back to his early years. Tilman had been a wild character back then, running black ops for the Agency when the whole thing was like a crazy game. Tilman's missions were risky, dangerous, but he always got the job done and he always treated his partners well. Regan and Tilman had become more than just business partners. They built a closeness that transcended money and political wrangling in backwater republics. They had been shot at and chased, almost captured, and even wounded together. Every time they had walked away intact.

As U.S. involvement in Central America was toned down, Regan and Tilman drifted apart. Not through choice. More through career expansion. In the end Tilman was pulled back to the States and handed an assignment in Washington. Regan, his own business growing strongly, found he lost touch with his CIA buddy on and off. But occasionally they would cross paths. And then the Shadow deal came along. Townsend, bankrolled by high flyers with political-military

tendencies, knew Regan had some Pacific Rim dealings. He had dealt with China on a few small deals.
When Townsend offered him the chance to come in on
the big operation Regan saw it as another expansion
opportunity. He was also surprised, though not exactly
impressed, when Tilman showed up on Townsend's
payroll. Regan's former CIA buddy was a different
man. He could still do his job and was pulling off some
risky deals for Shadow, but Regan saw a big change in
Tilman. He had lost some of his sparkle. It shocked
Regan a little, but in the end he accepted that time
changed people. Sometimes for the better, sometimes
not. Later when Regan learned about the killing of
three CIA agents who were on a stakeout trying to
catch Townsend's people during an exchange, he took
an educated guess that Tilman had done the shooting
on Townsend's behalf. He had been right. Tilman had
made no bones about it. It wasn't the first time he had
killed. He had done his share during the early years.
This time it was different. This time he had done for
no better reason than the money Townsend was paying him. Back in their early days Tilman had higher
ideals. He was a Company Man, no question, but right
or wrong in those days there was a pride in what a man
did. That had gone, leaving Tilman strangely reduced
in moral stature.

The abrupt change in the situation, with Townsend
and company showing up in Santa Lorca, hadn't concerned Regan too much. Problems that needed fixing
were all part of the business. He welcomed his working partners to his expansive hacienda, as he had in the
past. He saw it as an opportunity to work matters
through.

Now though, with Townsend's new man, Hawkins, being exposed as an undercover agent the picture had altered yet again. Enough so that Regan decided, mainly for his own protection, to call in reinforcements from his warehouse on Port Cristobal docks. That they were on their way made Regan feel better.

HAWKINS ROLLED THE SUV to a stop, raising a hand in greeting to one of Regan's security men. The man nodded and returned to his patrol of the grounds. Hawkins set the brake and switched off the engine. Climbing out, he turned toward the house, passing the identical SUV that had been parked alongside when he had left. Something clicked as he walked by and it was as he stepped inside the house, making his way to the open living area, that it registered. By then it was too late. He had made himself known to the group, still lounging around the room as he had left them.

Chomski glanced across the room as Hawkins showed.

"Hey, our very own scout. You spot anything out there, Tonto?"

Hawkins crossed to the bar and helped himself to a cold bottle of beer from the minichiller.

"Only the locals and a few oilmen spending their pay. Hell, Cristobal is one quiet town."

"Hear that, Rik?" Chomski said. "T.J. doesn't rate Port Cristobal."

"Maybe it isn't sophisticated for him," Brandt said.

The man was staring directly at Hawkins, a vacant smirk on his broad face, and Hawkins knew then what it was all about.

His instinct had been right all along. It had warned

him when he'd stepped out of his SUV, glancing at the other vehicle and observing that it was parked the opposite way around than it had when he'd left.

T.J., you walked into this like a dumb country boy, he berated himself.

"Something on your mind, son?" Townsend asked, rising from his seat to face Hawkins.

"Not really, boss."

The room had fallen silent. Out the corner of his eye Hawkins saw that Brandt was on his feet, too, edging wide to block off any passage to the door.

"I guess you'd better have your money back, Mr. Riotta," Hawkins said, easing his hand into his pocket for the roll of notes. "All I took was for a beer."

He showed the wad of money and tossed it toward Riotta, who caught it neatly.

"Got to hand it to you, T.J.," Chomski said. "You had them all hooked. I just never was a fan."

"We should have listened to Ralph," Brandt said. "He saw this fuck was a fake all along."

Hawkins was absently toying with the small change he'd pulled from his pocket. He was aware that matters were rapidly coming to a boil. His cover was disintegrating with each passing second.

"Should I know what's going on here?" he asked,

Brandt was the one who let it out, unable to hold back any longer. "Let's quit all this fucking around," he yelled. "We all know what this little shit has been doing. I told you I saw him in town talkin' with that mother who was in the gun store in Landry the day he was collecting the boss's shotgun. Then they met up with another guy and went to a hotel. He was in there for around thirty minutes. Came out and drove back here."

"Ouch," Chomski said. "I guess you fucked up there, T.J. You screwed us. Now it's payback time."

Hawkins gripped the coin-size device Lyons had given him and squeezed it. He felt the distinct click of engagement.

Brandt moved in fast, circling behind Hawkins to frisk him and remove his pistol. He snatched the bottle from Hawkins's hand and tossed it aside. Then he retrieved the cell phone Hawkins was carrying. The man paused, motionless for a second, then Hawkins heard the sudden intake of breath and the rustle of movement. He knew what was coming but prepared or not, the blow from Brandt's pistol drove Hawkins to his knees. He knelt on the floor, stunned, feeling the warm rush of blood from the gash in the back of his skull. It soaked into the collar of his shirt. He squeezed his eyes shut, trying to get them back in focus.

"Get him on his feet," Townsend said.

Hawkins felt himself being hauled upright and dragged backward, hands gripping his upper arms. He was slammed against the wall, his head bouncing off the stone. The shock cleared his vision and he found himself staring at Townsend.

"Goddamn you, boy. You'll suffer for this. Making me look a fool."

"It wasn't that difficult," Hawkins said, and regretted the words instantly as Townsend let go a wild yell, backhanding him across the side of his face.

"Think you're so smart, don't you? In that case why are you the one in the shit?"

"You want to reconsider that, Mr. Townsend? I'm not the one who stole top-secret U.S. material and sold it to the Chinese. I'm not the one about to go down the river for that."

"I hope you're not going to give me the 'do you love your country' crap," Townsend said. "Jesus, Hawkins, give me credit for some intelligence. I'm a product of America, son. I was born into a society that hammered it into me from day one. Land of opportunity. Riches for anyone if you're willing to work and work hard. Well, I was and I did, and I even served goddamn America. I fought her battles, killed her enemies, waved the flag. And while I was doing that the sons of bitches back home were growing fat on arms dealing and back-door politics. Selling us all down the fucking river so they could all keep getting richer and richer. And I went along with it all, just like the other suckers, until I got my eyes opened and decided well, hell, if it's good enough for them, then it sure is good enough for Oliver Townsend.

"As soon as I did my time I went right out there and sold my soul to the Devil and the mighty dollar. Now *I've* got a slice of the pie and boy does it taste good. You know what grieves those pious bastards in Washington? The fact I'm whupping their asses at their own game. Only I took it a step further and I jumped on the biggest gravy train of them all. And it hurts them, 'cause I went and shared out their fancy toys, sold 'em to the enemy. What fuckin' enemy? Last time it was the Russians. Now we're best buddies. Next year it'll be fuckin' North Korea. Hell, the Chinese are already doing multibillion-dollar trade with us. Damn me, son, it's just a big grown-up game of Monopoly. Buy and sell. Share and swap. Pull in the cash. Wake up and see the sky-writing, Hawkins. Global community means global economy. So let's pass around the goodies."

"Same old excuses I've heard from every crook I ever met," Hawkins said. "Never do understand why you try so hard to justify what you do."

"Must be some of that old-time religion my mother used to throw at me. Something about repentance? Or was it seeking spiritual solace? Never could make the difference. In the end, son, I really don't give a sweet fuck what you think. I don't owe you a damn thing, except maybe a bullet between the eyes for all the grief you've created. I had you figured for a genuine believer. Damn you, Hawkins, you know how hard it is to recruit really good men?"

"Maybe I could do weekends for you," Hawkins said, and immediately regretted his remark.

It got him a hard, full-on punch that split his lower lip and raised a bruise across the side of his jaw.

"No place for smart remarks, Hawkins. In your position I would keep very quiet." Townsend rubbed the raw knuckles of his right hand and watched as Hawkins spit blood from his swelling mouth.

He stayed silent, watching as Jack Regan crossed the room, a wry smile on his face.

"Bubba, choose what you say with your head, not your ass. This ain't your day."

"We should finish this now," Chomski said.

"No, no, no, Ralph," Townsend said. "I want to know who this prick works for. And how much information he's passed on to his people. Killing him in anger won't give us a thing. We need to assess the situation. Damage limitation is the watchword for the moment."

"Oliver, may I suggest we consider our options," Su Han said from the other side of the room. "This is exactly what this man wants. For us to lose control before we know exactly what the problem is. If we do that, then he has already achieved a small victory."

As Townsend let them consider his words, Han turned casually to stand close to a desk. Only Hawkins saw him reach out and close his hand over a pair of flash drives. The Chinese dropped them into the pocket of his jacket.

Regan turned and left the office. He picked up a transceiver from a side table and pressed the transmit button.

"Xavier, come in."

"*Sí.*"

"Keep it sharp. Tell the others."

"Is there are problem?" Xavier asked.

"Possibility. Hawkins might have been followed from Port Cristobal."

"How many?"

"Two we know he met."

"I understand."

Regan stood debating his next move. He sensed he wasn't alone. It was Su Han.

"He *may* have brought his contacts back with him?"

"Damned sure he didn't just pass the time of day and nothing else." Regan banged his fist against the back of a heavy chair. "Son of a bitch. Just when things were running smoothly."

"Good fortune can be a capricious mistress, Mr. Regan."

"You don't say. My old man always told me when things look good they seldom ever are."

He moved to one of the windows and peered out, nodding as he saw heavy drops of rain hitting the glass. In the few seconds he stood there the rainfall increased rapidly. In the glare from the security lights beaming out across the grounds he watched as the incoming rain swept through the foliage, bouncing as it struck the earth. Santa Lorca lay in the tropical rain belt and sudden unexpected rainstorms were the norm at this time of year. Which wasn't going to help matters right now.

The transceiver in his hand crackled and Regan raised it to answer.

"Boss, I can't find Rico."

"What about Delgado?"

"He is—"

The transceiver fell silent. Regan didn't waste time calling Xavier's name again. There was no point. A man like Xavier didn't break off in the middle of a conversation unless something—or somebody—caused him to.

Regan called in his house security, a team of seven men. Unobtrusive when not required, they emerged from their positions and joined him.

"Time to earn your pay, boys. I believe we have unwelcome visitors. Unwelcome and hostile. You know what to do. Go to it."

Su Han returned to the office, drawing his pistol. He indicated Hawkins. "It appears this one is smarter than we all have been led to believe."

"A burst in the head should change that," Chomski said.

He had armed himself with a Franchi SPAS shotgun and racked in a shell with a hard yank on the slide.

"I'm beginning to come around to your way of thinking, Ralph," Townsend said.

"Let me do it," Brandt said. "I never did take to this bastard."

"Rik, that hurts," Hawkins mumbled, his mouth swollen from where Townsend had hit him.

Brant found that funny, grinning. "Not as much as—"

The sudden rattle of autofire broke through the rumble of the falling rain. Bullets struck one of the windows, glass blew into the room and everyone scattered. A second burst followed hard on the heels of the first.

Hawkins was left alone in the confusion. He saw his chance, took it and launched himself forward, his target Su Han. The Chinese failed to see Hawkins until the last moment, and then it was too late. The Phoenix Force commando, powering across the empty space between them, hit Han hard, pushing him sideways. Han realized what was happening in the last second before they struck the window. The impetus took them through in a shower of splintered wood and broken glass. Han's terrified yell was drowned by the torrential rain. Hawkins maintained his grip on Han as they dropped to the ground. The Chinese gave an explosive gasp as the impact took his breath away and he lay on his back, trying to suck air into his lungs, momentarily paralyzed. The moment they landed Hawkins let go, rolling clear, then twisted back to snatch the SIG-Sauer Han still gripped in his right hand. Hawkins's free hand snaked into Han's jacket pocket and located the flash drives. He pushed them deep into his pants' pocket, then gathered his legs under him and sprinted for the closest cover.

Behind Hawkins the SPAS shotgun boomed repeatedly as Chomski shoved his head out the broken window and cut loose.

Stony Man Farm, Virginia

"We have incoming," Wethers called across the room.

"Patch me in," Kurtzman said, turning to view the wall monitor.

"Visual is from my Slingshot bird," Wethers said. "I've been monitoring Regan's place and ran an infrared scan. I did a perimeter and immediate area check. There's a vehicle approached from the direction of Port Cristobal, off the main road and moving down the approach to Regan's hacienda."

Kurtzman hit the magnification relay and increased the image, checking out the signatures.

"Open truck with at least half a dozen armed men in the back. Storm's making it difficult to sharpen the picture any further."

Wethers tapped in more commands and speakers became active.

"That's Regan calling on his land line about ten minutes back. I tapped in as soon as we knew T.J. was in the house. I've been recording Regan's calls ever since."

"We verified it's Regan from voice analysis," Delahunt said. "It was easy to pin them down after we ran comparison tests on those recordings Townsend logged onto his computer."

"Good of him to assist," Brognola said.

Wethers smiled. "He doesn't know yet. Now, we picked up on this latest call to someone identified as Manolo. Told him to gather some armed men and get out to the house fast."

"The number he called was local. We ran a trace," Delahunt said. She put up a map of Port Cristobal that was overlaid by satellite grid lines from the Slingshot system. "The phone is located in this building on the docks."

"Wasn't it the docks where Phoenix had their meet with Regan last time around?" Brognola asked.

"Where the contract with that Fedayeen representative was to go down? Yes."

"Regan had a warehouse there where he conducted his arms business."

"It seems he still does. Our Mr. Regan is a known figure in Port Cristobal. He's well-known for his entrepreneurial skills."

"Translated that means he probably has connections bought and paid for," Brognola said.

"Money and guns," Delahunt replied. "Nothing much changes."

"Look at the background. Santa Lorca as a country doesn't have a lot going for it at the moment. The current oil finds might pump some money into the state coffers, but the place has always been an open market for illegal trading of one kind or another." Brognola studied the satellite imagery. "Can you get a message through to Lyons? Warn him what's coming up?"

"I'll give it a try."

"Talking of money," Kurtzman said. "I've now frozen Townsend out of his accounts. I've changed his passwords."

"What next?" Brognola asked.

"All his data has been downloaded, so I'll wipe his hard drives and leave him with nada."

"So," Price said, "what are we going to do with all that illegal money?"

"It's a thought," Tokaido said with a grin.

"Aaron could buy a new coffeepot," Price volunteered.

"That suggestion sounds appealing to me," Brognola said. "Okay, people, fantasy time over, let's get back to work."

LYONS AND BLANCANALES HAD followed Hawkins back to Regan's hacienda. The old Renault they had rented in Port Cristobal looked like most of the other vehicles on the road. Sometime in the past the suspension had nearly quit, so the ride was heavy and they were able to count every rut in the badly maintained road surface. When Hawkins had turned in at the gates of the hacienda, Lyons had driven on and made it around the next bend before pulling off the road and driving the Renault deep into the thick shrubbery. He cut the engine.

"You see the size of that place?" Blancanales asked.

"We're in the wrong business if we want to make money," Lyons observed, reaching into the back to get to the large bag containing their weapons.

They were already carrying their handguns. From the bag Lyons extracted a pair of the new P-90s. He handed one to Blancanales and a web belt that held pouches for extra magazines. In addition the belts were equipped with magazines for Blancanales's 9 mm Beretta, and Lyons had a number of speed loaders for the .357 Colt Python.

The Able Team commandos were equipped with lightweight communication sets. They had already checked that the units were working.

Lyons heard the soft ring tone coming from the sat phone he was carrying. He took it out and flipped it open.

"Yeah?"

"Satellite scan has picked up an armed group heading your way. Be with you in a couple of minutes."

"I'm not sure I should thank you for that."

"If you don't, I'll understand."

Lyons cut the call and relayed what Wethers had told him.

"Sitting here isn't the best we can do then?" Blancanales said.

The receiver in Lyons's pocket began to beep.

"That answer your question?" He pushed open his door. "Let's go and haul T.J.'s ass out of there. I don't want to be the one telling David his boy got killed on our watch."

They cut through the deep foliage in the direction of the low perimeter wall, moving quickly but with caution, because both were clear on how penetration into hostile territory had a habit of escalating from zero to the top of the scale with frightening speed.

Crouching below the rim of the wall, they took the time to listen, hoping to pick up any peripheral noise. The night was alive with insects, all in the throes of making as much racket as they could.

"Why the hell do we always pick noisy locations?" Blancanales asked.

Lyons scowled at him.

The sound of a footstep caught their attention. It was coming from their left. The continuous tread told the Able Team pair they would have company within seconds. The aroma of cigar smoke added another indication the guy was almost on their position.

Blancanales risked a look over the top of the wall and saw a lean man cradling an AK-74 in his arms. The man wore dark pants and a loud colored shirt. The cigar that had betrayed his presence was stuck between his lips. As the guy moved past, they heard the soft hiss of a transceiver hooked to his belt.

Rising to his feet Blancanales hopped over the wall,

landing lightly. Yet even that was enough to alert the guard. He began to turn, unlimbering the cradled AK. Blancanales refused to give him any slack, slashing the P-90 across the side of the guy's head. The cigar flew from his lips, sparks trailing. The man followed them down, striking the ground hard. Blancanales stood over him and hit him again.

Lyons joined his teammate. Through the heavy spread of tropical, lush vegetation, they could see the outline of the hacienda, lights glowing behind the windows. They crouched and made for the foliage fronting the house. They had seen the spread of light from the security lamps fixed along the roofline, but as long as they remained within the cover of the vegetation they might remain unseen.

Raindrops slapped against the greenery around them. The drops were overtaken by a sudden, heavy downpour that increased the noise level intensely. It took less than thirty seconds before Lyons and Blancanales were soaked.

Lyons almost collided with the second guard as the man was talking into his transceiver Before he could complete what he was saying Lyons slugged him with the P-90. The man, Xavier, fell to his knees, blood pouring from his mouth. Lyons stepped behind him, dropped the P-90 over his head and yanked it back against the guy's throat. The Ironman slammed a hard knee into the base of Xavier's neck, crushing down hard with the rifle. Xavier started to gag, spitting blood, his arms reaching over his shoulders to claw at Lyons torso He fought for long seconds before his life ebbed away, kicking to the last. As the guy went slack, Lyons released his hold and Xavier collapsed to the rain-sodden ground.

YARDS AWAY Rosario Blancanales, moving closer to the
house, spotted a third guard. The guy had his weapon
in the firing position, and it was obvious he had picked
up on one of the transceiver bursts that something was
wrong. Crouching in the dripping foliage, rain pounding down out of the dark sky, Blancanales watched his
man get closer. He ignored the hard beat of the torrential downpour and let the guy come almost level before
he lunged to his feet, swinging the assault rifle up and
around to stun the man. He almost made it, but at the
last moment the target became aware of a close presence and jerked back.

Blancanales realized he wasn't going to get the right
amount of power to put his man down, but it was too
late to pull back. The impact of the assault rifle was reduced as the guard hauled back, and the blow was
more glancing than full impact. It knocked the guy off
balance, twisting him so he was facing away from
Blancanales when his finger jerked back on the trigger
of his AK, sending a sharp burst into the side of the
house and through one of the windows.

Blancanales sensed the guy pulling himself under
control, arcing the muzzle of his weapon back on line.
He dropped to one knee, swiveling the P-90 across his
body, and held the guy in his sights for scant seconds
before he pulled the trigger. The 5.7 mm slugs ripped
into the guy's torso, throwing him backward. He
thumped to the ground hard, his AK spilling from his
hands in his final moments before his ravaged body
began a rapid slide into death.

T. J. HAWKINS TOOK a running dive into the tangled foliage, landing and rolling under cover. He could hear the

repeated bursts from Chomski's SPAS. The shotgun charges ripped through the lush greenery, showering Hawkins with shredded leaves and twigs. He stayed on his stomach, dragging himself deeper into cover, knowing that pursuit would be hard on his heels.

Ralph Chomski wouldn't allow his quarry to get away.

Twisting onto his back, Hawkins sat up, peering through the foliage at the house. The sheeting rain blurred the image but it was no exaggeration to say Chomski was firing at everything he could see, whether it was a legitimate target or not.

Hunching over the SIG-Sauer, Hawkins checked the magazine. It was full. He eased back the slide to see if there was a round in the port. There was. Pushing to his feet, the Phoenix Force commando was about to move off when he caught a glimpse of someone with pale blond hair moving in his direction.

It was Carl Lyons. The head of Able Team, armed with a P-90, was soaked to the skin from the downpour. He took note of Hawkins's bloody features by the light from one of the security lamps.

"What did you do? Criticize the evening meal?"

"They're a touchy bunch in there."

"T.J., they have reinforcements coming in, right behind us."

Lyons moved forward as he caught a glimpse of Blancanales heading for the hacienda's front door.

"Hell, he must think you're still in there. Pol. Haul back. T.J.'s already—"

Lyons suddenly realized he was talking into a dead unit. He looked down and saw the loose, thin wire from the microphone. It had been pulled free and Lyons realized it had to have happened during his clash with the man he had taken down. He remembered the clawing hands of the choking guard, reaching up over his shoulders in a desperate attempt to stay alive. The man had to have hooked his fingers in the wire during the struggle.

Without another word Lyons cut across the open space between the foliage and the house, his P-90 up and ready.

"I can't believe I'm going back inside," Hawkins muttered as he angled around toward the side of the house.

BLANCANALES HIT THE FRONT DOOR with his foot, kicking it wide, then ducking inside as he scanned the interior. The moment he cleared the frame he dropped to a crouch and moved to one side, the muzzle of his P-90 tracking ahead.

A rush of sound caught his attention and Blancanales turned, picking up one of Regan's security men emerging from beneath an arch. The guy was equipped with an AK, and he swung the assault rifle in the direction of the intruder. Already on track, Blancanales's P-90 crackling sharply, the burst ripping into the guy midtorso. He fell back with a howl, his own weapon discharging into the ceiling.

Blancanales flattened against the inner wall, hearing the slap of feet against the tiled floor. Shadows bounced ahead of the rushing figures, signaling their approach.

To Blancanales's right Carl Lyons loomed large in the open doorway, his timing as perfect as it could be. He met the rush of armed figures as they came into view, and the area exploded in an exchange of gunfire that shredded any peace that might have reigned only minutes before.

"JESUS CHRIST," Riotta screamed.

He turned aimlessly, his arms flailing as he made uncoordinated attempts to ward off the sudden racket from weapons around him. He was the least experienced in the room when it came to being under fire. In fact he had never been under fire before in his life, and the experience unnerved him completely. Panic set in and Riotta tried to escape. He scuttled in the direction of the closest wall, huddling against it and attempted to slide toward the door.

AS HE SAW T. J. HAWKINS cutting around the side of the hacienda and realizing what he was doing, Ralph Chomski swung away from his firing point at the window and turned back into the room. The front of the house had become a combat zone, with a number of weapons firing at the same time. Chomski thrust his hand into his pocket where he had jammed extra shells for his shotgun and began to slot them into the SPAS. With the weapon reloaded Chomski chambered the first round, lunging across the room. He intended to be there to face Hawkins when he reentered the house.

Chomski crouched low, using furniture for cover, and crossed the room, finally ducking behind the cover of a room divider. He ran along the passage that would bring him to the door Hawkins might use to make his entry. He heard a footfall behind him and spun around.

It was Rik Brandt. The man held up a warning hand.

"Easy, buddy, it's me." Brandt held his pistol in his big left hand.

"Hawkins cut around this side of the house. If that bastard gets back inside, I want his ass."

"You and me both." Brandt paused, his slow thought process taking a moment to clarify. "They busted us, Ralph?"

"If we don't walk out of here alive, I'd say yeah. Now stop thinking and help me nail this little shit."

The target door burst open, rain sheeting in from the storm outside. Brandt turned his gun on the opening, triggering a couple of shots before he realized no one was there.

"Easy, Rik," Chomski warned.

His warning went unheeded. Brandt moved forward, his pistol probing ahead of him, caution cast aside in his need to locate his target.

"Rik," Chomski yelled.

A flicker of movement at the lower-left corner of the door preceded the muzzle-flash as Hawkins fired, the SIG-Sauer angled up at Brandt's bulk. The 9 mm slugs cored into the man's lower torso and up into his chest cavity, clipping organs and blood vessels. Bleeding internally, Brandt stepped back, fell against the open door and went down on his knees and onto his face.

"You son of a bitch," Chomski screamed, triggering the SPAS.

He saw the dark outline of Hawkins's body as the Phoenix Force pro pulled back from the door. Chomski held back, refusing to be drawn.

There was a scuffle of sound to his left. Chomski glanced around and saw Riotta. The man was in a total panic, his face sickly white, eyes wide. He came at Chomski in a rush, flailing the air with his hands as if to ward off the crackle of gunfire.

"Get me out of here," Riotta screamed.

"Find a fucking place to hide if you can't face it."

Chomski had no time for Riotta. The man wasn't going to be of any use. He was almost a gibbering wreck. As Riotta lurched up to Chomski, reaching to claw at his sleeve, Chomski reached out to push him away. Riotta stumbled against Brandt's slumped body. He looked down and saw the bloody marks of death.

Chomski saw what was coming as Riotta recoiled from the body, colliding with the door frame. He looked at the opening and before Chomski could make any kind of move to restrict him, Riotta pushed away from the frame and went out into the darkness.

HAWKINS SAW RIOTTA as the man burst through the door, reeling as the full effect of the downpour hit him. The drenching force of the rain halted Riotta in midstride, his mouth open as he reacted to the chill of the heavy rain.

In that frozen moment Hawkins caught a glimpse of Chomski behind Riotta. Chomski seemed to hesitate briefly, as if he was making a decision, then he ducked behind the blocking bulk of Riotta and Hawkins knew the guy was making his play. Chomski had chosen to use Riotta as cover while he broke through the door, his intention to catch Hawkins off guard.

Hawkins saw the man pushing through the open door, his SPAS arcing around to shoot as he cleared Riotta's covering outline. He might have made it if Riotta hadn't snapped out of his frozen pose, twisting his body as he made a dash away from the hacienda.

Chomski realized his cover had moved, leaving him exposed, and his intended action revealed. He shook his head to clear the rain from his face, eyes searching for Hawkins.

What he saw was Hawkins's SIG-Sauer, the muzzle dropping into target acquisition.

"You're mine," Chomski screamed, defiant to the last, and emphasized his words by jerking the SPAS toward Hawkins.

He was a microsecond too late as the P-226 exploded with sound. Hawkins fired hard and fast, triggering three shots that impacted with Chomski's skull. The force kicked him back and slammed him against the wall. The SPAS blew its shot skyward before the weapon slipped from Chomski's loose grasp. He toppled sideways and his already shattered and bloody skull thudded hard against the ground.

Moving forward, Hawkins scooped up the SPAS, working the slide to jack another shell into the breech, then turned on his heel and went in through the open door.

REGAN HEARD his transceiver crackle. He put it to his ear. "Speak to me."

"Manolo. I hear shooting."

"No shit, bubba, where are you?"

"Here. At the gate."

"There are three of them. They hit us hard," Regan stated.

Before he cut the transmission Regan heard Manolo yelling at his men. He dropped the transceiver and turned as he picked up sound close by. It was his surviving security man, clutching a shattered and bloody arm.

"They're inside. We couldn't stop them."

"Where's your fuckin' gun?"

"I lost it when I fell."

Regan backed away from the man, merging with the shadows, trying not to dwell on what was turning into one gigantic mess. His security force was decimated, his safe house turned into a battle zone. This wasn't the way it was supposed to happen. Up until a few days back the whole operation had been working well. His association with Townsend and Shadow had earned Regan a great deal of money, especially the Chinese connection. All the bases were covered. Which went to show nothing should be taken for granted. Now everything was going to hell in a hand basket, and Regan wasn't happy with that.

As Regan worked his way through the house toward the rear, his mind worked busily, calculating the odds of getting away free and clear. He envied Pete Tilman. Receiving Regan's call would have enabled Tilman to make his own break and get out from under with comparative ease. Regan hoped that Tilman made it. In a world of mistrust and divided loyalties Tilman was one of the very few Regan could call a real friend. They had walked through hell together and come out the other side virtually unscathed. No matter the divergence of their ways over the years, they always remained faithful to each other.

With the crackle of autofire in the background Regan pushed through a door that led off the kitchen, bolting it behind him, traveled along a narrow passage and down a short flight of steps. Another door opened to the garage. He secured the door once he went through. Regan flicked a switch and a single fluorescent flickered into life.

A black civilian Hummer was the only thing in the garage. It was fully gassed up, with extra fuel cans se-

cured in the rear, along with a pack of MREs—Meals
Ready to Eat—and water. On the rear seat were two
large carry-alls. One held clothing, the other a laptop
computer, its hard drive containing Regan's detailed
database. In there was a comprehensive list of his global contacts and sources. It made interesting reading.
Jack Regan had contacts in both high and low places—
industrial, military, political. Alongside the laptop were
a couple of extra pistols and loaded magazines. In a
sealed, solid package was a quarter of a million U.S.
dollars.

Regan climbed in behind the wheel and opened the
glove compartment, which held another pistol, a wallet with more cash and a small leather case that contained his passports, credit cards and a handheld
electronic organizer that held coded details of his various worldwide bank and investment accounts. There
were a couple of satellite phones, always on full
charge, each holding numbers Regan could call day or
night if he needed to call in favors.

He flicked on the power, checking the dash readout.
The Hummer was kept in top condition, battery always fully charged, oil and water topped up. He turned
the ignition key and the powerful engine rumbled into
life. Regan let it warm up, reaching out to pick up the
remote that would raise the garage door. He locked his
seat belt in place, placed his pistol on the seat beside
him, then pressed the remote and watched the garage
door slide open on oiled runners.

The garage faced out across what appeared to be a
patch of untended, thick foliage. It was in fact a solid
piece of ground that would allow him to drive clear of
the hacienda, then make a wide circuit and return to the

dirt road leading back to the main highway. Once through Port Cristobal, Regan would head due north, the narrow highway taking him up-country and to a border crossing. Once clear of Santa Lorca he would be able to make his choice of final destinations.

Regan drove slowly, without lights. He didn't need them, even in the savage downpour. The storm was working in his favor, covering the sound of the Hummer.

He reached the dirt road and swung in the direction of the main highway. The all-terrain vehicle had no problems with the muddy trail. Regan was able to increase his speed, and he decided it was safe to switch on the headlights. As the twin beams lanced into the gloom and the sheeting rain, the former CIA agent imagined he saw a dark shape stumble across his path. He thought he had imagined it until the Hummer's wheels bumped over something solid. Regan rolled on a few yards and braked. He sat for a moment, then reached into the back for a raincoat and struggled into it. A long peaked baseball cap completed his protection against the elements. He picked up his pistol and a flashlight, and climbed out, making his way to the rear of the vehicle.

The flashlight picked out the hunched figure, half submerged in the greasy mud. Regan used his foot to roll the body over. The Hummer's heavy wheels had burst the body open like a ripe melon. It was messy. Regan ignored that and turned the flashlight on the face, which was untouched, the rain sluicing away the mud to expose the dead features.

Joseph Riotta.

Townsend's moneyman had been thinking along the

same lines—get out before he walked into someone's line of fire.

Regan shook his head.

"You forgot the main thing, bubba," Regan said out loud. "Forward planning. Never pays to do anything without forward planning."

He turned and climbed back in the Hummer, driving off without another look back.

CHAPTER THIRTEEN

Regan's security force, reduced to the final two, tried to move Townsend deeper into the house, exchanging fire with the attackers. In the semidark it had become difficult to select and lock on to a target.

Townsend resisted their attempts to move him. He had his own weapon, and he had no intention of cowering in some dark corner. He had faced hostile fire before and though he never called himself a hero, he refused to retreat, preferring to make his own decisions. The security men broke away, leaving him to his own devices, and having seen the way matters were going, chose to save themselves.

They cut through the house, heading for the same door Hawkins had used in his confrontation with Chomski and Brandt.

The security men saw Hawkins at the last moment. He had pushed through the door, the SPAS tracking ahead of him. The sudden appearance of the two hardmen, their own weapons up and ready, drew a swift reaction from the Phoenix Force commando. He kept moving forward, dropping to the floor, the SPAS's muzzle angling upward. He heard the crackle of gunfire, the shots cleaving the air above his prone body, drilling into the wall behind him. Hawkins triggered the shotgun, feeling its recoil, then saw the charge rip its way into the closer of the two men. The deadly force picked the guy up and flung him back across the room, trailing a mist of blood. He slammed against a piece of furniture, unable to control his own movements as he toppled backward, landing hard. His left side from the waist up had been reduced to a bleeding mush, ribs poking through the tattered flesh.

As Hawkins turned his attention to the second guy he heard the crackle of the man's weapon, felt the slugs hammer into the smooth wood floor. Splinters peppered his sleeve, some digging in deep. Hawkins gasped, twisting the pump gun around and triggering a fast shot that clipped the target's shoulder. The minor injury didn't put the guard down but had the effect of making him pause and step back, allowing Hawkins the chance to adjust his aim and fire again before the hardman recovered. This time the commando was on target and his shot hit the guy in the center chest. There was no need for a follow-up.

THE SOUND OF THE SPAS made Townsend throw a glance over his shoulder, wondering who was triggering the weapon. He knew Chomski had armed himself with a shotgun, but the man had vanished, along with Brandt, and Townsend had no idea where he was at that moment. Come to that, where was Regan? He seemed to have quit the scene, as well.

Townsend suddenly felt very alone.

"The hell with this," Townsend muttered. "If the bastards want me, let them come and try."

He raised the pistol, turning in the direction of the main entrance, and in the shadowed confines of the room he made out a dark figure as it detached itself from cover.

Townsend leaned forward, trying to make out who it was. There wasn't enough light to distinguish the features, but he did make out blond hair. No one in Regan's group had hair that color, so Townsend had to take this man as one of the attacking force.

He didn't hesitate, though in retrospect he realized he should have taken a little longer to settle his aim. Instead he triggered a shot and gave a grunt of satisfaction when the figure spun halfway around and stumbled.

Got the mother, he thought.

Townsend stepped forward, going for the kill shot.

He missed the second man, who lined up the P-90 he was carrying and triggered a solid burst that took Townsend in the chest, burning pain searing his body. Townsend dropped to his knees, the pistol slipping from nerveless fingers. A second burst hit him and he arced over on his back, spilling his blood across the cool floor tiles. He heard rapid movement around him, the murmur of voices that were becoming dimmer and dimmer. The pain swelled, then the shadows closed in and enveloped him.

"T.J.?"

Blancanales held his P-90 on the advancing shape he half recognized.

"Ease off that damn trigger, Pol."

"I think we cleaned the nest in here, but we have more outside."

"Hey, did Carl take a hit?"

"Nice of you to notice."

Townsend's bullet had penetrated Lyons's upper right arm, lodging in the hard muscle. He was bleeding, his hand clamped over the wound, his P-90 dangling from its neck sling.

"We need to—" Hawkins began.

"What we need is to get out of here now that we're done."

"You forgetting the backup squad out there?" Blancanales said.

"Load up and let's do it," Lyons snapped. "I've had my fill of this backwater sinkhole."

They reloaded every weapon they carried.

"You going to be okay?" Blancanales asked.

Lyons snapped a fresh top-load magazine into his P-90.

"Don't worry about me," he said. "Worry about those suckers out there."

"You're the boss," Hawkins said.

"That's right. Now let's haul ass out of here."

MANOLO SPREAD HIS MEN as they went EVA from the truck with a sharp sweep of his arm. They all knew the hacienda and the grounds that were thick with greenery. Regan had allowed the vegetation to spread, hiding the frontage of the house and providing a natural barrier for anyone trying to take too close of a look. Manolo had pointed out to Regan that the barrier also served to prevent Regan from being able to spot any incoming and unwanted visitors. Regan had considered the point, but had chosen to ignore it as it could work both ways and he had to choose his way.

This night, with the near jungle around the house and the severe rain, Manolo understood the problems he and his men might face. He had noticed a wind starting to push in from the coast, its force driving the heavy rainfall in solid sheets across the earth. Even now, as Manolo stood partially sheltered by the greenery, the severity of the downpour didn't go unnoticed. As the reinforcements closed in on the hacienda, they were forced to shield their faces from the impact of the rain.

Salvanno, one of Manolo's lieutenants, edged up to him, his M-16 pulled close to his body.

"This is not good, Mano. It's hard to see where we're going let alone watch out for a target."

"We have no choice," Manolo said. "If we take Regan's money then we are obligated to do his work."

"That I understand. But in this?"

Somewhere off to their right a man shouted. The call was followed by the crackle of autofire. Other weapons replied in kind, the sounds dulled by the falling rain.

"Now is not the time to discuss the climate," Manolo said.

He took off across the sodden ground, in the direction of the gunfire, with Salvanno on his heels.

"There, there," a man yelled.

Weapons followed his pointing finger and gunfire erupted, the bright stab of muzzle-flashes breaking the gloom. The whip and snap of slugs cut through the falling rain, catching soft flesh and spilling men to the sodden ground in ungainly tumbles. On top of the autofire came the harsh crack of a powerful shotgun.

THE SHADOWS WERE LIT by the savage interchange of hard fire. Manolo's crew of local hardmen, far from being novices, found themselves face-to-face with three specters from hell.

The Stony Man trio emerged from the hacienda with weapons up and firing, and cut a bloody swathe through Regan's crew.

The 5.7 mm P-90s and Hawkins's SPAS shotgun returned the fire from Regan's crew in a hail of death. The Stony Man team emerged from the heavy downpour, seeking and finding targets with skills that were overwhelming in their ferocity. Bodies jerked under the impact of relentless fire. Punctured flesh spouted blood, bone splintered and numbing pain became the overriding factor in the swift decimation of the local hardmen. They crumpled like windblown chaff.

Hawkins lowered his shotgun, dropped the empty weapon and replaced it with his P-226 pistol. Only now, as the rush of combat began to slowly ebb away, did he feel the pain from the bloody and ragged tear across his left side. Even the sluicing effect of the falling rain failed to erase the warm sensation of free-flowing blood soaking through his clothing.

Across from Hawkins, blond hair plastered tight against his skull, Carl Lyons had refreshed his P-90 and moved forward to prowl the area in an ever-widening curve. His wounded arm still shed blood and he held it tight against his side, refusing to allow it to hamper his ability to operate.

Slightly to the rear, unconsciously taking the position, Blancanales made certain no one could take them by surprise.

The near immobile tableau held for some time, long

enough for the Stony Man team to be certain all threats had been dealt with.

Around them the tall trees swayed under the power of the storm. A wind had arisen and it pushed the rain across the terrain, rattling and slamming it against anything that stood in its way.

"How do we get out of Santa Lorca?" Hawkins asked.

"We need to get back up the coast where the Navy dropped us," Blancanales said. "We hid a signal device. All we need is to activate it and they send in a chopper from the carrier."

"Let's go," he snapped, and led the way across the grounds to the Renault they had used to trail Hawkins from Port Cristobal.

Blancanales got behind the wheel, started the vehicle and, after his companions piled in, drove steadily back along the muddy strip of the side road until they hit the main road.

The coast road was awash, deserted, and they reached the town without seeing anyone. Port Cristobal looked like a ghost town. The entire population had gone to ground to wait out the storm.

It was a good three miles to the turnoff that overlooked the beach. Blancanales drove the Renault deep into the undergrowth and they abandoned the vehicle, making their way down to the beach. Out beyond the shore, the ocean was a dark swollen mass of restless water, the wind whipping the waves into foam. They walked the beach until they reached the place where the signal device sat jammed beneath rocks. Blancanales activated the signal, then the three of them found a sheltered outcropping to wait for the Navy chopper to fly in and pick them up.

Less than forty minutes later the chopper arrived. Black and without lights, it swung in over the beach, hovered, then settled.

Hawkins and Blancanales helped Lyons to the open hatch. His arm was bleeding, despite the crude bandage they had fashioned from a strip of Blancanales's shirt. Despite his hardman act, Lyons was groggy and surprisingly offered little resistance when crewmen from the helicopter took over and helped him on board. As soon as Hawkins and Blancanales were inside, the hatch was closed and the chopper lifted off for the return to the U.S. Navy carrier out in international waters.

TWO HOURS LATER Lyons was resting, sedated following the removal of the bullet. He was in the carrier's sick bay, where Hawkins's side had been cleaned and stitched. He had been given shots against infection, and his other numerous bruises and gashes treated, too.

Apart from being wet and cold, Blancanales had come through unscathed so he was the logical choice to make a report to Stony Man.

Over the secure Navy communication system he updated Barbara Price.

"We should have code-named this Clean Sweep," Price said after hearing his field report.

"It needed doing," Blancanales told her. "If we don't make it clear how we view this kind of action, it'll keep on happening."

"Survivors?"

"We do know Townsend is dead, and so are his top

aides, Chomski and Brandt. They were the main Shadow people. As far as we're aware Jack Regan wasn't among the casualties."

"That's the second time he's walked away from us," Price said. "That man has a charmed life."

"T.J. said the Chinese guy, Su Han, was there just before the shooting started, but he seems to have fled the scene."

"Like you said, Pol, the main Shadow personnel have been accounted for. I guess we can mark that down as a success for the mission."

"T.J. got his hands on a couple of flash drives Han tried to walk away with. Could be we came away with a bonus."

"Unless they're just old family recipes."

"Barb, you spend too much time listening to the ramblings of that delinquent Briton, McCarter."

"You could be right."

"Any news on Phoenix?" Blancanales asked.

"On route from Bagram."

"They do the business?"

"If you mean did they level half of northern China in the process, then I have to say yes."

"Sounds as if we will be getting letters of complaint from Beijing," the Able Team commando stated.

"The way Hal tells it, if that happens, the President is going to go ballistic. Once we present him with the evidence Phoenix is bringing back, plus photographs of said illicit deeds, he can tell Beijing where to stick its complaint."

"Hey, we'll see you later," Blancanales said, and signed off.

He made his way back to the cabin he'd been assigned, sank down on the bunk and was asleep within minutes.

THE MANNER OF SU HAN's departure from the hacienda was far removed from that of his arrival. Recovering from his fall through the window, he had crawled into the undergrowth, with the increasing din of battle filling his ears, the torrential downpour soaking him through. He dragged himself as deep into the dense foliage as he could and lay in a waterlogged depression, cold and aching and not a little concerned for his own safety.

Any plan he might have been considering in partnership with Oliver Townsend seemed far from his grasp now. The attack on the hacienda seemed to go on for an eternity, though in retrospect the conflict didn't last that long. Even when it appeared over and a heavy silence fell over the place Han remained in his place of concealment, not risking showing himself until he was fully convinced he was alone.

He sank into an exhausted sleep and when he next opened his eyes the first pale slivers of dawn were edging through the thick clouds. It was still raining, though not as hard as earlier.

Sun Han, former Director of the Second Department, Intelligence, dragged himself out of the muddy water and took stock of his surroundings. The only sound was that of the rain. He moved, with great caution, in the direction of the silent hacienda.

He began to see bodies around the front of the house. He bent and picked up as discarded handgun, checking to see that the magazine was fully loaded, and held it in his right hand as he approached the house.

The main door stood ajar. He moved inside and found more dead. Among them were Chomski and the man named Brandt. He also found Oliver Townsend. There were also Regan's security team members. Regan himself was not among the dead, nor was Riotta, Townsend's financial expert.

Whatever had taken place in and around the house had in effect destroyed Shadow. If this was the work of the Americans, exacting justice against the people who had stolen their secrets, then they had accomplished it fully. This, along with the strike against Guang Lor, showed that the U.S. wouldn't tolerate such actions. They had their secrets and were willing to reach out wherever needed to protect those secrets. For that, Han understood and respected their dedication. Not that it did anything to solve his own personal position in the aftermath.

Han was now on his own, a fugitive from his masters in Beijing and now without the protection of the people he had joined to foster fresh business relationships.

He wandered around the house and found himself in the room Regan had used as an office. He located his own attaché case on the floor beside Regan's desk. Opening it he found the contents secure. He closed the case, then paused and reached into his pocket for the two flash drives he had taken possession of just before the American, Hawkins, had pushed him through the window. His fingers closed over empty air. The flash drives were gone. Han moved to the window and examined the ground outside. Splintered wood and broken glass lay where he had fallen. It was light enough now for him to be able to see the ground clearly.

The drives weren't there. Even when he climbed outside, got on his knees to search, he found nothing. Han returned to the house and took his attaché case back to the room he had been using. He quickly removed his wet clothing, dried himself and dressed in clean clothes and shoes. He took his attaché case, tucked his acquired pistol behind his belt and made his way from the house. Passing through Regan's office he noticed a cell phone on the desk. He slipped it into his pocket.

The SUVs were still there. Han took one and drove away from the house, along the muddy access road that would take him to the main highway. As he drove, his mind was working busily. He had accepted the loss of the flash drives, and as important as they might have been to his future, they were lost to him now. There were still substantial cash amounts in various accounts, so money wasn't an immediate problem. His first priority was to get out of Santa Lorca. Sooner or later the incident at Regan's hacienda would be discovered. Han didn't want to be around when that happened.

Jack Regan's disappearance intrigued him. Where was the man? From his association with Regan it had become clear to Han that he was a survivor. Understanding Regan the way he did, Han imagined the man would have had an escape plan prepared. If he had seen the way things were going, Regan might easily have put his plan into action and quietly slipped away. If Han was right, Regan was probably already out of the country. There was another possibility. Perhaps the Americans had captured him, spiriting Regan away to some secure place where they could interrogate him over the affairs of the Shadow organization. Of the two options

Han somehow believed the former was the most likely scenario.

He drove around Port Cristobal, heading for the border that lay to the north along the coast road. In the early morning he pulled over and took out the cell phone. Su Han needed help getting clear of Santa Lorca, and at this moment in time there was only one person he could think of who might be able to help. Checking the phone, he was relieved to find it was tri-band. He dialed a number that was forever imprinted on his memory and waited for several rings. The connection finally clicked over to the message service and Su Han spoke quickly in his own tongue. He placed the cell phone on the seat beside him and continued driving north. He passed through a couple of small fishing villages, stopping once to buy bottled water and packages of crackers. His dollars were accepted readily.

Han also received curious stares, wondering why until he realized that Chinese travelers were probably not seen very often in Santa Lorca. That concerned him a little. If the authorities started to investigate the deaths at Regan's hacienda, it would come out a Chinese national had been seen in Port Cristobal before the killings and then moving around the country after the event.

Han's concern traveled with him. There was little he could do about his appearance, and trying to abandon the SUV at this stage would only leave him stranded.

The return call on the cell phone solved all his problems in a single stroke.

"Director Han? Why have you called me?"

"Listen to me, Sammo. There have been disturbing developments here in Santa Lorca. The Americans tracked down our Shadow friends. There was a strike at Regan's house, and they were all killed. I barely escaped with my life. Where are you?"

"At a small airstrip just across the border. I have been trying to make contact. There was supposed to be transport here to pick me up."

"It won't be coming. You must stay away from Santa Lorca. I am on the run myself, driving north. I ask a favor. Wait for me before you leave. You are my only hope of escape."

There was no hesitation in Sammo Chen Low's voice. "Of course I will wait. How long will you be?"

"Three hours maximum. I am on the coast road. It is the way I was brought into the country myself."

"Was it the crossing at La Cruz?"

"Yes."

"I will be waiting."

"You will not regret this, Sammo."

SAMMO CHEN LOW closed the cell phone and slipped it in his pocket.

"Understood, Director Han." He turned and smiled at the Chinese who had traveled all the way from Beijing with him. "He says I will not regret having helped him."

"How would you regret carrying out a great service to your country, Sammo?" The slim, soft-eyed operative from the enforcement section of the Second Department, Intelligence touched the heavy, suppressed pistol that lay in his lap. "It seems that your forward planning has paid off. Instead of *us* having to go all the way into Santa Lorca to confront Han, *he* is coming here."

Sammo Chen Low nodded. This was turning out better than he had expected. He hadn't been looking forward to going all the way to Regan's hacienda and play-acting until he managed to get Su Han on his own. This way it would be quicker and cleaner. Beijing would be satisfied that Han had paid for his incompetence, Chen Low, as a loyal member of the Party, would receive his promotion, and the crisis would be over.

He sat back, prepared to wait, and was already envisaging the expression on Su Han's face when he realized what was going to happen to him. By that time it would be far too late.

Far, far too late...

EPILOGUE

Mission Debrief—Stony Man Farm

"Why don't we look at the negative aspects of the mission first," Hal Brognola said, taking his seat at the conference table.

Both teams were in attendance, including Carl Lyons. Despite being in recovery, his arm heavily bandaged and in a sling, he had insisted he be here. Refreshed and rested, in clean clothing, they were all showing the physical effects of the mission.

Jack Grimaldi was here, too.

Mei Anna had moved on from Bagram with Loy Hung to a secret location in Hong Kong, with the assurance she would be in contact with McCarter soon.

There was a definite air of tension in the room.

"There was too much screwing around on this one," Brognola said. "Your foray back into China went against every rule of engagement we have. It was damn foolish and it could have cost us."

McCarter held his gaze, keeping himself in check.

"The whole team could have ended up in prison, or worse, and you blatantly ignored my concerns."

"Tough," McCarter said.

"What?"

"Hal, you heard. I told you exactly what I intended at the time. We had a team member in jeopardy and there was no way we were leaving her behind."

"Officially, Mei Anna isn't a member of Phoenix Force."

"Oh, come on. That's a cheap shot and you know it. She was enough of a member when you recruited her to go along. Bloody hell, Hal, you can't just muck around with the rule book when it suits you and the big chief, then renege once the deed has been done. Remember what was said at the start of this mission? Anything and everything is considered okay, just as long as we get the electronic gizmo back. Well, we did just that and we put Guang Lor out of action. To do all that we made an illegal incursion into Chinese territory, engaged their military and killed a fair few, caused damage. And all with presidential sanction. So quit shaking the big stick at me, because it doesn't bloody well scare me."

"You done?"

McCarter considered, then shook his head. "One, Mei Anna took a hell of a lot of hard treatment on this. She could have simply directed us into China and waited with Jack. But she went in with us. That made her a paid-up member of the team. Hal, you bloody well know we never leave anyone behind. You knew bloody well we couldn't abandon her. Two, lay off Jack. In the field he's under my command as head of Phoenix Force. He had no choice. I ordered him to take us back over the border to pull Anna out. He was obeying orders. My orders. Right, Jack?"

Grimaldi looked blank for a moment.

"I…yeah, that's right. David ordered me in."

"This has been a weird one all the way down the line, Hal," Lyons said. "Teams split up. T.J. going under cover. Gadgets getting himself caught up in that mess on the train. We were up against more than one group. But we delivered in the end. If I remember, there was a suggestion of 'whatever it takes to get the job done' back at the start. So what's the beef? We got the job done. End of story."

Brognola stared around the table. They were united on this. He could sense it.

"So this is how it's going to be, huh? Making up and breaking the rules when it suits? Doing it your way, even if it leaves me having to explain it to the President?"

McCarter nodded. "That's the way it has to be, Hal. Take it or leave it."

Brognola leaned forward, hands flat on the table. "It doesn't give me any other options then." He paused, maintaining his blank expression. "I'm just going to have to ask for a raise. The money I'm getting isn't enough to cover this kind of crap."

He let it go at that, relaxing, and waited while it sank in.

Kurtzman broke the silence. "Coffee all 'round?"

"What the hell," Brognola said. "Count me in."

He opened the mission file in front of him. "Shadow as we know it has been broken up. Townsend and his chain of command is gone. Jack Regan has slipped the net. No trace, but I guess he'll surface somewhere else.

He has too many contacts to stay out of business for long."

"Su Han's body was found two days ago just over the border from Santa Lorca," Price said. "Two bullets in the back of his head. Execution-style killing."

"His own people catching up with him?" James suggested. "The Chinese don't forgive lightly."

"We may never know," Brognola said, "but I have a feeling you're not far off the mark."

"Let's stay on Han for a while," Kurtzman said. "Those flash drives you picked up, T.J. They held a mass of data. The guy must have downloaded his computer before he skipped China. Contacts. Background on Guang Lor and the missile development program. Detail on bank deposits. The involvement of high-ranking officials from Beijing. I figure he must have been hoping to start up again someplace else, so he compiled a little dossier of his own. Names and faces. With that information he would have been able to run one hell of an operation. The data is going to keep our intelligence agencies busy for weeks."

"Any of it cross-reference with Townsend's data?" McCarter asked.

"Yes, plus Townsend's own collection. That guy was an information freak. Once we broke his encryptions, the stuff just kept coming."

"Not just his Shadow backup," Brognola said. "Townsend had detail on people in high places in positions that might be regarded as overly sensitive. Government, military and industrial. Some nasty surprises, too. People you wouldn't expect to be involved with someone like Townsend and his business."

"Has the President seen these names yet?" Blanca-nales asked.

Brognola nodded. "Oh, yes, he's seen them. I'm surprised we can't hear the heads falling into the Potomac from here. He's made it this week's top of the list. Expect to see some resignations any time now."

"So what have these people been doing?"

"Back-door deals. Laying foundations for future business deals. Political chicanery of the highest order. These people are amazing. They rant on TV about facing our common enemy, then go and arrange a deal with the same people through their front men. Oliver Townsend was just a small cog in their machine. They're carving up Asia and buying favors in Beijing futures. Military ordnance has become one of the growth industries worldwide. Sons of bitches don't give a damn that the technology they're trading could be used back at us. All they see is if *they* don't sell to the Chinese someone else will."

"Market economy gone mad," Manning said.

"And what about this deal with Tilman?" McCarter asked. "This hit team Gadgets tangled with?"

"The girl, Hendrick, was put on Tilman as a watcher. Her employers, the same ones we've just been discussing, were aware of Tilman's influence within the CIA. They wanted him on their payroll for the word he could get for them on CIA global policy, but once he started to waver they must have decided to cut their losses and remove him before he had a chance to spread any gossip about them. Hence the hit men sent to join the woman on the train. If Gadgets hadn't been around, they would have succeeded and the attaché case he had with him would have vanished."

"As it turns out, Tilman had a real bag of tricks there," Kurtzman said. "Names and faces on disks. A neat little history that sums it all up for us."

"I guess Tilman couldn't drop his CIA training," Brognola said. "He naturally created a file on everyone involved, all summarized and ready to point the finger."

"Professional to the last," Price said.

"More than his employers," Brognola added. "Washington P.D. were called when someone spotted a break-in at Tilman's apartment. They got there before the perp got away and found him in possession of a suppressed Uzi. He'd found it in a concealed compartment. Tilman's CIA connection was flagged up later and the Uzi was checked against the bullets from the three dead agents. They matched."

"So Tilman did ice his own buddies," Lyons said. "Nice guy."

"That's the icing on the cake," McCarter said. "What I want to hear is the Chinese reaction to our little sojourn in their territory."

"What do you think happened?" Brognola asked.

"Indignant red faces. Accusations of illegal incursions into peace-loving China. The destruction of an innocent fertilizer plant and the wholesale slaughter of indigenous peasants going about their daily tasks for the good of the Party. Outrageous propaganda lies by the warmongering U.S.A. Faked photographs. No missiles. No stolen technology."

"And it's goodnight from *60 Minutes,*" James said. "Or in this case, five seconds."

"Pretty well what happened," Brognola said. "A delegation had a meeting with the President. They made demands, and he showed them the circuit board and the photographs. Denial. More accusations. Threats. The President lost some of his cool and told them if they wanted to make an issue of it, then okay. He would take everything he had and go public on a global scale. He added that he would also be exhibiting the data files we got from Su Han's flash drives and expose names and identities of Beijing individuals involved. He dropped a couple of names just to show he wasn't running a bluff. Apparently that had some kind of calming effect on the delegation. They backed off and said they needed to consult with Beijing themselves. A meeting was arranged for later that day, but the delegation didn't show. By that time they were on a plane heading home."

"And nothing since?"

"Our intelligence sources say the bamboo curtain hasn't rattled once."

"Is the Man still rattled?" McCarter asked innocently. "Or are we still in his employ?"

"He sends his thanks."

"I should bloody well hope so. No bonus then?"

"Pushing it again, David."

"Somebody around here has to. The rest of these old women will just sit here and not say a word."

Brognola closed his file. "Time you people got out of here. Go where you need to be. Make sure your phones are on standby. Just in case."

McCarter was first on his feet. "I'm off then. First plane to London."

"I wonder who he's going to meet?" Hawkins said knowingly.

"A certain young Chinese lady," Encizo suggested.